GAYLE CALLEN

REDEMPTION
OF THE
DUKE

AVON

An Imprint of HarperCollinsPublishers

This is a work of fiction. Names, characters, places, and incidents are products of the author's imagination or are used fictitiously and are not to be construed as real. Any resemblance to actual events, locales, organizations, or persons, living or dead, is entirely coincidental.

AVON BOOKS
An Imprint of HarperCollins*Publishers*
10 East 53rd Street
New York, New York 10022-5299

Copyright © 2014 by Gayle Kloecker Callen
ISBN 978-0-06-226796-2
www.avonromance.com

First Avon Books mass market printing: May 2014

Avon Trademark Reg. U.S. Pat. Off. and in Other Countries, Marca Registrada, Hecho en U.S.A.
HarperCollins® is a registered trademark of HarperCollins Publishers.

Printed in the U.S.A.

10 9 8 7 6 5 4 3 2 1

To Carol Lombardo, my dear Purple friend.
Writing may be solitary, but brainstorming is not.
I can't thank you enough for your generous help
in the birth of my stories, and for allowing me
a glimpse into your graceful handling
of the next exciting stage of our lives.
I'm taking notes. ;)
Your wit and your insight brighten my every day,
and I will always be grateful.

Chapter 1

Adam Chamberlin sat alone in his London study, preoccupied once again by the astonishing realization that he was now the Duke of Rothford—he, the youngest of three sons, who'd been called a scoundrel and a rake and worse by his own brothers. For many years he'd taken great pleasure in living up to that. He and his younger sister were the offspring of his father's second marriage to a much younger woman who'd brought little but beauty to the family, not property or connections. Adam's brothers had never let him forget it, although always out of earshot of their father.

He'd deserved Society's scorn once upon a time; he'd even reveled in it—anything to prove to his brothers that their threats and their condemnation didn't matter to him.

Before joining the army, he'd never been responsible for anything or anyone. But the Eighth Dragoon Guards had shown him that a man could be judged on his honorable deeds, not his ancestors or his money. He'd been able to start over, to support himself instead of holding his breath waiting for his father to die and his brothers to make good on their threats of cutting him off.

But that hadn't happened. Fate had intervened in a way impossible to predict, and he'd had to resign his commission. And now he, who'd never once even been allowed to know the responsibilities of a duke, was saddled with all of it, homes and estates and servants who all depended on him not to make a mistake.

He was very good at making mistakes.

Suddenly, he heard a sound, something tipping over on a shelf. He stilled, thinking that although Rothford Court, a palatial pile of rocks on Belgrave Square, was so cold as to be a cave in winter, it would hardly be permitted to have rats.

And then he heard a sneeze.

He relaxed back in his father's big chair. "Would you like a handkerchief?"

After a long moment, he saw her little head first, dark hair in a braid, face pale at her discovery. It could only be Lady Frances Chamberlin, his eldest brother's child, hiding underneath the long table behind his sofa. She was ten, and had been away in the country on his return to England a few months back. Now she stared at him with the wide blue eyes of the Chamberlins, and it was like looking into his brother's eyes. But instead of condemnation, he saw innocence and wariness and curiosity.

He stood up and gave her an exaggerated bow, hand sweeping across his stomach. "Lady Frances, it is so nice to see you again."

She bit her lip, and if possible her eyes went larger. But there was a hint of humor there, as if she found it silly that an adult would bow to her.

"I barely remember you," she said at last, voice hesitant and quiet.

He seated himself behind his desk slowly, not wanting to frighten her off. "You were four when I left. What do you remember of me?"

She was holding something clutched in her hand, working it between her fingers nervously. "Mother says you did bad things and that I should not em—emu—"

"Emulate me?" he finished for her.

She nodded. "How could I be like you? I'm a girl."

"Very wise. I certainly made mistakes when I was younger, but I hope I've grown up and learned my lesson."

She took several steps around the sofa and stopped. "You were grown up when you left."

"Some people don't think so," he said dryly. "Even I don't think so. I could be foolish. But not to you, I hope."

She shrugged. "I remember you putting me on your shoulders once and romping around like a horse."

He grinned. "I remember that, too."

"And Father caught us and scolded me."

Adam's smile faded. "He was scolding *me*, child, not you."

"You sent me a letter when he died. My governess, Miss Hervey, said I should keep it hidden from Mother, and I do so although I don't know why. It was quite nice."

How could Adam tell her that her mother believed every word of the hatred her husband, the ducal heir, had harbored for Adam? For no other reason than that he hated Adam's mother, that he feared Adam was their father's favorite as a child, until the two older brothers had conspired to turn their father's approval to dismay and then terrible disappointment.

Like so many people, Frances's mother thought he was worthless. He'd never felt that way about himself, had done his best to become a better man. He had so far to go.

"I had the fever, too, you know," Frances said solemnly, running her finger along the bookshelves that lined one wall.

"I didn't know. I am so glad you returned to health."

"Not my father or Uncle Godfrey or Grandfather. They all died."

"I'm so sorry, Frances." Adam nodded, not knowing what else to say. It still seemed so unreal that he was now the duke, the man with the power and the wealth, who'd once thought his army career the only thing that would keep him from genteel poverty when his brother inherited the dukedom. That power couldn't bring back the dead, couldn't absolve him of the guilt that lingered on the edges of his dreams. He still lived with the memory of unexpected battle, the emotions of fighting for his life, the triumph of winning—and then the vivid images of his men dead and dying.

He was trying to put it in his past. The investigator he'd hired was due to arrive any moment with the details that would, hopefully, give Adam some measure of peace.

Frances now stood at the edge of his desk. "You look sad, Uncle Adam. Father died last year. Great-Aunt Theodosia says we mustn't worry about him, that he's at rest."

"You're a brave girl," he answered, smiling at her.

There was a polite knock on the door. Frances stiffened and looked over her shoulder warily.

"I can't let you hide," he said with regret, "but if anyone asks, I will say I requested your visit."

She brightened.

"Come in," he called.

Seabrook, thin white hair combed meticulously across his pink scalp, bowed his head after he entered. "A Mr. Raikes to see you, Your Grace." He glanced at Frances, and if he was curious, he'd long ago learned not to show it.

"Thank you for answering my questions, Frances," Adam said. "You may go now."

She gave him a brilliant smile that Seabrook couldn't see, then skipped from the room.

Raikes stepped in after she'd gone. A private investigator, he was plump and bald, with a neatly trimmed beard—a man who looked so normal no one would give him a second glance. Adam assumed he was very good at using that to his advantage.

"Your Grace," he said, bowing his head.

Seabrook closed the door behind him.

"Sit down, Raikes." Adam leaned forward. "Did you find Miss Cooper?"

Raikes allowed himself a small, pleased grin as he sat. "I did, sir."

Adam let out his breath, then said mildly, "It took you long enough."

The man smiled, unperturbed. "That it did. It wasn't easy to find her."

"But I told you her brother's name and shire."

"Given that you served with him, it's a shame you couldn't come up with more, Your Grace."

Adam arched a brow at the man standing up for himself, letting his amusement show. "Yes, well, we were comrades, not close friends."

"And it would have helped if the lady would have stayed put. But she couldn't, Your Grace." Raikes cleared his throat, his frown marking his uneasiness. "She had to work to support herself and her mother after Sergeant Cooper's death."

Adam felt a stillness inside him, a disbelief and a gaping hole of guilt. It was his fault a gentlewoman had had to lower herself to earn her living. "What is her position?" he asked, trying not to imagine the worst. A desperate young woman could sink so far . . .

"She is a lady's companion, sir, hired earlier this year by Lord Warburton of Durham for his daughter."

Adam understood the plight of a lady's companion, the endless hours at the whim of another person. More than once his Aunt Theodosia had spoken of her disdain at the way some of her friends treated the unfortunate women they employed. He eased his stiff fingers, surprised to find he'd been clutching the arms of his chair. "That is not the worst employment a young lady can have."

"No, sir. And you're in luck. Her family has come to London for the Season."

At last, something was finally going his way.

"Tell me where she lives."

Miss Faith Cooper, unusually young for a lady's companion at twenty and five, was dressed in her usual dowdy, bulky clothes designed to hide that fact. But today she was feeling conspicuous; in fact, had been feeling followed from the moment she'd entered the curving pathways of Hyde Park. Pulling her cloak tight about her to combat the chilly temperature of the early Season in London, her entire focus was on her eagerness to be with the Society of Ladies' Companions and Chaperones, as they'd laughingly called themselves. Who else could understand and commiserate better than others who had to endure the whims of elderly ladies who could never be too warm, or the whims of selfish young girls who believed the search for the proper husband was the worst dilemma a woman could face? Sometimes one just had to laugh.

Faith had once known all about real dilemmas: dwindling money without dowry or the handsome features that might make up for it. All of this she'd overcome on her own, by means both scandalous and necessary. And though it was hard work helping a self-centered young woman during her first London Season, Faith relished the challenge of guiding the girl to maturity and happiness. Sometimes she felt like she was guiding the baron and his wife, too. They had been social leaders in their quiet village, and were now at sixes and sevens in Town.

All of these thoughts were on her mind when a boldly handsome man stepped into her path and forced her to come up short in surprise. Though he was tall, it was not his height that was overwhelming; it was his very presence, as if he knew he commanded attention and used that to his advantage. He wore snug trousers, polished boots, and an expensively tailored greatcoat that she suspected did not need padding in the shoulders. To her surprise, he doffed his top hat and gave her a brief bow, which so shocked her that she almost turned around to see if someone stood just behind. He had light brown hair that could almost be called sandy, tousled artfully by the wind. His chiseled face had harsh lines where a woman's would have soft curves, a nose that commanded attention, and lines about his eyes as if he smiled much of the time. Those eyes were blue and alive with interest and amusement as they took all of her in.

She hugged her cloak tightly, and though she was far too curious, she attempted to move around him. "Excuse me, my lord." For he had to be a peer, of that she had no doubt.

He grinned. "Miss Faith Cooper, I believe?"

She drew herself up, forcing down a frisson of nerves. "We have not been introduced, sir. This is most improper. Please step aside."

"Then allow me to introduce myself. I am Rothford. Have you by chance heard of me?"

In that moment of charged expectation, she thought she sensed a faint feeling of uncertainty emanating from him, but that had to be wrong. For he was Rothford—the *Duke* of Rothford—and such a man was at the top of the social ladder, of the House of Lords, and even of life itself.

She sank into a curtsy, but could not resist glancing up beneath her lashes to stare at him once again. Why was such a man introducing himself to a lady's companion? "Your Grace, surely you have me confused with someone else."

"You *are* Miss Cooper?"

"Yes, but . . . why would you know of me? I am newly arrived in London with my employer and his family."

She glanced around, certain that people must be staring. Strangely, the two of them seemed to be almost alone on this path. And since he knew of her, this could not be accidental.

"I have made it my business to find you, Miss Cooper," he said, still in that amiable tone of voice.

He came no closer, so she did not feel she had to run, but could only stare at him with growing confusion. "To find *me*, Your Grace? But why?"

"I served in the Eighth Dragoon Guards with your brother."

His voice gentled with regret and sorrow. Faith inhaled at the twin stabs of grief and frustration that always battled within her. Mathias's death more than two and a half years ago had stripped away the one source of income she and her mother had lived on. And then memories of her brother's rare letters flooded back. He'd mentioned the duke by name more than once.

"I see by your expression that I have the correct Miss Cooper," the duke said kindly. "I have spent the six months since my return from India looking for you. I knew the northern shire Cooper was from, but not the parish, and it took some time for my man to locate your village. But of course, you were already gone."

Her village? she thought, as a cold shiver of

wind seeped inside her cloak. What had he heard about her there?

"I offer you no cause for alarm," he insisted.

She schooled her features into impassivity, something she was usually so good at. "You have confronted me in a public park, Your Grace. That is suspicious enough."

"True," he said with regret. "But once I discovered your place of employment, I thought it would seem unusual if I were to call upon a woman employed by Lord Warburton. Would you have preferred that?"

His tone was wry, and she knew he teased her.

"Such behavior on your part could very well have jeopardized my position," she responded coolly. "But so can meeting a man alone in Hyde Park."

He looked around. "I did not think we'd be quite so solitary, that's true."

"Then let us be brief. You have not answered my question, Your Grace. *Why* have you been looking for me?"

"To offer my condolences, of course."

She blinked at him. "You could have written a letter."

The warmth in his eyes faded into sobriety. "That would be far too easy, Miss Cooper, and in no way respectful to the memory of your brother. We served together, and I was lucky enough to survive. Sometimes I believe I'm too lucky," he added with faint sarcasm.

Faith could only stare at him. Whatever was he talking about? Why would a peer question the blessings in his life while blindly risking her very reputation? "Thank you for your kind thoughts, sir. If that is all . . ." She gathered her skirts and made to step around him.

"Wait," he said, reaching out as if to take hold of her arm.

She pulled back, frowning, and he put up both hands.

"I don't mean to be rude or cause you problems, Miss Cooper. In fact, I want to help. I'd like to offer my services in any way that would be beneficial to you."

"Your services?" she echoed, almost gaping at him. This all felt so very wrong. "I need nothing from you, although I do appreciate the offer."

She didn't need a man to save her—that was in her past. She stood on her own now. He didn't try to stop her as she sailed past him, head held high.

"Miss Cooper," he called, "this will not do."

She paused and glanced back at him over her shoulder. "It will have to, Your Grace. Any further meetings between us would be highly inappropriate and unnecessary. Thank you for your condolences. Good day."

She walked off, her stride brisk and direct, that of an accomplished servant rather than the gentleman's daughter she had been raised to be. As she followed a curve in the path, she risked a look behind her. He hadn't followed, but he was still standing there, watching her, his expression bemused but determined. She should probably worry about that show of determination, but couldn't believe he was serious.

Yet her mind was flooded with curiosity. He'd been a cavalryman, she realized, her pace slowing as her mind settled. Why had a duke—or the heir to a dukedom—bought a commission in the army?

She tried to put away her interest when she reached the bench where her friends sat. Their expressions lightened with welcome upon seeing her, and relief flooded through her.

They were impoverished gentlewomen just like her: Jane Ogden, with a slight limp since childhood, worked as companion to an elderly woman; and Charlotte Atherstone, a chaperone nearing her middling years and well respected for her unmatched ability to keep her charge protected, even as she guided her into a proper marriage.

Faith liked Charlotte's work best, and aspired to such a position. It felt . . . motherly or sisterly to help a young lady find the perfect man, the perfect life. It was almost what she was doing with Adelia, but she herself didn't have the vast understanding of the peerage that Charlotte had, her own mother being so disinterested. So they had long discussions where Charlotte talked and Jane and Faith absorbed. Relationships among the peerage could be so complicated, but it was the sort of puzzle Faith enjoyed.

They all had the same afternoon off each week, Wednesday, and had randomly met in Hyde Park when a chill wind had blown off Charlotte's bonnet, and the younger two women had ended up chasing it. It had been refreshing for all of them to meet like-minded souls. Though they'd only met two months before, they felt almost as close as sisters.

Charlotte smiled serenely as Faith approached. "We feared we would not see you today. So Miss Warburton could do without you after all."

Faith sat down on the same bench as the two women, trying hard not to look back the way she'd come. If the duke had followed her, she didn't want to call attention to him—and surely he wouldn't approach her in front of witnesses.

"Miss Warburton is attending a musicale at her aunt's this afternoon," Faith said. "Plenty of relations for her to talk to. But tonight, the family and I will be attending the Earl of Greenwich's ball, her first engagement of this kind. Miss Warburton is understandably excited. I had much to prepare this morning before I could leave."

"You are her companion, not her lady's maid," Jane said disapprovingly. "I cannot believe they did not bring enough servants to London with them."

Faith shrugged. "I am grateful for the work, even if it goes beyond what I was told. And I've told you how satisfying it will be to me to help the girl find maturity and happiness."

"But without the extra salary, I'm sure," Charlotte said, frowning.

Faith was glad for the sympathy of her friends, but she steered the conversation away. They discussed Jane's elderly employer having her first visit from a relative in more than a month—the three of them occasionally visited the woman together, cheering her up—and how Charlotte's young lady had received a second inappropriate proposal that had to be turned down.

"She is devastated, of course," Charlotte said. "She doesn't understand that these men are beneath the expectations of her family, beneath her in means and in placement in Society. I heard the poor girl crying in her bed last night. She's afraid she will never find a husband, and doesn't want to hear that I believe she simply needs be patient. To a fresh young girl, who am I but an aging woman who never managed to marry?"

Though they gave each other sympathetic nods, Faith was having a hard time concentrating. She couldn't forget the strange meeting with the Duke of Rothford. She wanted to question her friends about him, but how to bring him up without sounding suspicious?

"Who do you think will be at the ball this early in the Season?" Faith asked, feeling foolish and curious all wrapped together. "I heard the Duke of Rothford has come to Town." *So very subtle,* she told herself with an inward wince.

Charlotte stiffened. "The Duke of Rothford? What do you know about him, Faith?"

"Nothing much," she answered truthfully.

"Though he'd been with the army in India for many years, people still whisper about the exploits of his youth," Jane said eagerly.

Alone much of each day, Jane loved to gossip good-naturedly whenever she had the chance. But then a chaperone or companion needed to know the background of every eligible man her charge might meet.

"I forgot you have only recently come to London," Charlotte said to Faith. "Perhaps word did not spread so far north about the faithless young man who gambled and spent money on entire wardrobes of garments that he boasted he only wore once or twice before casting them off. He participated in drunken duels, wild horse races, and hosted legendary parties."

Such a man had tracked down the sister of a fellow soldier to ask how he could help? It made no sense. Unless of course he had other reasons . . .

"And there were women," Jane said in a breathless, low voice. "Indecent women who became his mistresses—not that he ever had one for long."

A coldness settled deep in Faith's bones at the thought of those desperate women cast off at the duke's whim. "But . . . if he was such a wild young man, heir to the dukedom, why did he purchase a commission?"

"Because he wasn't the heir," Charlotte explained patiently. "He had two older brothers."

"I'm certain his father insisted he join the army," Jane said firmly. "How else to control such a young man? He could hardly be a minister."

"But how did he inherit the title with two brothers ahead of him?" Faith asked.

Charlotte's expression faded into sadness. "A truly tragic story. Last year fever swept the Chamberlin household, and both the duke and his two older sons died within hours of each other, while the youngest son was still in India."

The three women sat quietly for a moment in solemn thought, even as birds trilled around them and distant voices were raised and lowered as if floating on the wind. Faith understood what it was like to be told that your only sibling was dead. But did Rothford feel the same sorrow as she? How could he—he'd ended up with the title of duke, in control of vast estates occupying far corners of Britain and the world.

While she'd had to make a decision that banished her from home forever.

Chapter 2

But the following Wednesday, just when Faith had practically forgotten about the duke, he was there in Hyde Park again on her afternoon off. He was alone, both hands resting on the head of his cane, and he was watching her.

She saw him from a distance, standing exactly where they'd met the week before. Her heart started to pound—with anxiety, she assured herself. He looked tall and dashing, the sun glinting off the embroidery of his red waistcoat, his striped morning coat emphasizing the width of his shoulders, the narrowness of his waist. Faint amusement curled one corner of his lips, but those blue eyes were full of determination. She almost turned and ran.

But she'd never backed down from a challenge, had met every adversity with acceptance and resolve. Whatever he wanted from her—whatever game he proposed—she would make him understand she wasn't playing.

Keeping her steps short and ladylike, Faith approached him, then curtsied. "Your Grace," she said coolly. "I do not think our meeting again is accidental."

"Indeed it is not, Miss Cooper."

His voice was rich with assurance and confidence, the voice of a man used to getting what he wanted, used to command. She tried to imagine him in a life-or-death situation and could not.

"Have you given thought to my offer of assistance?" he continued.

She arched a brow. "There was no need to consider what I'd already politely turned down. Did you forget?"

"No, Miss Cooper, but I cannot disregard the fact that because of your brother's death, you, a gentleman's daughter, were forced to accept a position of employment. And I feel responsible."

She heaved a sigh. "That is entirely wrong of you, Your Grace. Unless you shot the rifle yourself—"

"I might as well have," he interrupted quietly, soberly.

The words of dismissal died in her throat, replaced by a lump of dismay and sadness. "What are you saying?" she whispered, forgetting that she stood in a public park with a man.

His eyes met hers with directness. "Miss Cooper, I have lived with the knowledge of my mistakes for well over two years now. Guilt and sadness mar my every day."

"Mistakes?" she echoed.

"I and two of my fellow soldiers made a decision that cost three men their lives, one of them your brother."

"What decision?" she demanded in confusion. She didn't know what to think, as everything she'd been through the last two and a half years seemed to mock her with futility. Had her brother died for nothing? It seemed appalling and infuriating, and so terribly, terribly sad.

"The words are indelicate to a lady's ears," he began.

"Do continue," she said between gritted teeth. "Death is an indelicate subject."

He bowed his head a moment too long. "It is. My explanation will sound as if I'm making excuses, but you wanted the truth. My regiment was escorting prisoners to a detention facility where they were to be . . . questioned."

"Interrogated, you mean, even tortured," she said indignantly.

"We believed so, yes."

"I know how to read, sir, and because my brother was involved, I learned to understand the meaning beneath the pretty words."

"In times of war, such measures are often necessary," he explained, "but these men seemed like starving villagers, and were in the company of their women and children. I was convinced that the information supplied by our superiors was wrong, and I persuaded my friends of this. We looked the other way as the prisoners escaped. These same men returned with reinforcements and attacked. Your brother and two other men died because of my judgment."

"Your judgment?" she said in a choked voice. She tried to put herself in his place, but she couldn't see starving villagers, only killers who'd taken Mathias away. "More than one person in London has believed your judgment suspect, sir. Do they not hold you accountable now?"

"Strangely enough, Miss Cooper, people seem determined to believe that mistakes happen. That is too easy a way out."

"And now you try to salve your conscience?" she said, appalled that her voice was shaking. But the enormity of the consequences of this man's actions seemed to be strangling her. Everything in her life had changed because of him. "Another easy way out?"

"You cannot believe this is easy for me, Miss Cooper."

There was sadness and weariness in his voice, but she had no sympathy for him. "What do you want from me?" she demanded, her own voice low and hoarse. "Forgiveness? You shan't have it. My brother is dead, and you are alive and dressed as London's finest dandy."

"No, not forgiveness. But allow me to help you in some way."

She drew her breath in harshly. "Help me? You

cannot. You cannot bring my brother back, can you?"

She saw a muscle clench in his jaw, but his voice was mild when he spoke. "No, and I regret that every day. But you are in need of assistance, and I can offer that, in memory of your brother."

Assistance? She wouldn't accept that from a man again.

"No, thank you," she said tightly and swept past him.

And then she saw her friends staring at her in shock, and she had no idea how long they'd been there or what they'd overheard. She hadn't known them long—what would they think about her? What would they say?

Jane took a limping step toward her. "Faith, that man . . ." she began, before trailing off.

Faith glanced over her shoulder, but saw only the duke's back as he walked away.

"He is the Duke of Rothford," Charlotte said slowly, her brows lowered in concern.

"I know. He introduced himself."

Jane's mouth sagged open. "Introduced himself . . ."

Faith would not hide this truth from her friends, especially since his behavior had made her look suspect. And he had not asked her to keep his secrets. "He believes his misjudgment in battle caused the death of my brother, and he offers his condolences and his help."

Charlotte narrowed her eyes. "That is quite the revelation."

"I refused him, of course. That would only make my position even more precarious."

Jane licked her lips. "Does he want you to . . . consort with him?"

Both Faith and Charlotte shot her outraged glances.

"Of course not!" Faith insisted. "He cannot possibly help me, and I would not accept."

"Still," Charlotte mused, "I am reluctantly impressed that he has a conscience after all."

"A guilty one," Faith insisted. "My brother . . . my brother knew he risked his life for the Crown, I know, but to think he might be alive today—" Her voice caught on her grief and her regrets. She and her brother hadn't been close, with parents who raised them without any discipline, in a manner that seemed uncaring. Mathias had had his friends and his own life, and left her alone. He hadn't consulted anyone when he'd impulsively joined the army. She'd felt surprised when he remembered them each month with a portion of his earnings. That had made her feelings soften toward him. But his death had put an end to any chance they might reconcile as adults.

"You cannot live in peace wishing the past were different," Charlotte cautioned.

"I know. But I can put it behind me and move ahead. I wish the duke would."

Jane cocked her head. "You almost sound as if he's being persistent."

Faith hesitated, then admitted, "He is. He tried

to offer me his help last week, and seems to want to ignore my wishes in the matter."

"Oh dear," Jane breathed, glancing with worry at Charlotte.

"I will ignore him," Faith insisted. "He will come to realize he must look to God for forgiveness, not me."

"But . . . he is a duke," Charlotte reminded her. "They are creatures who believe they can always have their way."

"Not this time."

But her friends didn't look convinced.

Adam watched Miss Cooper with her friends from the concealment of a wooded copse. He logically understood that he'd offered his help—twice—and been refused.

He couldn't blame her—and he couldn't accept it, either. Maybe he'd thought it would be simple: settle a sum of money upon her and ease his conscience. But from her every expression, he knew she would not accept that kind of help.

There was something about Miss Faith Cooper that seemed . . . fascinating. Approaching her friends, she'd moved with a calm grace that to him seemed to signify great control. As the three women spoke, their expressions ranged from serious to concerned, and he knew that was because of him. She had no reason to fear him, and neither did they. He would find a way to make her realize he only meant to help her.

Yet she seemed accepting of her life, the life he'd helped bring about. Well, he couldn't have it.

She was younger than he'd first thought, and he wondered if she took pains to appear other than her true age. Her black hair, already the severe color of night against her pale complexion, was pulled back simply at the base of her neck, no girlish curls above her ears. Her face was thin, her body well hidden in voluminous garments that protected her from the late winter cold of London—or protected her from other things.

But that face—cheekbones that emphasized the hollows beneath, darkly arched brows above pale gray eyes that flashed silver at him when she was angered. She was no great beauty, but her features were arresting when she wasn't in control.

But he suspected she was in control much of the time.

She and her friends walked away together, and he watched until they were out of sight. After that, he had no choice but to go home.

Seabrook took his greatcoat, hat, and cane in the entrance hall, which soared up three stories and ended in a domed stained-glass ceiling.

"Good afternoon, Your Grace. Your mother and sisters are in the drawing room preparing for callers."

"Then I should escape," he said, trying to get a smile out of the old man.

But Seabrook had been with the family for three generations now, and any humor must have long ago been extinguished.

Adam sighed. "Then I shall be the good son and brother and greet them."

The drawing room had frescoes on the ceiling and several fireplaces along the length, with groups of sofas and chairs scattered about. It was easy to pause on the threshold and not be seen, since he wasn't formally introduced.

His mother was still a beautiful woman, with blond hair that had already been so light that the whiter strands of age simply blended in. She was vain enough that she now used makeup to enhance her features, but her maid was so skilled it was hard to discern. She had a generous mouth made for smiling, and Adam's blue eyes, more beguiling and innocent on her. Not that she was all that innocent anymore, but she played it well. Men still regularly proposed to her, but as a duchess, she reigned supreme. He knew she'd never marry again, though he thought she might dally on the side.

His sister Sophia was the attentive daughter because she knew it was her duty, rather than experiencing a deep connection with their mother. Sophia was blond as well, a shade of honey, her eyes their father's green, her figure displaying the voluptuous curves she'd inherited from their mother. But her disposition was all her own: sweet-natured and kind, bright with opinions, and always generous with her thoughts. Sophia had written to him faithfully in India, letters he read over and over again in soggy tents while his candle sputtered. Once he'd inherited the dukedom, other women of his acquaintance began to write, but he valued them little compared to his deep tenderness for his sister. Even their older brothers could not fault her, and had let her be during her childhood. She'd been no threat to them, and there was plenty of money for her dowry. Of course, her beauty and disposition would bring the right sort of man to the marriage. Now that Adam was in charge, he would make sure she married the man she wanted, not the one who best suited the family.

"Ah, Rothford, you have returned in time to greet your legion of female admirers!"

Adam turned to the writing table, his aunt Theodosia's favorite place in the drawing room, where she kept up the connections that spanned the Continent. She was his father's only sister, long a childless widow, free to live her life as she pleased. She answered to no one's authority but her own, and her eccentricities were legendary, from gardening at night to protect her skin (even though the poor servants had to man the lamps to light her way) to cold baths in country streams to invigorate her heart. When their servants at their country seat heard that she was coming, none of them set foot in the woods for fear of encountering the naked elderly lady.

His mother had been a distant, beautiful woman he'd only seen after dinner each night of his childhood, but his aunt had been the one to see to his education, to scold his mistakes, to laugh at his foolishness, to be wounded by his thoughtlessness as a young man. And if she knew what his mistakes had cost in India, he might never receive her good humor again.

"Aunt Theodosia," he said, "you know my female admirers do themselves no favors by pretending to call upon my sister and mother only."

"Some girls are foolish in their youth," she insisted, her turban a crown upon her head, her necklaces stacked upon each other so much that only perfect posture could keep her from slumping forward. "You cannot hold that against them."

"And some *men* are foolish as well."

That subtly bitter voice could only be his sister-in-law, Marian, Marchioness of Tunbridge, his eldest brother's widow, who'd been betrothed to the heir in childhood, and had reigned in her mind as a future duchess. But his brother Cecil had died an hour before their father, never having inherited the title. Adam would pity her crushing disappointment if she weren't so effortlessly disagreeable. Marian was too thin, as if she starved her life away for an enviable waist. Her dark hairstyles, elaborate as cake decorations, sometimes left the maids in tears. But Marian did her best to seem regal and stoic, the tragic heroine of a novel.

He glanced at her, his mouth curved with amusement. "Do not paint all men with the same brush, dear sister. And I will do the same for your fair sex."

"Oh, I do agree that there are foolish women, Adam. Look how many pretend to call upon you?" she said in an overly sweet tone.

She'd never once called him by his title, and he knew it was deliberate. It didn't bother him, which secretly bothered her.

And suddenly it seemed very petty and pointless, especially when he thought about Miss Cooper, who worked to earn her keep. But not much longer, if he could help it.

Sophia approached him, took his arm, and led him toward the window. "You're frowning, Adam. What's wrong? I don't think I ever saw you frown when you were younger."

He patted her hand on his arm. "A title and its responsibilities will do that to a man."

"War will, too," she said softly, studying him with true concern. "You don't talk about it much. Nor did you write about it. From your letters, I would have thought you were marching through jungles to sketch the scenery."

He smiled. "It is in my past, not something I want to dwell on. And I certainly don't want my lovely sister knowing of the dark side of life."

"I'm not *that* sheltered," she insisted. "Aunt Theodosia takes me with her to her charities, and it's not all about sipping tea and discussing what balls to host. I've been to the East End. I've held babies as their mothers died. I've—"

He frowned down at her. "Where have you been, Sophia? If Aunt Theodosia thinks this is proper for a young lady—"

"Adam, helping people is important to me. Having the funds to do so only makes it imperative. I just want you to understand that you cannot always protect me, just as I can't always protect you. Although I wish I could have . . ." She trailed off, still gazing at him as if she could read into his soul.

He briefly glanced out the window at the carriages passing by. His little sister wanted to protect him. The sweetness of it tightened his gut. He remembered being twenty to her ten years, and leaving the room instead of punching his elder brother, only to find out later she'd been eavesdropping and rushed in to kick Cecil hard in the shin. Cecil turned her over his knee for that, and she hadn't made a sound—or so his other brother Godfrey had told him, enjoying Adam's fury that their little sister had been the subject of their punishment of him.

"We want to protect the world, Sophia," he said quietly. "Sometimes all we can do is one little piece of good." He thought again of Miss Cooper, and knew that Sophia would understand his focus, his need to make amends for all he'd cost this one lonely woman.

"Lord Shenstone left his card for you, Adam,"

Marian called as if she'd just remembered. "You and he used to make quite the fools of yourself. He says you have avoided his invitations. But we all know it's only a matter of time before you enjoy the pleasures of London again," she added lightly, perhaps slyly.

Adam thought of Shenstone, the scrapes they'd gotten into, the women they'd corrupted, the gaming hells where all of it had taken place. He didn't want to go back to those places, but in some ways those were the innocent, exciting times of his life. Now he dutifully escorted his aunt and mother to balls and musicales, where even touching a woman's bare hand was practically a proposal of marriage. Once he'd been ignored as a younger son; now he was the focus of the marriage-minded mamas and their eager daughters, even as others whispered behind his back. It almost made him long for the old days of excitement and temptation.

But he wasn't going to be that man again. The army had taught him honor—or at least he thought it had, until his terrible mistake. But he didn't just have Society to focus on. He'd taken his place in the House of Lords, and soon he'd convince them all that he had knowledge of the world, that his experiences would be useful. He'd find something meaningful to do with his life, to fill the void of something . . . missing.

"How concerned you are about others, Marian," Aunt Theodosia said, not looking up from the letter she wrote in her slow, laborious hand. "Do you have so little to focus on that you can call your own? Perhaps your daughter would like more of your time."

"You know she's in the schoolroom yet," Marian said. "She and I walk the park when her governess has her afternoon off. We have lovely discussions about her future."

"Or rigid outlines of rules," Sophia murmured for Adam's ears alone.

And that made Adam melancholy. He didn't want his niece raised to emulate her mother, who was fixated on her own life and still full of self-pity. She was out of mourning, yes, but she was looking backward, and that couldn't be good for her daughter.

Then with a sigh, Sophia rested her head against his shoulder. "I hear others talking about you."

"Still eavesdropping?" he teased.

"How can it be eavesdropping when they're speaking in normal tones? But I am not the only one who noticed the change in my big brother when he returned home from India. They keep asking when the real Adam will return."

"Never," he said simply.

"I don't know about that. I'm not sure you've quite found the *real* Adam."

He frowned and would have questioned her, but the first callers were introduced by the butler, and he had to don the face of the duke. His mother brought him forward, full of pride and delight, as if he could do no wrong.

She didn't want to hear the wrong he'd done—had never wanted to hear it, even in the old days. Then, she'd called him high spirited. What would she have said about his thoughtless confidence in India, where men had died because he was convinced he was right?

Chapter 3

Two days later, Adam was strolling Bond Street, waiting for his sister to emerge from the dressmaker's shop, when he saw the familiar bonnet of Miss Faith Cooper. He found his boredom gone, his mind alert for how he could approach her. He watched her enter a bookshop, and while he knew she didn't wish to be accosted by him again, he was convinced she was wrong to decline his help. It was up to him to change her mind.

She emerged onto the street again at the side of a delicate young lady, who immediately loaded a package wrapped in string into Miss Cooper's waiting arms, even though several packages already dangled there.

As if Miss Cooper was a servant, rather than a companion. He felt affronted on her behalf, guilty that her predicament was partly his fault, then filled with renewed determination to make things better for her. His own sister would never treat a companion that way—

And that was the perfect solution, he realized. Miss Cooper would not accept money or an open-ended offer of help, but perhaps she would accept a new position, a gentle one where she would enjoy his sister's companionship—and he could make sure Miss Cooper wasn't worked too hard.

He watched as she deposited the parcels in a carriage with the help of the coachman, then rushed to catch up to her young charge, who was entering a milliner's shop.

Adam made sure he was right in Miss Cooper's line of sight before she entered. He rested his shoulder against the brick wall, arms crossed over his chest, and grinned. She pulled up short upon seeing him, eyes wide and distressed, and he tipped his hat to her.

Pressing her lips together, she focused on the doorway as if she meant to go through, then whirled toward him. She passed by without speaking, stopped near the street as if looking for someone, and spoke quietly over her shoulder.

"What are you doing here, Your Grace, following me?"

When he straightened, she immediately said, "Do not dare to act as if we're speaking!"

He went back to lounging against the wall. "Very well, but I do assure you, Miss Cooper, that I did not follow you. Your appearance was simply fortuitous."

He nodded at two women who strolled by and blushed upon seeing him.

"If you're not following me," she continued softly, "then I suggest you turn around and leave."

"I cannot do that. We have unfinished business."

"We do not, sir. I want nothing to do with your halfhearted apologies and offers of assistance. As if I'd take money from you!" She inhaled a gasp and looked around as she realized her voice had risen.

Adam understood her anger—hell, he was angry at himself. But he wouldn't let that anger keep her from seeing what was best. "I promise I do not offer money, Miss Cooper, but a chance at a better life. I see how Miss Warburton treats you, like a lady's maid."

She stiffened with each word, until he thought her shoulder blades would meet, her back was so straight.

"My position is none of your business."

"Except that I can offer you better. Come work for me. My sister is in her first Season, and often feels lonely away from our country seat." That was an exaggeration—his sister made friends everywhere she went. "There are servants aplenty to deal with her clothing and her hair."

Miss Cooper blushed, proof that she'd been assigned such chores.

"I'm sure you believe you know what's best for your sister," Miss Cooper said impassively, "just as you seem to believe the same about me. I assure you that you're wrong. Good day, Your Grace."

She marched into the milliner's shop without another glance at him, and he almost followed her inside before catching himself. Such an error in judgment would not win her over.

"Adam?"

Upon hearing the call from behind him, he realized he'd almost forgotten his sister.

With a cloth wrapped about the handle, Faith guided the iron and pressed it against the skirt of Adelia's gown. She sucked in a breath at the sudden sting as she burned herself. Carefully, she set the iron back near the hearth instead of throwing it, like she wanted to.

She wouldn't have burned herself if not for the duke and his proposal. Who'd have thought she'd find another position alluring and forbidden all at the same time?

But all day long, as Adelia prepared for a dinner party and had Faith changing her gown and gloves and slippers over and over again, Faith had thought of nothing other than the duke's offer.

She imagined he would pay her more, too, and his guilt would keep him from overworking her.

She sucked on her burned finger and silently berated herself. She could not allow herself to be dependent on one man again. Oh, Lord Warburton was certainly her employer, but it wasn't the same thing as having a young, handsome bachelor take control of her life.

Handsome? Where had that come from? What did his looks matter, compared to what his behavior had wrought in her life? And now he was trying to make it worse.

But he thought he was trying to make it better.

That night, Faith almost begged leave to stay home, but for some reason Adelia seemed to need her nearby early in the Season, and Faith could not resist being needed. Young women at this stage of their lives could be so fragile. Occasionally, a title name slipped Adelia's tongue, or she couldn't remember who was related to whom and needed Faith's growing expertise. Adelia was the little jewel of her very plain family, the one upon whom all expectations of family prominence rested. For that, Faith pitied the poor girl and thought she could make things better.

Sometimes Faith found her own in-between status awkward, but she was learning to deal with it. If she were a lady's maid, she'd have eaten with the servants, but as a companion, she sat with the guests, where occasionally, no one spoke to her. She didn't mind; the food was usually delicious and listening in on conversations was the perfect way to learn more about Society. She planned to become the most sought after chaperone.

But that night would be different, because while she was seated with an elderly lady in the corner of the Randolphs' small drawing room discuss-

ing needlework, the Duke of Rothford was introduced. The whispers buzzed outward from him
like the rays of the sun. Charlotte, standing with
her charge, shot Faith a wide-eyed look.

"I did not think I could be surprised anymore,"
Miss Bury mused upon seeing the duke. "But then
again, I did not think this party could be anything
but dull."

She tittered and elbowed Faith, who forced a
pained smile to her lips.

"He's trying too hard to be good," the old
woman continued in a loud whisper that could
surely be heard by the next couple. "It won't last
long—it never does with young bucks. Perhaps
he's just trying to get himself a wife."

Or perhaps he's trying to prove something to
himself, Faith thought. Was Miss Bury right? Was
it only a matter of time before something bad
happened? If she went to work for him, she'd be
caught right in the middle.

Three women entered with him, two blondes
and a brunette. As if Miss Bury read Faith's
thoughts, she said, "Those women are his mother,
sister, and sister by marriage."

"Oh," Faith murmured, eyes widening.

The youngest woman must surely be his sister,
and Faith watched as she was surrounded by
other young ladies and led away, laughing.

And he thought she needed the help of a companion? she wondered cynically.

And then his gaze swept the crowd and

landed right on her. She flushed with heat as if he'd touched her. No, surely it was the worry that others had noticed. How would she explain herself?

But even the old woman at her side noticed nothing, so focused was she on the duke himself. Faith couldn't even look at Charlotte, who knew all about her improper meetings in the park with the duke.

"Faith!" Adelia hissed as she approached. "I caught my hem and tore it. I need your help sewing it."

Faith followed her out of the drawing room to the ladies' retiring room with relief. By the time they returned, the duke was already leading their hostess in to dinner, and everyone else followed according to rank. She trailed at the end along with someone's young male cousin from the country, who blushed to the roots of his hair when she smiled absently at him.

She sat on the far end of the table from the duke and his family, and she couldn't quite hear what was being said, only the laughter his words evoked. For a man concerned about mistakes he made in war, he put on a good show, entertaining the guests, flirting harmlessly with elderly women, and behaving more reserved with the debutantes. Faith overheard his mother praising his attributes, the seriousness with which he'd returned from war. Faith cynically thought the duchess didn't have to work so hard. When the ladies retired to the drawing room, leaving the men to their port, they could talk about nothing else but the Duke of Rothford. Everyone was ready to believe him reformed and eligible.

But she knew better, especially when Adelia sent her to retrieve her reticule and the duke appeared out of the shadows when she emerged into the corridor.

Faith gasped and put a hand to her chest, glancing up and down to see if they were alone before frowning at him.

And they *were* alone, more so than they'd been in the park or on Bond Street. They were dangerously alone.

"Can Miss Warburton work you any harder?" he asked softly.

She took a step backward. "Believe me, Your Grace, I would fetch a reticule for a sister or friend, why not Adelia? You make too much of how I help her."

"I don't think so. I saw your bare hands at dinner."

She clutched them together, though they were now hidden under gloves. "You could not have—we were too far apart."

"Not that far. You are embarrassed about their roughness, embarrassed about what you do."

"I may not like the look of my hands," she insisted, "but I am not embarrassed by respectable employment."

"I've offered you *better* employment."

"And I've refused."

He took a step closer. "I could push the matter."

She groaned and wished she could childishly stomp her foot. "And I will still refuse. I cannot make you feel better about yourself."

"That is not the point—*I* can make your *life* better."

She stared up at him in confusion, wondering how long it would be before he'd take her at her word. And then she realized she was standing too close, that he was leaning over her to make his point, that if anyone saw them—

And worst of all, she was actually *flattered* by his persistence.

Outraged at her own ridiculous sentiments, she mustered her dignity, stepped away, and said coolly, "No, thank you, Your Grace." What was wrong with her? The man's folly had caused the death of her brother, had made her what she'd become. "I do believe it's time you return to your triumphant tour of London. You are the talk of the town, which you must certainly enjoy."

He shrugged and leaned against the wall with that indolence that grated on her nerves.

"You know it is meaningless and it will soon die away. No one discusses anything of importance with me; after all, I was a scapegrace before India, and returning as the duke is of more interest to them than anything I might have experienced in the jungles of a foreign country."

She hesitated. "Anything you experienced— you mean anything you did."

"Yes, as you know, there are things I don't wish to relive by speaking of them," he said somberly.

She didn't want to hear that he suffered for what he'd done—it shouldn't matter to her. She took her leave, but couldn't get away from him, certainly not that evening, when the carpets had been rolled up in the drawing room for the dancing to begin. Adelia was flushed with excitement and happiness, more than once gushing into Faith's ear about possibly dancing with a duke. Faith at last moved away from Lady Warburton and her daughter and retreated to the row of chairs that followed one wall into the corner. It was the wall-flower row, where girls without partners waited with the elderly, the chaperones—and the companions. Charlotte was already there, an open seat waiting for her.

Sweet Miss Bury, the wispy-haired lady she'd conversed with before dinner, patted a chair beside her and Faith smiled as she sat, sending an "I'm sorry" glance at Charlotte. Not that Charlotte would stay seated for long. Her respectful employers consulted her frequently for her knowledge of eligible men, the best families, and everything Charlotte had learned over a lifetime in London. She was in demand and respected—the things Faith wanted for herself.

"I see your Miss Warburton is all atwitter about the Duke of Rothford," Miss Bury said conspiratorially.

"Yes, she is." Even a woman hard of hearing would have understood Adelia's words.

"He cuts a dashing figure." Miss Bury clucked her tongue and shook her head as the duke swept past, partnered with the prettiest girl there.

Faith nodded, but found herself reluctantly watching them. He knew the steps of the quadrille as if he hadn't been an army officer for several years—she wasn't sure how long he'd actually been gone.

They made a handsome couple, and many people seemed to be watching them, even though others lined up in the dance. Then he "graciously" offered his skills to other young ladies, including Adelia, who flushed and seemed to be breathing so rapidly she might have set off a swoon.

Then he started on the wallflowers, coming closer and closer to her chair with each dance. Miss Bury was beside herself at his generosity and consideration, talking about each young lady's future delight at being so singled out.

But Faith's unease and trepidation was growing as he came closer. He wouldn't—he wouldn't dare ask *her* to—

For a moment, a sense of exhilaration swept over her, the feeling of being the focus of a man's attention, something she'd seldom experienced.

Then she caught site of Charlotte's white face, the way she pressed her lips together in disapproval. At the duke's outrageous behavior? Or did she think that Faith had somehow called it down on herself?

Two seats down from her, His Grace bowed over

the hand of a plump girl whose mother swooned into her husband's arms at the honor of it all.

The duke met Faith's shocked gaze and smiled. She inhaled sharply, then escaped the instant they stepped onto the dance floor.

In the corridor near the ladies' retiring room, she leaned against the wall and simply breathed, her eyes closed with exhaustion—mental and emotional exhaustion at least.

Why was he focusing on her like this, teasing her—practically *flirting* with her? Of course he wanted his own way, a salve for his conscience, but was this how rakes got whatever they wanted?

And she wasn't innocent, though she was not married. As an adolescent, she'd become close to her neighbor, Timothy Gilpin, son of a baron. She'd spent her childhood exploring their library, and later, she'd explored more than that with Timothy. She'd been without a dowry, not pretty, with no prospects for the future. And her curiosity—and his—had led them both to an afternoon concealed near the river.

Closing her eyes, she dropped her chin to her chest and sighed. She'd always been too curious for her own good. But she didn't think her curiosity had led to her problems with the duke—no, that was all on his head. Surely he would grow bored with her soon enough.

At last, she reentered the drawing room—where the duke wouldn't dare to approach her, where she was free to watch him—and attached herself to Adelia. He spent much of the next hour with his sister and mother. His sister had a pretty vivaciousness that attracted much male attention. It was obvious that his mother still possessed the same lure, for she was no matron in a lace cap. Yet, she was still a mother, doting on the duke, and bringing him to the notice of her friends and their daughters.

Faith was very glad when the Warburtons decided to leave for home, so she no longer had to watch the duke and his family. But later that night, as she was washing out Adelia's chemise, she found herself imagining having a houseful of servants to help her with such tasks.

No, she would not think of such temptations.

At Rothford Court the next afternoon, Adam almost escaped his sister. She'd watched him curiously at dinner the previous evening, but they'd had little chance to talk since. He'd breakfasted before her, and she'd had a luncheon elsewhere. But they passed in the entrance hall when she was on her way in with their sister-in-law, Marian, and he had no choice but to allow her to drag him into the small family drawing room, with its more intimate seating that encouraged confidences.

He didn't have any confidences he wished to share, especially not in front of Marian, who had long ago mastered the art of looking bored and overly curious at the same time.

"You were quite the dance partner last night," Sophia said.

"After six years in India and Afghanistan, you surely cannot blame me for enjoying such pleasures." Adam walked to the window to stare out nonchalantly, making sure the women knew he had to be elsewhere soon.

"I hear the British Society in India is tolerable." Marian sniffed.

"Bombay and Calcutta have dances and musicales, all the usual entertainments, but sadly, I was not often in those towns."

"You wrote me from places with exotic names, like Mehmoodabad"—Sophia stumbled a bit over the word—"and Dubba."

"Believe me, the names are the most exotic things about them. You don't want to hear about such places," he chided. He thought of the dirt and blood and death, Afghani mountains, Indian jungles—all things he'd put behind him.

"Then tell us about your dance partners," Sophia said sweetly.

Trapped, he thought with admiration.

Marian eyed him. "You had a number of them, none of which were suited to your attention."

"Marian," Sophia said with mild reproof.

She shrugged. "It's true."

Sophia bit her lip.

"Ladies," Adam said, "I danced with the women who seemed the most eager to dance."

Sophia clapped her hands together. "It is rare

to see the other men disgruntled because you showed them up so. I thought you were kind to dance with the wallflowers."

He inwardly winced. He was glad to seem kind, when really he'd wanted to bother Miss Cooper, to force her to consider him and his offer. In the end, he *was* being kind, at least to her.

Or was he growing obsessed?

He glanced again out the window, wondering how much longer his sister would continue to tease him—and saw the actual object of his campaign. Miss Cooper was walking slowly past Rothford Court, staring up openmouthed, but not stopping.

He felt a rush of triumph—and attraction, which no longer surprised him. Miss Cooper was not your ordinary woman, though aligned with the wallflowers of Society.

"Ladies, excuse me," he said, heading swiftly toward the door.

"But Adam," Sophia called, "I wanted to ask you about Miss Fogge!"

"I'll return later!"

He hurried past the footman, who betrayed no emotion other than a widening of the eyes.

"Your Grace, shall I fetch a cloak?" he called as Adam opened the door.

"I won't be gone long."

Outside, he hurried down the marble stairs and the walkway to the gates. The wind picked up near the street, penetrating his coat, but he didn't mind the chill, because Miss Cooper had seen him. And increased her speed. The chase was on.

He glanced at the house once more, and saw the curtains move in the family drawing room. At the pace Miss Cooper was setting, he'd thankfully be out of sight of his sister before catching up with the woman.

Because who knew what Sophia might see?

And Adam felt himself coming back to life.

Chapter 4

He was coming for her—and Faith felt like an utter fool. What had possessed her to go out of her way to walk past Rothford Court?

But there was also a dangerous excitement making her breath come quickly, her heart pound, as she glanced over her shoulder and saw him threading his way through the light crowd, making people stop and gape at him. He wasn't chasing *her*, she told herself. He was chasing the terrible mistakes of his past. She was a means to an end.

If she rationally understood this, why did she feel this way?

Because he was a man, and he was showing interest. She was disappointed in herself. The duke's focus on her was bringing back excitement, the dark world of desire.

She was carrying a set of handkerchiefs wrapped in paper and string, finished with her errand for Adelia. Where else could she go? The duke was gaining on her slowly, as if he was enjoying himself, drat him.

The only safe place was the Warburton town house. When she reached the front door, she turned to give him a triumphant smile. It faded away when she saw him opening the gate. With a gasp, she fled inside, then managed to walk sedately past the butler and up the stairs toward Adelia's room, even as she heard a knock at the front door.

She swallowed hard, but could not believe he'd ask for her. That would cause too much talk, even for a duke.

She knocked on Adelia's door, and when the girl called for her entrance, she found her holding two different necklaces up in the mirror.

"Oh, Miss Cooper, do give me your opinion. I'm to have luncheon with Mama and her friends, and one of them is the mother of an earl and—"

Her flow of words was interrupted by another knock, and Faith hesitated before opening it.

The maid bobbed a curtsy and looked past Faith to say excitedly, "Miss Adelia, you have a very important visitor—a duke!"

Faith gritted her teeth even as Adelia's mouth dropped open and the necklaces fell unheeded to the floor.

"Shall I tell him to return when your mother is at home?" the maid continued.

"No! Oh, dear, Miss Cooper, whatever shall

I do? Mama would hate for me to miss such an opportunity—what if he never came again because I would not see him? Oh, oh, yes, I have you to sit with us, do I not?" she said with an eager smile. "I cannot believe it—a duke, come to call upon me!"

And what could Faith say to that? It seemed a cruel trick upon the girl, and Faith felt a party to it, which irritated her no end. She'd led the duke on a merry chase, and now she would be punished for it.

For punishment it was. Soon, she was curtsying before Rothford, allowing Adelia to introduce them as if they'd never met. Her cheeks were hot with a blush, and she imagined Adelia must think her flustered to be meeting such a lofty personage.

And what was the duke thinking? Surely he was pleased with his teasing—perhaps he thought all of this would make her simply give in to him. And *that* would not happen.

Like a good companion, Faith tried to pick up her needlework and retreat to a chair near the window, away from the two of them.

"Come, come, Miss Cooper," Rothford said, "I shall feel cruel to ignore you, is that not right, Miss Warburton?"

"Of course," Adelia gushed. "Miss Cooper is my dearest companion."

Faith reluctantly sat on the sofa next to Adelia, whose smile was so bright as to be brittle, while the duke took his seat in a chair opposite them.

He and Adelia exchanged remarks on the weather until the maid brought a tea service, which Adelia poured prettily. She was trying so hard and Faith felt worse and worse that the duke might simply be using her.

Or maybe he was using Faith to see Adelia—why did that give her thoughts of ill humor? But he'd been known to be in a fast crowd, to do reckless things, had he not? Perhaps he did not care if he hurt a girl's feelings. Everyone had flaws, including her—and her flaw seemed to be liking men such as he. She'd never known that about herself, had never met a rake and scoundrel before.

But he'd seemed so sincere in his grief at her brother's death, in his need to make amends. Which was the true man?

"Is this your first Season in London, Miss Warburton?" he asked after taking a sip of his tea.

"It is, Your Grace. If not for the trains, it would have taken us so dreadfully long to arrive. Are not modern conveniences wonderful?"

"I must certainly agree. Before the steamship, it took six months to reach India a few years ago. Imagine my delight on returning home, it took only six weeks."

"India must be a beautiful country," Adelia said dreamily.

Faith could not help glancing at Rothford's face, knowing what she did about his experiences in that country.

"I was not prepared for its beauty," he said

solemnly. "There are temples within the mysteries of mango groves, boating along the river at night, colored lanterns at the prows on the return, like many-colored fireflies. The native people often had their women dance for us, nautch-girls draped in scarves and jewels that winked in the torchlight."

Faith felt under the spell of the images he wove in her imagination, and saw that Adelia was all agog.

Then the duke's gaze focused back on them, and he cleared his throat before sipping again at his tea.

Was he embarrassed? She could not believe it of him, he of the bold, teasing words, and the determination to have his way, regardless of what she wanted. Didn't most men simply talk of their horses and carriages? That seemed the normal conversation Adelia had with her occasional young man.

But Rothford had found something to admire in India, even though it had cost him the lives of friends—although she couldn't quite imagine Mathias good friends with a *duke*.

"You make me quite want to visit India," Adelia said politely.

"Many young ladies do. There is a whole British Society in Calcutta and now Bombay."

"The heat, though—I do not do well in the heat. I much prefer the English countryside at the height of summer."

"And what about you, Miss Cooper?" the duke asked.

She pricked her thumb with the needle at his question, then hid it in her skirt pocket with her handkerchief. He smiled at her knowingly.

"Forgive my concentration, Your Grace, but what was your question again?"

Adelia shot her horrified look, as if Faith's conduct toward a duke shamed her.

"I wondered if you like the heat of summer or prefer the cool countryside?"

"Why . . . I imagine I do not have a preference. The summer's warmth can feel lovely after a long winter, but a woman's garments do not make the enjoyment of it easy."

Color stained Adelia's cheeks, and Faith realized it might be improper to discuss clothing with a man.

"Uh . . . I mean—I meant—"

"No, no, I understand your meaning," he said heartily. "Wool can be deuced uncomfortable in a man's suit, as well. A refreshing honesty you have there. Miss Cooper must be easy to talk to, eh, Miss Warburton? But then that's why you chose her as your companion."

"Very true, Your Grace," Adelia said softly. "Might I pour you more tea?"

He took his leave after the appropriate quarter of an hour, bowing to them both, until Faith could have rolled her eyes. After the butler saw him out, the maid pressed herself to the window of the small entrance hall to watch him walk away, until the butler sent her off with an ominous frown of disapproval.

In the drawing room, Adelia, too, was standing at the window, and Faith half expected a scolding.

"The Duke of Rothford visited me," Adelia said on a dreamy sigh.

Faith gave her a gentle smile. "He is a very polite man."

Adelia eyed her. "Even with your foolishness. Really, Miss Cooper, should not a companion be less easily flustered?"

Faith nodded soberly.

Adam was not going to abandon the notion of helping Miss Cooper, even though his impromptu visit at the Warburtons' town house had caused Lady Warburton to trumpet the news all over London, as if he were actively courting her daughter. Three days later, at another ball, he escorted his aunt, who gave up plans for the opera when he insisted she attend the ball with him. She studied him with narrowed eyes, then did not question him, only refused to change her gown, though Marian professed that it was completely wrong for a ball. But fashion had never concerned Aunt Theodosia.

In the carriage, his aunt studied him openly, and he wondered if she was looking for a weakness to exploit, so she could discover his purpose. That amused him, but he concealed his smile.

He shouldn't be enjoying the chase of Miss Cooper so much, especially since it all began with a tragedy he helped cause. It wasn't like the pursuit of a lover, full of intrigue and desire, but it was almost taking the place of that, which even he found strange.

At the ball, he remained at his aunt's side, though her friends tried to draw her into the refreshment room, and his tried to draw him to the card room. Lord Shenstone stood watching him, curly auburn hair somewhat subdued by Macassar oil. He didn't talk, only smirked, like Adam's fall from grace was only a matter of time. Adam nodded politely, but he wasn't ready to deal with the friend who'd once accompanied him to the worst places in London.

He spotted Miss Cooper standing with a group of dowdy-looking women near a wall, trying to look older than she really was. He ducked behind a column and pulled his aunt with him.

She rapped his forearm with her fan. "What is so important that we must be concealed?"

"I need your help with a young lady," he said. He'd given up thought of using his sister to lure Miss Cooper. Sophia was too obviously good at making her own friends, and Miss Cooper had seen that.

"Who are you talking about?" She blinked at him, then lifted her monocle and studied him like a bug disturbing the butterfly collection she'd created when she joined the Entomological Society.

"Miss Faith Cooper. But if she knows I've put you up to it, she'll refuse, and I can't have that."

"Do not tell me this is an amour of yours."

He raised both hands. "She is not. But there is a connection, and she has refused all of my offers of help."

"Of course she has. It is highly improper for a woman to accept help from a man unless she's of service to him."

He winced. "I don't wish to discuss that with my aunt. Just let me point her out to you, but don't let her see you're with me."

"Is she a shopkeeper you'd like to elevate?"

"Aunt Theodosia, you do not have to believe the worst of me anymore," he said sternly.

She eyed him with twinkling eyes. "I do not, believe me. But you were always such a scalawag, and since you've returned from India, some of the . . . spark has gone out of you. This is the most excitement you've shown since you returned. Perhaps you should explain."

He exhaled. "Just look at her first, will you? She's not a shopkeeper, but a gentleman's daughter from the North who fell on hard times because of me. She's the companion to the daughter of Baron Warburton. Do you know of him?"

"I know of the family, but he seldom comes to London, so I would not recognize him on sight."

He peered around the column and spotted Miss Cooper. "She's seated with the other wallflowers, third from the corner, ridiculous clothing and dark hair pulled back severely to make her look older."

Aunt Theodosia displayed her fan again and fluttered it before her face, leaving only her eyes visible between her turban and the fan. "Ah, I see who you mean. Quite a plain creature, for you."

"I've told you I'm only interested in helping her."

She leaned back against the column and gazed up at him. "Why?" she asked simply, all amusement gone from her wrinkled face.

The truth tumbled out, and he told her everything. Her eyes grew moist, but she did not cry.

"Oh, Adam," she murmured when he was done. "Surely in your heart of hearts, you know this was an accident of war, that you made the best decision you could, with the only information you had available."

"That doesn't matter, does it?" he said bitterly. "Her brother is just as dead, and she lost her only means of support. My actions have kept her from marrying, have forced her to work for a family that uses her as a lady's maid, for God's sake, when she's a gentlewoman. Three men died, Aunt; my friends Knightsbridge and Blackthorne are doing what they can to help the other two victims' families. I will not fail to do my part, even though Miss Cooper resists everything I try."

"Does she know why you want to aid her?" she asked gently.

"I told her the truth, and of course she's furious

with me, but . . . her rejection isn't all about that, I think, although I do not know its true source."

She nodded and peered back to the crowded ballroom, where Miss Cooper still sat, surrounded by older ladies and plain-faced sad girls.

"I'm glad you finally told me everything, Adam. It has been a black cloud hovering around you. Maybe now it will begin to lessen its hold on you."

"Three men are dead because of me, Aunt. I don't think that's something you leave in the past, like forgetting a friend's birthday."

She shrugged. "In my long life, there have been many tragedies I thought I would never get past, but in the end, our nature is such that the mind allows forgetfulness, that we might find happiness again."

He shrugged, unconvinced. "The death of a spouse must surely be one of those events. I know you loved Lord Duncan."

"Yet that is a sadness that women know most of us will eventually endure. But, Adam, I bore five babies that were either dead at birth or died within hours."

Shocked, he gazed down at her with wide eyes. "Aunt Theodosia, I am so sorry. I never knew."

"You were very young, and such things weren't discussed. But I found happiness again, Adam, and you will, too."

He didn't say anything, because he couldn't believe that. But helping Miss Cooper would go a long way toward restoring some of his equanimity. "So you will help me?"

"Of course I will. She looks like a fine young lady. Explain your plan."

And so he did.

She tapped him with her fan again. "Then I'm off. But I'll choose the moment I wish to approach her, so do not rush me."

He smiled. "I trust you."

She rejoined her friends and Adam found himself the recipient of welcoming smiles from mamas and their daughters. Not so much the fathers—until their wives elbowed them. He didn't blame them. He wouldn't want a man with his past courting his sister.

He had vowed to dance as much as he could to raise the spirits of young ladies—but it also had the side effect of unsettling Miss Cooper. She seemed to think he might embarrass her by asking her to dance, and although he knew it a bad idea, he wished he could. He wondered how she would feel in his arms, imagined her to be light on her feet, if her stride escaping him the other day was any way to judge. He hadn't bothered to catch up with her, because it was so enjoyable to watch the swish of her skirts from behind, and to realize those bulky skirts subtly disguised her as much as that severe hair. Where at first he'd thought her Cooper's elder sister, he'd since changed his mind.

"So you're finally away from the skirts of your family."

Shenstone's voice was soft and wry near Adam's ear, and he turned to find his oldest friend standing close, arms crossed over his chest, expression cynical and sardonic and vastly amused.

For a moment, Adam felt like time had not passed, that the two of them still ruled the underworld of London, where there were no rules.

But six years ago, Adam had broken away from his family, believing he had to support himself before that day when his brother inherited the title and showed Adam exactly what he thought of his "half" brother. Instead, Adam had made terrible mistakes, become the duke, and was now trying to be a different person.

He clasped Shenstone's hand firmly, and they grinned at each other. "Good to see you, old man," Adam said.

"Rothford." Shenstone looked him over. "I never thought I would call *you* that. Does the mantle of near royalty rest so heavy on your shoulders that you could not come among your lesser friends?"

"You know that's not true."

"Do I?" his friend said lightly, but his eyes showed no amusement. "I've heard you've been back as long as six months."

Adam blinked at him a moment. "I hadn't realized so much time had passed. I had pressing business to finish up after resigning my commission, and was in the North for some time." Chasing a woman—how Shenstone would laugh at that, especially since it wasn't for the usual reasons one needed a woman.

"I do understand that things have changed for you," Shenstone admitted, sounding almost reluctant. "You were never bred for the ducal 'honor,' and I imagine there might be a lot to discover."

Adam shrugged. "My father always believed in hiring the best men of business, including his steward, bailiffs, and land agents. They're still doing their work, leaving me with little to do to assist."

"You make that sound like a bad thing."

It was. Adam still had yet to find a way to be a part of his dukedom. He didn't want to simply benefit from the money and prestige. There had to be something else for him to do. He'd gone into the army looking for a purpose, and now that he'd had to give that up . . . well, he had yet to find a true substitute.

Except, of course, for his obsession with Miss Cooper. He forced himself not to glance in her direction. Nothing got by Shenstone, and Adam wasn't about to betray his interest—his purely professional and helpful interest.

"Together, we can find much to occupy your time," Shenstone reminded him. "In fact, tonight there is a particular hell that needs our attention."

Adam remembered the smoke of the dark rooms, the vivid décor, the roulette and dice tables—and the women. There'd been times, in his spiting of his father, that he'd disappeared into one for several days, and the memories were still not all present.

But now he was the face of his family, with duties to uphold, women to protect and guide, including his unmarried sister. He didn't want Sophia married to anyone like himself—or Shenstone. She deserved an honorable, educated, respectable man, who hadn't squandered parts of his life in the worst sorts of behaviors. And he would see that happen.

"I don't know when I'll next be able to visit our old haunts," Adam said.

"The Crown weighs heavy upon your brow?"

Adam chuckled, but Shenstone's smile was cool.

"The fate of my sister concerns me, the honor of my family. I seem to have to be a different sort of man now." India and Afghanistan had begun the transformation, but how could he explain that to Shenstone, whose only hardship had been getting ejected from Oxford, to his father's displeasure? "But just because the gaming hells cannot appeal to me anymore does not mean I'm against joining you at our club or the fencing academy."

"At White's? With the old men?"

"They're not all old," Adam said quietly.

"Next you'll be saying you're looking for a wife."

"Eventually I'll have to, shan't I? The heir, and all that."

"You're *choosing* this, Chamberlin—Rothford,"

Shenstone corrected himself. "Remember sweet Louisa, the actress you used to consort with?"

He did, and the memories were uncomfortably erotic. "She's in the past now."

"I refuse to allow you to do this to yourself," Shenstone insisted.

Adam eyed him. "I don't believe you have a choice."

"We'll see."

Chapter 5

Faith forced herself to relax when she did not see the Duke of Rothford. She saw his sister, sister-in-law, and mother, but if he was around, he was remaining in the card room with the other gentlemen. So as she watched Adelia and performed her duties as occasional sounding board and rest partner—the young woman never liked to be alone!—Faith also studied the dancers, especially enjoying the gowns of the women. Maybe she should make a study of fashion as part of her quest to become a chaperone . . .

And then, from across the room, she saw a face from her past. And he was watching her, too.

Timothy Gilpin, once her childhood friend, and then more.

She had come to him when her brother had died, when they were selling the paintings off the wall and poverty beckoned. She'd asked him if he would mind if she requested a letter of reference from his father, a respected baron whose library she'd spent hours in every day.

But Timothy, then engaged to be married, had thought her request would call attention to their past relationship. Faith had bowed to his wishes, owing him loyalty since he'd kept secret their relationship. But without references, she'd been unable to secure a position a gentlewoman would aspire to.

Did Timothy wonder where she'd gone when she'd left their village? Did he suspect the lengths she had to go to, in order to survive?

Now he was staring at her a bit wide-eyed, his face its usual paleness beneath his shock of red hair. And then he inclined his head toward her, and she did the same. He seemed to take that as permission to approach. After everything they'd once meant to each other, she wasn't sure what she felt upon facing him again, except wariness.

She rose to meet him, giving him a faint smile. "Good evening, Mr. Gilpin."

"And to you, Miss Cooper." He glanced around. "I had not thought to see you in London."

At such an exclusive ball, were obviously his unspoken thoughts.

"I am employed by Lord Warburton as a companion to his daughter."

"Ah, I see."

They'd once been close friends, and to see now by his smile that he was conscious of his superior station as the heir to a barony, made her sad.

When the silence stretched out, she said, "I remember that you were engaged."

"And I did marry."

"Is your wife in attendance?"

"She is not," he said swiftly, lowering his brows.

As if he wanted to make sure Faith didn't meet her. Very well, she understood that.

Or did he know what Faith had had to do to survive after her brother's death?

No, how could he? She'd moved to another parish, and her mother would certainly never tell people.

"Well, please give her my congratulations," Faith said.

Timothy nodded. "My thanks. A good evening to you, Miss Cooper."

He moved away, and she sat down, feeling a mixture of several emotions, but the predominant one being relief. What if she'd had to marry that man?

Oh, but in his youth, he'd been a fine companion, eager to run about the village exploring frog ponds and collecting unusual pebbles. They'd both loved to read, and the hours in his family library were some of her more precious memories.

And then in their adolescence, they'd begun to see each other as a man and a woman. Their first kiss had almost been accidental, both of them bent over a particular book in the library, then practically bumping heads as they turned to discuss it. She wasn't even certain which of them kissed the other first. After that, they were different with each other, aware of feeling an attraction, desperate to be alone to talk, hold hands, and steal more kisses.

It wasn't much later that the kisses became more.

"Miss Cooper?"

She blinked and brought herself back to the present. Before her stood a tiny elderly woman, and when Faith rose to her feet, the woman barely came up to her chin. She wore an empire-waist gown from another era, plenty of necklaces that jingled together with her slight tremor, and a turban wrapped about her head. She now studied Faith through a monocle that dangled from a jeweled chain.

"Good evening, ma'am," Faith said, curtsying. "Have we met?"

"No, we have not, young lady, and I decided to remedy that. I was looking for a place to sit and someone pointed out the open chair next to you."

Someone? she thought, but didn't question her.

"I am Lady Duncan. Do sit beside me and keep me company."

Faith waited until the lady sat down slowly, using her cane, before she took her own seat.

Sighing as she stretched out one leg, Lady Duncan said, "Ah, that is better. These sorts of events are such a crush, and I find it difficult to stand so much. People talk over my head, of course, and it grows most tiresome asking them to repeat themselves with all this loud music. You speak right into my good ear, Miss Cooper, and we'll get along famously."

Faith smiled at her. "May I fetch you a drink, my lady?"

"Oh, no, then I'll have to be in the ladies' retiring room all the time."

Faith blinked and hid a snort of laughter at such refreshing honesty.

"Eh, I look at all these foolish young girls, pining away for a dance, and I feel sorry for them."

"Why, ma'am?"

"Today's young man is too interested in himself, flitting about from his horse racing to his gambling to his pugilism. They don't wish to find a nice wife—they want to enjoy themselves until they're too old to make a girl a good husband."

Faith chuckled.

"Ah, but I am hurting your feelings, Miss Cooper. You are unmarried, and perhaps you wish it were not so."

"I am a realist, my lady. My features did not attract a young man in my youth, and without a dowry, I had to work for my living. No young man here would be interested in a lady's companion."

"Your youth? Are you an ancient, then?"

Faith looked around at all the delicate young women. "Sometimes I feel it."

"Do tell me your age."

"Twenty and five, my lady."

"Pshaw, I did not marry Lord Duncan until near thirty. I turned down seven proposals before him, and a few after."

"Seven proposals?" Faith exclaimed, delighted.

"A woman must be careful to find the man who will be indulgent to all of her activities. And my activities have always gone far beyond morning calls and the opera."

"And what activities do you pursue, my lady?" Faith asked.

"Women's rights!" Lady Duncan clapped her hands together, drawing several startled looks. "Did you read Mary Wollstonecraft's book, *A Vindication of the Rights of Woman*?"

"Yes, ma'am, I did. A fascinating study about women's education and upbringing limiting our expectations, not our gender."

Lady Duncan patted her knee. "I knew I was going to like you!"

They conversed for the next half hour, their topics ranging from women's rights to industrialization's effect on landowners to the latest novel. Faith forgot about the party, her duties, and just enjoyed the eccentric old lady's forward-thinking views and clever responses.

"Oh, it is difficult to have such conversations at home," Lady Duncan said, sighing heavily.

"I feel the same way, ma'am."

"There are too many silly women in your house, too?"

They shared grins.

"My dear, I think you should come accept a position with me."

Faith's smile died and she stared into the old woman's bright eyes. "Oh, ma'am, you are kind, but—"

"Do not think I'm being impulsive. Although I will not tell my family this," and she leaned closer, "but it is getting more difficult to write all the letters and speeches required of me. My hand tires far too swiftly these days, as do my eyes. Cursed old age, yet I am glad to still be suffering through it, instead of in the ground. I am not so anxious to join my late husband yet."

"You've made a generous offer, Lady Duncan, and I am flattered, but I certainly cannot leave my charge in the middle of the Season."

"And why not? Are you a poor relation?"

Faith grinned. "No, ma'am, I have no attachment except that I've given my word."

"Are you happy there?"

She hesitated, and then said nothing.

"So you are not happy, and from the looks of the Warburton girl, I imagine she's not good company for a mind like yours."

Faith blushed. "That is a generous compliment, ma'am, but I am in training—of sorts."

"In training? Do explain."

"I wish to become a trusted chaperone, not simply a companion. Surely it will be best if I remain with a young lady to learn more of what I need to know."

"I like a girl with plans. A chaperone first and foremost needs to understand *Society*, and I can teach you everything you need to know. Leave it to me, young Miss Cooper. I will see to our mutual happiness."

She started to rise with the aid of her cane, and when Faith jumped up to take her elbow, Lady Duncan peered up at her.

"One thing you can learn—unless I ask for help, I do not need you to offer it."

Faith quickly pulled her hand away. "Forgive me, ma'am."

"Of course I do. You act with sweet kindness. Until we meet again."

She limped away, crossing the middle of the dance floor, not even looking both ways. People cleared a path, even if they had to bump into each other in the middle of the waltz.

Faith covered her mouth to hide her laughter. She slowly sank back into her chair, dazed and hopeful, but she was used to not expecting much. And then she had a thought—she hadn't mentioned her employer's name. How had Lady Duncan known it?

Oh, whoever had pointed out Faith must have told her.

"Miss Cooper, please come with me to the ladies' retiring room," Adelia called, moving past Faith's chair without even stopping.

Faith rose up, trying not to sigh.

And trying to remind herself that for all she

knew, Lady Duncan would entirely forget their conversation by the next morning.

But instead of forgetting the conversation, Lady Duncan arrived midmorning, before the Warburton ladies had even gone shopping, let alone were expecting visitors. Faith heard about her arrival while she was working on Adelia's hair.

Lady Warburton came into the room, wearing a pinched frown. "We have a visitor, Adelia, the Countess of Duncan. Do hurry preparing her hair, Miss Cooper."

Faith's hands had slowed to a stop on hearing the name of their visitor, but she quickly pinned up the last curls, leaving a few to dangle artfully near Adelia's ears. Her pulse was fluttering with excitement, even as she told herself to calm down.

The young woman frowned, but her mother snapped, "It will have to do. Ladies? The countess is waiting."

But to their surprise, Lady Duncan was not in the drawing room, where the butler had left her. Faith let out her breath, not believing that she'd come all this way just to change her mind.

And then they heard voices, and followed the sound downstairs to Lord Warburton's study.

Lady Duncan was seated before his desk, hands clasped on her cane. She turned her head and smiled. "Ah, your lovely family. Do introduce me, Warburton."

Standing up, he cleared his throat, giving his wife a frown as he said, "Lady Duncan, may I introduce my wife, Lady Warburton, and our daughter, Miss Adelia Warburton. And of course, you tell me you've already met Miss Cooper," he added coolly.

Faith bit her lip and curtsied with the other ladies.

"I did not realize you had met my daughter's companion, Lady Duncan," Lady Warburton said.

"Oh, yes, just last night at the ball. We had a lovely conversation. I was just telling your husband that I wish to hire her away to work for me."

The stark silence was only broken by Lord Warburton's harrumph. Lady Warburton's eyes were narrowed as she focused on Faith.

"Miss Cooper, you wish to leave us?"

"Oh, no," Lady Duncan interrupted. "She was quite loyal. But I insisted. I have quite the connections at the registry office. I have already alerted them to expect you, and to recommend their best companion and even a lady's maid, if you'd like."

Faith tried not to flinch. She did not want her employers to believe she had complained about the amount of work she'd been given.

"They'll even grant you the same wage price they guarantee to me, since I have hired so many servants."

The Warburtons exchanged a meaningful glance.

"But I've grown quite attached to Miss Cooper," Adelia said stubbornly.

"And I can understand why, my dear," answered the old lady. "But Miss Cooper is an ardent believer in women's rights, and I have use for such a mind."

"Women's rights?" Lord Warburton said, his nostrils flaring.

Oh, Lady Duncan was playing this perfectly, Faith thought with admiration.

"Have you expressed such sentiments to my daughter?" Lady Warburton demanded.

"I have not, my lady," Faith quietly said. "I did not think you wished me to converse about my beliefs."

"And you thought correctly," the woman retorted. She turned to her husband. "I believe Miss Cooper might serve Lady Duncan well."

"But—" Adelia began, only to be shushed by her mother.

Faith gave her a regretful look. Perhaps the girl really did value her opinion and assistance. But Faith's hands were chapped and painful, and she fell into bed exhausted each night.

"Will you mind if I take Miss Cooper with me right now?" Lady Duncan asked.

"Oh, no, my lady, I couldn't," Faith insisted. "Miss Warburton has an outing with friends at Vauxhall Gardens tonight, and I must help her prepare."

"You, a lady's companion, help her to dress?" Lady Duncan said doubtfully, eyeing Lady Warburton.

"No, no, of course not," Lady Warburton hurriedly said. "Lady Duncan, if you'd like Miss Cooper's companionship this evening, I'm certain it can be arranged."

"Very good," Lady Duncan said, rising to her feet. "I'll send my carriage around for Miss Cooper and her things this afternoon."

She limped from the room without waiting for an escort, leaving Faith standing alone with the Warburtons looking at her. The baron's expression was disgruntled, as if only the extra work of hiring a new servant bothered him. But Adelia and her mother looked both betrayed and suspicious.

With a huff, Adelia turned her back and flounced out of the room.

Lady Warburton said stiffly, "Have you been so unhappy with your employment, Miss Cooper?"

Without having to lie, Faith said, "Ma'am, I have not been looking for another position. Lady Duncan's offer was just as surprising to me as to you. I did not wish to offend you in any way."

"I would have said you could have refused the offer, but Lord Warburton does not care for servants with ideas of equality, so this is for the best. Do go pack your things."

Faith didn't bother to bristle at the label "servant." She was simply happy for so little drama with her departure. She curtsied again. "Thank you for your kindness, my lady."

Not six hours later—and after being ignored

by Adelia all day—Faith was in an expensive carriage alone, being driven to her new home.

She was having second thoughts, only in that she hadn't even done any research, had simply accepted Lady Duncan for what she seemed to be. But the Warburtons had obviously known of her, and she'd attended an exclusive ball. So if things turned out badly, Faith had only herself to blame.

But the carriage was soon driving through Belgravia, then stopped on the square itself. Faith eagerly opened the door before the coachman could—and saw Rothford Court looming up before her. Her mouth sagged open, and she prayed the traffic was so bad that the coachman couldn't pull up before the house next door.

And then she realized that the coachman was waiting for the gate to be opened, and she had to close the door as she was driven within the grounds of the duke's home.

She felt sick inside at the manipulation. Obviously, Lady Duncan was acting on the duke's behalf. Were they related? Faith should have studied her *Debrett's Peerage* better, but she was always so busy. If he had coerced an old woman to do his bidding, why, that was simply terrible.

And this was what Faith's carelessness had wrought: she was out of a perfectly acceptable—if overworked—position. She felt trapped by the duke, ready for pride's sake to simply quit. But of course she had her mother to support, and although she had her initial letter of reference, she was certain the Warburtons would not give her one for abandoning them. If she begged for her position back, things would be even worse for her.

Faith reluctantly decided to play the hand she'd been dealt, to see what Lady Duncan had to say for herself.

Though she did not enter through the servants' door, the coachman did drive up to the side entrance rather than the main portico of the mansion—no town house, this, though it be in the middle of London. Once she was inside, a smiling middle-aged woman greeted her, wearing a plain black gown with a lace collar, a large ring of keys dangling from her belt.

"Miss Cooper, I am Mrs. Morton, the housekeeper. Lady Duncan told us to expect you. Welcome to Rothford Court."

"Thank you, Mrs. Morton. Would Lady Duncan be available?"

"No, she is out paying calls, but she assures me you will be having dinner together. I'll give you a brief tour of the house while the footmen see to your trunk, and then you can relax in your room until dinner is announced."

"Would you mind if I ask you one awkward question?"

"Of course. I will do my best to answer."

"How is Lady Duncan related to the duke? She never quite said. She might simply be a distant relation, for all I know."

Mrs. Morton nodded. "A wise question. Lady

Duncan is the older sister of the late duke, and therefore the aunt to the current duke."

"I see. I never thought to inquire myself," she added, trying not to blush.

Faith did her best not to gape as she followed the housekeeper through the public rooms, the drawing rooms, gallery, public and private dining rooms and breakfast room, and so many others that her head spun from trying to keep the layout straight in her mind. Everywhere were marble columns and frescos, gilt trim, fan-vaulted ceilings, and medieval tapestries.

And the library—it rose two stories high, with little secluded window seats and cozy, deep chairs. The smell of leather was intoxicating, and she inhaled deeply. Mrs. Morton smiled.

Faith was looking forward to the solitude of her own room until the housekeeper led her into a room nowhere near the servants' quarters, with a massive four-poster bed hung with curtains, gilt furniture, and embroidered curtains on the windows, all styled in soothing blues and creams.

She didn't want to appear provincial by asking if this bedroom was really for her, for obviously Mrs. Morton knew where she wished to put Faith. But she must have looked a little dazed, for the housekeeper smiled at her.

"You must be a special young woman, because Lady Duncan has never tolerated even the suggestion of needing a companion."

Or the duke was a persuasive man, Faith thought with frustration.

"You will find yourself well treated, Miss Cooper, although there is always a . . . personality or two among the family. As for dinner, I will have someone bring you down in time to meet the family. You'll be dining with them."

Of course she would, Faith thought, trying not to wince.

"Shall I send up a maid to help you unpack?"

"No, thank you for the kindness, Mrs. Morton."

"Then have a good rest."

And Faith was soon alone. She walked slowly to the window and stared out at the beautiful garden within the walls that encircled the mansion. She sat in the window seat and surveyed everything that was being offered to her.

To appease a guilty man's conscience.

She tried to tell herself that this was no different from being under Lord Warburton's control—it was probably better, for the duke wished to help her.

But she hadn't heard promising things about his past. What if he hadn't changed? Could she count on Lady Duncan to protect her? Everyone in the household was a stranger, none of whom cared about her.

And none of them knew what scandalous deeds she'd committed in her past. She'd be unceremoniously banished from the house if they knew.

She closed her eyes. The weight of the secret was sometimes so heavy.

Chapter 6

Faith had always been careful not to own any flattering gowns—she'd always wanted to project the air of an aging spinster, so she wore gowns a few years out of date, extra petticoats to give herself a fuller waist, and all of them could easily be removed alone. She changed into a fresh gown, and was waiting when a maid came for her.

The maid introduced herself as Ellen, but didn't meet her eyes. She was a short, pale girl with limp hair, so blond as to be almost white, pulled back beneath her cap. Her lashes were pale, her eyes water green—she could have been a ghost, especially with the white maid's uniform and apron. She silently led Faith down through the house, while Faith congratulated herself on remembering the way. She led her toward one of the smaller drawing rooms, obviously for the family, and Faith found herself tensely awaiting an introduction—

and bracing herself for her first proper meeting with the duke.

Ellen gestured through the open doors, but did not precede Faith inside. Taking a deep breath, Faith stepped into the doorway and paused. She had only the briefest moment to take in the scene, several women standing and sitting as they awaited their meal, the seated ones chatting, one lounging on a chaise, another standing near the window. The Duke of Rothford was nowhere in sight, thank God. Faith was worried she'd be unable to hide her anger.

"Miss Cooper!" cried Lady Duncan, using her cane to rise slowly to her feet. "I am so glad you arrived without any problems. Come, do come in and allow me to introduce you to the family."

Faith thought her anger might arise toward Lady Duncan, but she found it dissipating in the face of the woman's cheerful, pleased expression. She was only doing the duke's bidding, and he ruled the household.

Lady Duncan turned to the woman leaning back on the chaise longue, who idly lowered her book to her lap. Faith recognized her as the duke's mother.

"Damaris," Lady Duncan said, "please welcome my new companion, Miss Faith Cooper. Faith, Her Grace, the Duchess of Rothford."

Faith sank into her best curtsy. "It is a pleasure to meet you, Your Grace."

"Likewise," the duchess answered, then flicked

a lazily interested glance at Lady Duncan. "Your new companion?"

"She will be living with us here, yes. I've already discussed it with your son."

"I never thought you'd admit to needing help, Aunt Theodosia," said the thin, brittle woman standing near the window, her elaborate hairstyle seeming to defy physical laws.

"Marian, this is Miss Cooper. Lady Tunbridge is the duke's sister by marriage."

"A pleasure, ma'am," Faith murmured, feeling pity for the woman whose husband had died.

Lady Tunbridge nodded coldly and went back to looking out the window. The duke's young sister was introduced last, and she rose to her feet to give Faith both her hands, as if they were equals in Society.

"Miss Cooper, I am Lady Sophia. What a pleasure it is to meet you."

Faith couldn't help giving the woman a warm smile. "It is the same for me, Lady Sophia."

"Now you must not feel neglected," Lady Sophia said in a conspiratorial voice, her eyes twinkling at Lady Duncan. "My aunt Theodosia is quite proud of her independence. You might end up reading away your days, waiting for her to need your help."

Lady Duncan waved a hand, with a "Pshaw," but she seemed pleased with the observation.

"I'll gladly keep her company if that's all she

wishes," Faith insisted, "just in case she needs something of me."

"Quite obliging, aren't you?" Lady Tunbridge said. "But then, you're being paid for the position."

"Marian," Lady Duncan said coldly. "Not everyone is as fortunate as you are."

"I, fortunate?" the woman shot back. "I am a widow whose husband died tragically. Where is my good fortune?"

The duchess frowned and kept reading her book, even as Faith schooled her features to impassivity.

"I believe you had many fine years with my nephew," Lady Duncan said sternly, "and the result is a beautiful daughter. Will she be joining us for dinner?"

"Of course not," Lady Tunbridge said with exasperation. "She has many years left in the schoolroom. She ate in the day nursery with her governess. I will see her before she goes to bed."

Lady Duncan and Lady Sophia exchanged a glance that seemed to pity the little girl. But Lady Tunbridge had already turned back to the window and missed the exchange.

And then with no fanfare or introduction, the Duke of Rothford stepped into the drawing room. Faith didn't know where to look, so aware was she of their improper, private conversations, her anger at his highhandedness—and how very masculine he was in a room full of women. His light brown hair was rumpled, as if he'd run his hands through it. She couldn't believe he was nervous upon facing her—no, he'd gotten what he wanted.

And when his blue eyes alighted on her, she kept herself from flinching by sinking into another deep curtsy.

Lady Tunbridge made a muffled sound very like a snort, then turned away again.

"Adam, we have a new member of our household," Lady Duncan said. "Shall I introduce you?"

Faith knew the coincidence would be too great for the duke not to be involved, but perhaps Lady Duncan did not know they'd already met. Faith took the reins into her hands so he couldn't make things worse than he already had. "The duke and I have briefly met, my lady. He once called upon Miss Warburton. I was her lady's companion," she explained to the others in the room. Not a lie, but not the whole truth either.

"Adam," Lady Duncan continued, "Miss Cooper is my new companion."

Rothford gave her a brief nod, his smile pleasant but distracted, as if politeness were necessary, but nothing else. As if he didn't really need to notice her. Part of her was relieved—if he could carry this off, then maybe she wouldn't have to leave with no position to go to—but part of her was offended.

And why was she offended? She certainly didn't want the duke to treat her as anything other than his aunt's companion, a woman who meant nothing to him. She'd never wanted to be the symbol of his guilt he'd made her out to be.

Or did she want him to notice her because he was an attractive man? And that was ridiculous. She'd seen many attractive men, and she was beyond their notice, a creature from the wallflower row along the ballroom. And he was a duke, for heaven's sake, the highest aristocracy next to royalty. Now that his conscience felt appeased, he would stop noticing her, too. He already had.

Dinner was announced before another word could be said—the butler had obviously been awaiting the duke—and the family entered the private dining room in no formal order. Lady Duncan took Faith's arm and brought her near the far end of the table, and gestured for her to sit beside her. The duke sat at the head, of course, his mother on his right, his sister on his left. Lady Sophia sat on the other side of Lady Duncan, and across from her, Lady Tunbridge.

Course after course was served, and Faith listened to the flow of conversation, even as the exquisite taste of each dish seemed to cause a little burst of awareness in her mouth. The food was far superior to the Warburtons'. There had never been an extravagance of money when she was growing up, so as an adult out in the world, she'd first noticed the differences in the variety of foods. She had to go on long walks to keep her figure.

And she was still obsessed by the food, the

crimped cod and oyster sauce, grilled mushrooms and partridge breasts at the duke's table.

"Miss Cooper?"

She suddenly realized that the duke himself had spoken her name, and she looked up from her plate, wide-eyed. "Yes, Your Grace?"

He must have called her name more than once, for Lady Duncan gave her a friendly, amused smile to counter Lady Tunbridge's disdain.

And then she was the focus of the duke's blue eyes, which revealed nothing but polite interest, when recently they'd smiled into her own with wicked deliberation.

"Miss Cooper, since you were working as a companion for another family you must have made quite the impression for Aunt Theodosia to be so bold—because she's never bold," he added, smiling at his aunt.

Faith felt awkward, guessing he'd put her up to it. And she certainly hadn't made the right kind of impression on him!

Lady Sophia tried to reassure her. "Aunt Theodosia is the boldest woman I know. She's been to Egypt—twice! Nothing can stop her once she sets her mind on something."

"Miss Cooper and I had a lovely discussion about the place of women in Society," Lady Duncan said, a napkin tucked into her neckline. "I immediately knew we would relate well to one another."

"Are you still fixated on this women's-rights issue?" Lady Tunbridge asked, frowning.

"Do you not care that we cannot control our own property?" Lady Duncan demanded. "That we cannot vote for our country's future, that a man can beat his wife and be within the law, but beat his friend and be arrested?"

"It has always been like that," Lady Tunbridge said, pointing with her spoon, "and yet we women find a way to get what we want."

"Not the vote," Lady Duncan said. "Not the property that was mine. When I married, my husband was granted all of my property—not my dower property, of course," she said in an aside to Faith. "And then he died without issue, and all of the land that was mine went to his heir. Yes, he could have provisioned better for me, but we never thought he would die so young."

"He had sixty years," said the duchess for the first time. "I don't believe he was all that young."

Lady Duncan sighed, her wrinkled face relaxing into a reminiscing smile. "He seemed young to me."

"He only seemed foolish to the rest of us."

Faith could have sworn Lady Tunbridge mumbled those words, but Lady Duncan only cupped an ear and said, "Eh, what?"

Lady Tunbridge blinked at her. "Nothing."

The duchess's stare at her stepson's late wife was confused, but it cleared as she turned back to Lady Duncan. "You had us to help you, Theodosia."

"And I was one of the lucky ones," Lady Duncan

insisted, then beamed a smile at her nephew. "And you've all been good to me. But not every woman is so lucky. And that is just criminal."

"But not a crime," Lady Sophia said on a sigh.

"It should be, do you not agree, Miss Cooper?" Lady Duncan asked.

Faith glanced at the duke, uncertain of her place here. He'd wanted to hire her to soothe his guilt, but she was still closer to a servant in this grand household. How freely could she speak?

But then again, it wasn't her choice to be here after all—the duke had taken away her choices, because as a man and a peer, he could.

Clearing her throat, she spoke calmly. "I do believe women should have the same rights as men. Of course, some men treat their wives well, but too many do not."

"Here, here," said Lady Duncan, lifting her wineglass as if in a toast. She took a deep sip. "Ah, that goes down well."

Faith smiled at her, then looked around the table. The duchess looked bored, Sophia approving, Lady Tunbridge disdainful, and the duke—she wasn't sure what she was supposed to read from his expression. She might well be a very interesting insect, so far beneath him was she in Society.

But she had to admit that thought did not do justice to the man who thought he was helping her.

Who thought he knew best, she reminded herself.

He'd thought that once before, and men had died. Had he not learned his lesson?

"Where are you from, Miss Cooper?" Lady Sophia asked, leaning forward to see Faith on the other side of her aunt.

"The far north, my lady, a small village near the Scottish border."

"You came very far for the opportunity of a position," she responded.

"I was hired by the Warburtons in Durham, and came south with them for the Season."

"So you are relatively new to our fair Town," Lady Sophia said with obvious delight. "Are you enjoying it?"

"It has pleasant entertainments, of course, but it is so very crowded."

"And let's not forget dirty," Lady Tunbridge added.

"You could remain in the country, Marian," the duke pointed out.

"Even the dirt is better than such a solitary life year round," the woman conceded.

"Do you prefer the country, Miss Cooper?" Lady Duncan asked.

Faith smiled. "It's what I've known the most of. Please do not take offense, Lady Tunbridge, but I do enjoy the peacefulness, the scents of the garden, my hands in the dirt—"

"Don't forget the farm odors," Lady Tunbridge interrupted.

"I don't even mind those."

"Wait until you see Rothford's country seat this autumn," Lady Duncan said, patting her arm. "It is so restful and lovely, you will never want to leave."

Lady Duncan was making plans for months ahead, when Faith still didn't know if she could work for a man who'd manipulated her. But it would be Lady Duncan she'd be spending time with, she reminded herself, not the duke.

"Do you have family, Miss Cooper?" Lady Sophia asked.

Trying not to feel tense, Faith answered, "I do, my lady. My widowed mother still lives in our village."

"And you probably provide some of her support," the young woman said with sympathy.

Faith nodded.

"Any siblings?"

She didn't look at the duke, she couldn't, because suddenly she thought that his sister still had him, and Faith had no brother to grow old with.

"My brother died serving in the army, Lady Sophia," Faith said quietly, "just over two years ago."

And then she felt a new grief, of being unable to speak of his regiment, for all would know he'd served with the duke, and that Faith's employment could be no coincidence.

The young woman inhaled. "Oh, dear, I am so sorry to remind you of your sorrow, Miss Cooper."

"I am not alone in having lost loved ones, Lady

Sophia, especially not as this table. I know you all understand how I feel."

And although her words had been about the three widows sitting at the table, she couldn't help noticing that the duke set down his fork just after picking it up, then took a healthy swallow of his wine. She almost felt like she was throwing her brother's death in his face, but she hadn't been the one to bring it up—nor should she feel bad for discussing it.

But guilt and remorse were powerful emotions, and she'd felt them herself. She wanted to hold on to her anger over her brother's death, but she couldn't. The duke hadn't wanted him to die, hadn't deliberately made it happen.

But that didn't mean she could forgive him for forcing her out of one position and into another.

The conversation drifted to other topics, and Faith ate mostly in silence, glancing at the duke on occasion. This was her first time seeing him interact with people other than herself. He seemed so polite and friendly with all the women of his household, even tolerant of Lady Tunbridge. He was the one they deferred to, but he did not allow that to make him seem arrogant. No, he hid that part of himself well, maybe even from himself. His sister and aunt genuinely liked him, and his mother seemed to dote on his every word, asking about the women he'd recently danced with as if they were all future marriage options.

"He can't marry most of those women," Lady

Tunbridge said. "He's avoiding the ones he should be courting, and dancing with the ones who only exact pity."

Faith almost flinched. She was one of the ones he pitied, for her wallflower status as well as because of her brother's death.

"Everyone enjoys dancing, whatever their status," Lady Sophia said coolly. "I think it's wonderful that Adam is dancing with so many women who truly appreciate it."

"He never did that in his youth," Lady Tunbridge pointed out slyly.

"You can actually speak directly to me," Adam said in a dry tone. "I am sitting right here. And yes, I've matured in the army. It tends to do that to a man. I'm trying to make up for the mistakes of my past."

Faith kept her gaze on her plate.

"You have nothing to make up for," the duchess insisted. "You were a young man then—we were all young at some point. You were the heir to a dukedom, and that makes a man feel—" She suddenly broke off, and her pale cheeks reddened.

"He was not the heir," Lady Tunbridge said tightly, "much as you always wished otherwise. My late husband was. *He* should have been the duke."

The room was full of strained silence.

"I misspoke," the duchess said quietly. "Forgive me."

But Lady Tunbridge rose to her feet with stiff dignity and walked out of the dining room.

Lady Sophia said, "I'll go to her, Mama, if you don't mind."

The duchess was in the process of draining her glass of wine, then lifted the empty glass to her daughter as a permission of sorts. When Sophia had gone, the duchess stood up and said, "I will retire to my room to nurse my aching head."

She kissed the duke on the forehead as if he were a little boy, then lightly touched his shoulder. "I am so glad you're home," she whispered fiercely.

He touched her hand, then let her go.

Faith was left alone with the countess and her nephew. "I'd like to talk to you in private, Lady Duncan."

The footmen were waiting at the door to clear the table, and both Faith and the countess rose to their feet.

"Don't bother leaving," the duke said, and with a hand gesture sent away the footmen, who shut the doors behind them. "I imagine you have some things to say to me, as well?"

Chapter 7

Adam almost felt guilty at how much he enjoyed watching the many expressions of Miss Faith Cooper. He guessed she thought herself so very calm and professional, but for some reason, he could read every emotion that crossed her face and, strangely, so much of it was by the tilt of her head. Her head sank back in awe at the home he used to take for granted; her chin dropped as if to hide her uneasiness dining with a duke's family when she came from a humbler background; she held her head rigidly to control anger and indignation whenever she looked at him. Spots of color bloomed in her cheeks, and her gray eyes flashed almost silver in the lamplight. With her heightened emotion, he was surprised to find her pretty, when he'd thought her quite plain upon first seeing her in Hyde Park. She had this way of tilting her head up when intrigued, as if she was ready to face the world to appease her curiosity. But he was beginning to think she took great pains to seem other than she was.

"Your Grace," Miss Cooper began coolly, "I—" Then she faltered, glanced at Aunt Theodosia again, then let out her breath. "Oh very well, I could ask these questions in front of you both. Lady Duncan, how did you come to hire me? And please do not say we simply had an easy conversation and think alike."

"But we do, of course," Aunt Theodosia said, smiling almost innocently. "I took an almost instant liking to you from the moment . . ." Her voice faded.

"From the moment the duke pointed me out," Miss Cooper finished for her.

"Yes, I did that," the duke said, lounging idly back in his chair. "You would not see reason, insisted on keeping that position with the Warburtons—who took advantage of you—just because it was I who wanted to offer you help."

"You are a powerful nobleman, Your Grace," she said between gritted teeth. "Do you not think it looks suspicious for you to *help* me?"

"You know that's not why you rejected my help. My aunt knows as well—I told her everything."

Although he hadn't told his aunt how he felt lighter, more aware of everything, whenever he was near Miss Cooper—Faith. Even if only in his mind, he liked to think of her name, for it evoked her to him. She kept the faith of her brother's memory; she fulfilled her mother's faith in her by supporting her at great cost to her own dignity.

But did she have faith in herself? What did he sense beneath the cool, unflappable surface of Faith Cooper?

She turned to stare at Aunt Theodosia, who nodded and put her faintly trembling hand on Faith's.

"He told me of his part in your brother's terrible death, my dear. I was not there, I cannot excuse whatever behavior provoked him—"

"Arrogance, dear aunt," Adam said, feeling suddenly very weary. "Arrogance and the belief that other people make mistakes, but not me. That my gut was always right and I should never second-guess myself. But you don't need to hear my excuses," he said, looking directly at Faith.

Her eyes widened even as her gaze stayed fixed within his. He thought she might remain silent, because he was saying the truth, wasn't he?

"But don't you see you've done it again?" she demanded, glancing from him to Lady Duncan. "You're arrogantly believing I need you to rescue me!"

"But you do—you did." He leaned forward. "I didn't act rashly. I've given this *years* of thought. You, a gentleman's daughter, had to become employed because of me."

"No, I took a position because of my brother's death—and unless you killed him yourself, the world doesn't revolve around you and neither does the entire blame for his death."

He sat back again, staring at her in surprise. "Of course it's my fault—you agreed with me."

"I've thought better of it since we first met. My—my grief and anger welled up within me when you told me everything, made me relive his death all over again. Perhaps I would not have fueled your need to assuage your conscience if I'd been allowed to walk away. But no—you wanted more from me. And now you have it. Does it make you feel better?"

He frowned at her. "This is a trick question."

She groaned and got to her feet. "Lady Duncan, I will bid you a good night."

"But my dear, will you remain here at Rothford Court with us? I do look forward to spending time with you, to sharing my causes and perhaps passing on the fervor to someone who will appreciate it."

Adam watched Faith look down at Aunt Theodosia's hand, thin, frail, blood vessels like a mark of a long life—and that hand trembled now from age, not from emotion, and somehow that was worse, at least to Adam.

Faith must have thought the same. She smiled at his aunt. "If you still want my companionship, then yes, I'll remain."

She shot Adam a narrow-eyed look that Aunt Theodosia missed by sitting back and clapping her hands together. And that look said, *I have no choice—and it's all your fault.*

And he was content with that. She could not

talk him out of believing he'd done the right thing by assisting her, by bringing her into his own household where he could protect her. Nothing would happen to Cooper's sister now.

But as he watched her take her leave, found his gaze dipping to her hips once again, he wondered if he'd done what was best for *him*. She was not a willful, romantic actress, once his favorite type of woman. She was a gently bred lady living in his household, under his care. He'd once thought such a woman boring, conservative, and uninteresting.

And yet he had been anticipating their first dinner together, the conversations that might be battlefields. He desired her in a way that crept up on him slowly, so subtle he hadn't seen it at first, but now he couldn't deny it.

But he could never have her, could never dishonor her or her brother's memory. Maybe that would keep him from acting on impulse, from turning back into the boy he used to be, rather than the man he wanted to be, the man who had a reputation to uphold, the honor of a centuries-old title.

"Adam?"

He almost started at the sound of his aunt's voice. "Yes, Aunt Theodosia?"

She was watching him intently, then she glanced at the door Faith had just disappeared through. "Be careful, my dear boy. I know you want to help her, and now you have. Let me take care of her from now on."

"Thank you. I appreciate it."

His aunt left, and Adam pushed down his uneasiness.

Faith had slept fitfully in her new bed, and it wasn't out of discomfort. She should get up, could see daylight through the curtains, but the maid she'd asked to wake her hadn't come yet, so she lay there, feeling utterly lazy and almost content. She'd had a hard time falling asleep, still overly alert after the awkward dinner with the Chamberlin family.

And she had to admit—overly alert from being across the table for an entire evening from the Duke of Rothford. He was the powerful center of the family, made so by the deaths of his brothers, true, but she could imagine how it must have been with three young Chamberlin men vying for control. This massive mansion probably hadn't been big enough to contain them all.

But now it was just him, the duke, and revolving around him the women, each with her own very unique personality. Faith may have been overshadowed by the forceful women, but she hadn't minded watching them interact.

But now that they'd all met and begun to relate, surely things would settle down.

There was a knock at the door, and Faith sat up and let the blankets fall to her waist. "Come in, Ellen."

But Mrs. Morton came in instead, her expression more reserved than the previous evening. "Good morning, Miss Cooper. I do understand your exhaustion, moving to a new household, but I do think from now on you should attempt to join Lady Duncan as she takes breakfast."

Faith gasped. "But—I had no idea I'd overslept! Do forgive me, Mrs. Morton. It will never happen again."

Mrs. Morton nodded, her expression easing. "You do not work for me, Miss Cooper, and owe me no apology. But I appreciate the offer. I'll send Ellen to you, since she'll assist you dressing from now on."

"I don't need the services of a lady's maid, Mrs. Morton. Believe me, I'm perfectly capable of taking care of myself."

"Lady Duncan insisted, Miss Cooper. Have a good morning."

When the housekeeper had gone, Faith jumped out of bed and saw from the mantel clock that it was almost ten o'clock. Her mouth dropped open. She'd never slept so late in her life. And what had happened to Ellen? She hadn't told Mrs. Morton she'd requested the girl wake her—no need to get her in trouble on Faith's first full day.

She pulled a gown from her wardrobe, and was already brushing her hair when Ellen at last scratched on the door. Faith called for her entrance, and the girl walked—no, she sauntered toward the dressing table.

"Shall I do your hair, miss?"

"If you could bring me some warm water to wash with, Ellen, that would be a good start." She hesitated. "I know you are not in my employ, but if you offer to awaken me, please remember to arrive on time."

Ellen blinked her pale eyes, and her expression didn't change. "I didn't offer to wake you, Miss Cooper."

"Then you must have forgotten," Faith said patiently. "I promise, I don't need much from you, and I know you have other duties."

Ellen didn't say anything, only bobbed the tiniest curtsy imaginable and left the room. Faith grimaced and continued to brush her own hair. Did the girl think Faith wouldn't complain because she was barely above a servant herself?

And she was right, Faith thought grimly. It would not do to get the staff in trouble on her first day at Rothford Court.

By the time she reached Lady Duncan's sitting room, where she wrote most of her letters, Faith was feeling flustered. Lady Duncan, ensconced in bed with a writing desk across her lap, glanced up at her, then glanced again, pressing her lips together, probably to hide her amusement.

Faith knew what she looked like, hadn't had the heart to tell Ellen her hair-styling skills left much to be desired. A curl was already beginning to slide down her ear in a maddening way that made her want to itch—not that curls ever lasted long in her hair, but Ellen hadn't listened to her, had simply done what she wanted to do. Perhaps using a turban was a smart idea, she thought, eyeing the elaborate sky-blue turban Lady Duncan wore to match her dressing gown.

"Good morning, Lady Duncan," Faith said, sitting down abruptly in a chair beside the bed. "Please forgive me for being late." She glanced around at the feminine, intricate carving on all the furniture, the soft upholstery, the framed landscapes. This was a comfortable, soothing lady's retreat.

"We had not set a time to be together," Lady Duncan said, eyeing Faith through her monocle as if she wanted to see the hairstyle close up.

Faith resisted the urge to check her hair. "Perhaps not, but you told me you wrote letters in the morning when you were in residence, and I wanted to be here to help. I promise I will be tomorrow."

"Moving to a new home and meeting new people is always exhausting, my dear. And I am no greeter of dawn myself."

Faith usually was, but she stayed quiet, for today was no proof of that.

"Unlike my nephew," Lady Duncan added, shaking her head. "He used to be quite the lounger in his youth, not awake until almost noon from late-night revelry. But since his return . . ." She let her words die, and for a moment her eyes were touched with sadness.

Faith didn't want to know more about him, didn't want to encourage his aunt, but part of her employment was providing companionship and conversation to the elderly woman.

"Surely awakening earlier than before is also a sign of maturity," Faith offered hesitantly. "As a duke, he has much to do."

Lady Duncan seemed to brighten. "That's true. I would not want to think that he had trouble sleeping at night, although you are one of the rare people in whom he confided why."

This was beyond uncomfortable, but Faith could only nod.

"Plus, I do believe his insatiable need to fence might make him tired enough to fall sleep early at night."

"He fences?" Faith said, then inwardly winced. Of course he fenced—he'd been a military officer.

"He loved it as a boy, and returned home with even more of a fascination with it. He goes to a fencing academy nearly every day."

No wonder he seemed in . . . fine physical shape. She thought of the width of his shoulders, the way his trousers fit snugly to his thighs. And then a blush had her looking anywhere but in Lady Duncan's eyes.

"I am not certain how you wish my help with your letters, my lady," Faith said brightly. "Writing them for you, reading them . . . ?"

"Today you may read. What do you think?"

The first letter was to a women's group that was

forming in industrial Birmingham, with suggestions for speakers at their meetings, as well as the best way to advertise their events.

"You aren't just a supporter, my lady, but you are active in the formation of like-minded support groups."

Lady Duncan beamed at her. "I do my best. How else will women know how to band together and accomplish important things, if we don't help each other?"

They spent another hour on the letters, and Faith was more and more impressed by the lady's convictions. It was wonderful to speak so freely, to be unafraid to voice her own opinions. She and Lady Duncan seemed to relate on a level of deep friendship right from the start. It was refreshing and gratifying for Faith, who hadn't had many friends, except for the Society of Ladies' Companions and Chaperones.

And that reminded her. As she was taking away the writing desk from Lady Duncan's bed, she said, "I know we have not discussed my hours, ma'am, but might I continue to keep today, Wednesday, as my afternoon off?"

"Of course, of course, that will do well. I am certain I can find other free times for you."

"I have friends I regularly meet. But since it is my first full day, I will not desert you."

"But you must! You cannot change an appointment so late."

"That is too generous, my lady. It is hardly work to spend time with you."

"Good, then you won't mind accompanying me on a shopping trip in the next hour."

"Shopping?" she said doubtfully, thinking of the lady's advanced age and use of her cane.

"Do not be fooled into thinking I'm infirm," Lady Duncan insisted, sliding from bed rather dexterously. "I may need my cane for balance, but my legs are healthy enough to walk, so walk I do, most frequently. You might accompany me occasionally, and we'll see who has the strongest constitution."

Faith smiled. "You seem to like competition. Remind me not to play cards with you."

"Oh, you'll be playing."

The two women laughed together.

"Now go find your cloak and bonnet," Lady Duncan said. "It's still winter out there, though the sun is out. We will meet in the entrance hall."

And by "we," Faith found out that Lady Duncan meant the entire household of women, including Lady Tunbridge's daughter, Lady Frances. The girl, ten years of age, had her mother's dark hair pulled back in a braid, and the blue eyes of the Chamberlins. She was eager to attend with the ladies, but shy when introduced to Faith, and even shyer when her mother spoke gently to her, correcting her posture. So far, Faith had not heard Lady Tunbridge speak civilly to anyone in the household other than her daughter. As they walked out to the carriage, Lady Sophia took Frances's hand, and they swung their hands together happily.

They rode in the largest coach of the estate,

with the ducal insignia displayed on the side. On Regent Street, that insignia seemed to clear the way for them, and many people pointed at them from the pavement as they disembarked. Faith was used to being anonymous in a crowd, and it was disturbing to feel stared at. It didn't help that she was self-conscious about her hair, which the bonnet only worsened. She caught little Frances trying not to stare at her, and once, giggling behind her hand.

But Faith didn't mind. It was best that she be thought older and out of style. She hadn't realized she might not like being so on display with the duke's family, and it reminded her that Timothy Gilpin was probably still in town. She didn't want to give him any reason to think about her, to wonder why she had to run away to London to take a position, rather than simply stay home.

They walked along Regent Street, spending the most time in their dressmaker's shop, but also visiting a milliner, a cobbler, and a bookshop. Faith wasn't required to do much of anything except offer an occasional opinion, and it was relaxing.

The strangest thing was that every time she was on the street, she had a prickly feeling at the back of her neck, an . . . awareness that something wasn't quite right. She'd look around but see nothing more than other shoppers enjoying their day, ladies strolling arm in arm, gentlemen carrying their parcels, the occasional servant scurrying to a waiting carriage. She kept dismissing this foolish notion, but every time they reached the street again, it came back. Faith had the unusual sensation that someone was watching them—but of course, people were always watching aristocratic families. She simply wasn't used to it. And she never could discern one single person with his eyes on them, so at last, she forced it from her mind.

"Oh, it is Rothford!" the duchess suddenly exclaimed, waving at her son and a friend, who were about to enter a coffee house.

Faith slipped quietly to the back of the group, where she preferred to be anyway. The two men crossed the busy street and approached the ladies. She wanted to feel indifferent toward the duke's arrival—good Lord, she lived with him now—but she could not. There was something about him that drew the eye, that made one think of vitality and fitness and . . . oh very well, his handsome features could surely make a lady swoon. But not her, of course.

Everyone knew everyone else, until the duke's friend spied her.

"And whom do we have here?" he asked.

She could feel his gaze touch on her ugly hair, her bulky clothes, and instead of being embarrassed, she felt safe in her subtle disguise.

Lady Duncan said, "Lord Shenstone, may I introduce my companion, Miss Faith Cooper."

Faith curtsied. Lord Shenstone had the arrogance of a man who knew his good looks and his situation of birth gave him all the advantages he would ever need. He had reddish-brown hair that curled about his head, and the darkest eyes, which seemed unreadable. They should show happiness, but she couldn't be certain. He was more slender than the duke, but she did not assume that meant him to be weaker.

"Lord Shenstone and my nephew have been friends since their days at Eton," Lady Duncan continued.

"Friendship—is that what they're calling our years apart these days?" Lord Shenstone said with sarcastic amusement.

The duke smiled. Faith felt him glance at her only briefly, and she was relieved.

"Your letter-writing skills *were* sorely lacking," Rothford said to his friend.

"But I thought of you often." Lord Shenstone turned to Lady Duncan. "If you needed a companion, ma'am, why did you not ask? I have so many cousins I know not what to do with them."

Like they were all pieces on a chessboard for his amusement, Faith thought, keeping her annoyed frown at bay. But apparently, she was more transparent than she thought.

"Ah, your new little servant is not impressed with me, Rothford."

She felt her cheeks heat, but how could she defend herself without making things worse?

"Miss Cooper is not my servant," the duke said. His tone was a bit too sharp, and she wanted to wince—and she wanted to stare at him in surprise. His mother did that for her, and perhaps that was worse.

Lord Shenstone laughed. "I did not know being a servant was such a bad thing."

"I cannot imagine you wanting to be a servant," Lady Sophia said, lifting her chin.

"You are correct, of course, Lady Sophia," Lord Shenstone answered, bowing to her. He turned to Faith. "Forgive me if I offended you, Miss Cooper, although I'm still uncertain how I did so."

She glanced at Lady Duncan, who did not seem like she would restrict anything Faith would say. To Lord Shenstone, Faith answered, "I simply feel sorry for your cousins, my lord, since you do not seem to hold them in high esteem."

"That's very true," he agreed, "but since you have not met them, you cannot understand, can you?"

She nodded. "Then perhaps I am simply sensitive on behalf of companions and women everywhere."

Lord Shenstone studied her, that condescending smile still in place.

"I like the way you think, Miss Cooper," said Lady Duncan. "You and I will do so well together. Now tell me, Adam, what were you two gentlemen about today? Fencing?"

"Of course," Lord Shenstone answered. "And though I used to occasionally defeat him in our misbegotten youth, no more. Now it is like taking lessons from a master."

The duke shrugged. "I have simply had more practice."

He made it sound like he'd been sparring genial friends with wooden swords or buttoned points all these years, instead of opponents trying to kill him. He'd once been like Lord Shenstone, she suspected, a ne'er-do-well, a scoundrel—she found herself wondering how he'd first taken the reality of the army.

"It is called skill, Rothford," Lord Shenstone said genially. "I promise I will try to give you decent competition again someday." He glanced past their little group. "Today is truly the day to run into acquaintances on Regent Street. I do believe my vicar is in town."

Lady Sophia gave a little gasp and turned her head away with a blush.

Faith understood Lord Shenstone to mean the vicar of his local village, but she wasn't sure about Lady Sophia's reaction.

"Do you know this man, my lady?" Faith asked softly.

"He is Mr. Percy." Lady Sophia saw her brother watching, pressed her lips together, and said nothing more.

Then Faith saw the vicar in question and understood immediately. He was a handsome young man, plainly dressed but with a lively step. His chestnut hair gleamed in the sun when he doffed his hat, and his dimples winked into view as he smiled upon spying their party. By the time he slowed to a stop, he'd concealed those dimples, as with a respectful expression he bowed to the duke.

"Your Grace, the pleasant morning has only increased upon seeing your party."

"Mr. Percy," the duke said, with a brief nod.

"And what are you doing so far from Lichfield?" Lord Shenstone asked.

Mr. Percy smiled. "I am visiting my sister, my lord. Do not fear, I will be back home for the Sunday service."

"You are always the model of duty, Mr. Percy," Lady Sophia said.

There was an interesting edge to her voice that had Faith giving her a second glance.

Mr. Percy bowed to her. "Lady Sophia, I always wish to do what is expected of me."

"Of course." Her voice grew even cooler, and she suddenly took Frances's hand and drew the little girl toward the window of a pastry shop.

Faith saw the duke watching his sister, brows slightly lowered, even as Mr. Percy gave his regards to the other ladies of the party. He took his leave, and his last regretful glance was for Lady Sophia, who only gave a distant nod, then ignored her brother's direct stare.

A young woman emerged from a nearby shop, her head turned away as she spoke with a companion, and ran directly into the duke.

"Oh dear!" she cried.

The duke grabbed both her arms before she

could tumble to the pavement. The woman looked up at him from beneath her stylish hat, her expression full of surprise and then delight.

"Your Grace, how wonderful to see you again! And to think I once called you Lord Adam, but now you have a far loftier title. How things change, although I regret that a tragedy was the cause."

"Lady Emmeline, good day to you," the duke said. "And I appreciated your note of condolence."

Lord Shenstone, though he eyed the young lady with interest, gave a smirk when Rothford glanced his way.

"Your Grace, London has long missed you these many years, but I do say, you seem the picture of health after your heroic sojourn on the other side of the world."

Rothford gave her a smile, and although Faith had seen a more wicked one, it certainly worked its effect on Lady Emmeline, who blushed and giggled.

Lord Shenstone openly rolled his eyes behind the woman's back, although he did say, "You're looking particularly sunny this day, Lady Emmeline."

She made a great show of acting like she hadn't seen him. "Lord Shenstone, imagine *you* blending into a crowd like that. Do forgive my silliness and accept my wishes for a good day."

"Of course," he said, nodding, a muscle in his jaw clenching.

Lady Emmeline looked at their party. "Greetings, my ladies!"

Lady Duncan chuckled at the young woman's exuberance, Lady Tunbridge looked bored, but to Faith's surprise, the duchess smiled with sunny pleasure. Faith hadn't often seen the woman look interested in anything but her son.

"Rothford, is your dear sister—Sophia!" Lady Emmeline cried. "I've been so long in the country. Thank goodness the Season has brought us together!"

Lady Sophia took her friend's gloved hands and they smiled at each other. "Emmeline, it's been too long since your last visit. Please say you have time to come calling on me."

Faith couldn't miss the shy, blushing glances Lady Emmeline cast upon the duke, while he looked on with a bland smile.

"Of course, dear friend, I had planned to come today!"

Sophia turned to Faith. "Emmeline, here is one member of our party you have not met, Miss Cooper, my aunt's new companion."

Faith curtsied. "Good morning, my lady."

Lady Sophia caught her friend's arm in her own. "Emmeline and I have been friends our whole lives, school and holidays together. I know her family as well as she knows mine."

"How wonderful to have a friend as close as a sister," Faith said.

And by the way Lady Emmeline glanced at the

duke, perhaps the woman wished to be Sophia's new sister in truth. It was none of Faith's business, but she was surprised to feel vaguely bothered by the idea. The duke had to marry *someone*, after all. Perhaps Lady Emmeline just didn't seem . . . mature and sensible enough. He obviously needed a woman who could take him in hand.

After a few more pleasantries, Lady Emmeline reluctantly left them, the gentlemen took their leave and headed back to the coffee house, and Faith was able to linger at the rear of the party.

Lady Duncan allowed the others to stroll ahead and fell back to walk at Faith's side. "That must have been interesting for you, Miss Cooper. Quite an introduction to our complicated relationships."

"Doesn't every family have its complications?" Faith answered, smiling, tamping down her curiosity.

"Of course, of course, but ours . . . well, our family is far too special."

"Lord Shenstone seems fond of Mr. Percy," Faith began, hoping to seem polite rather than overly curious.

"And who can blame him? Such a congenial young man one might never meet again. Hardworking, respectful—such a shame he has nothing to his name beyond that." She shook her head.

And that was all Faith needed to know about Lady Sophia's response to Mr. Percy. If there was a depth of feeling between them, it was surely being discouraged by her family. Even Mr. Percy seemed accepting—it was Lady Sophia who appeared to bear ill will.

"Lord Shenstone is an interesting fellow," Lady Duncan continued. "The friendship between my nephew and him began at school."

"Many find their life's friendships that way, do they not?"

"But I have never been certain Lord Shenstone is a suitable companion. As youths, they did wild things together, as typical young men do. Adam had a difficult childhood, and it was only natural that he find some freedom and release on his own at school."

"A difficult childhood?"

"He was not the heir, you know, and his two older brothers—not of the same mother—did not offer brotherly love. I still had my own household then, and was not around enough to offer my support to Damaris and her children. But regardless, Adam decided that drawing attention to himself in outlandish ways was the best way to keep his father's notice."

"And did it work?"

"It did. His father was amused by his 'exuberance' for life, his pranks, his popularity. Lord Shenstone contributed much of that, of course, and their escapades only became more . . . adult as they grew older. The army changed all of that for Adam. He found purpose and maturity."

But he didn't let go of "arrogance," Faith thought sadly.

"I am not certain that during the intervening years of Adam's absence, Lord Shenstone changed in any way except to become more dissolute."

"Surely the duke will realize that himself."

Lady Duncan shrugged. "I hope so. It would be a shame if Adam allowed that man to bring censure on him after all this time."

Faith was surprised at Lady Duncan's tone. The woman had seemed so open and unencumbered by prejudices of any sort. Apparently, not where Lord Shenstone was concerned. And Faith's only thought was that both friends had courted trouble, and Lord Shenstone could not be blamed for what His Grace had willingly done.

Chapter 8

After a quiet luncheon with Lady Duncan, Faith was glad to escape Rothford Court. She headed for Hyde Park, her usual rendezvous with the Society of Ladies' Companions and Chaperones, feeling trepidatious, and not just because of the dark, low-hanging clouds over London.

Jane was the first to wave to her, and Faith waved back. "So sorry I'm late. I shared a meal with my new employer, and she was gracious enough to allow me to have this afternoon off, though I only just started with them yesterday."

"You have a new situation?" Charlotte asked, eyebrows raised. "When I last saw you with the Warburtons, they seemed content with your services."

"Oh, they were, but as you know, I was not happy with all the work they'd assigned me."

"Our position as lady's companion should not include laundry and hairstyling," Jane said, shaking her head with a tsk. "I am glad you made the change."

But Charlotte was watching Faith closely.

Faith sighed. "I did not initiate the change. I struck up a conversation with Lady Duncan, and since we shared many of the same philosophies, she asked me to be her companion."

Jane smiled innocently.

Charlotte frowned. "Jane, do you not realize that Lady Duncan is the aunt of the Duke of Rothford?"

Jane's smile faltered. "Oh dear."

Faith forced her own smile. "Sadly, I was in Jane's shoes, and did not realize the truth until I had already left the Warburtons' employ. I certainly don't know my peerage well enough yet. Lady Duncan has promised to help me with that."

"Then you're living with the duke?" Jane asked in a faint voice.

"I am employed at Rothford Court," Faith corrected. "And if you've seen the mansion, you know one could easily get lost in there, let alone see the same people each day."

"I believe I should have resigned upon hearing that I'd been deceived," Charlotte said.

Faith studied her for a moment. "Perhaps in your situation, with your connections, that would be feasible, Charlotte. But I know no one else in London, and, of course, the Warburtons would not give me a reference since I'd left them so quickly. How would I support myself?"

Charlotte gave an aggrieved sigh.

"And frankly, I enjoy every moment with Lady Duncan. It is a far superior position for me. And if it doesn't work out, I trust that she will give me a good reference."

"So you plan to leave as soon as possible?" Charlotte asked. "The duke's motives are highly questionable, given his conduct and his secrecy."

"I understand your concern, dear friend"—and she partially said that to remind Charlotte of their relationship—"but he has distanced himself since he feels he's now done what he must for the sister of a man he'd wronged."

They all fell silent for a moment, and Faith regretted the strain on their once-easy friendship. Another wrong to attribute to the duke. She brought up the health of Jane's employer, and the woman launched into a long-winded recitation. But Faith saw that Charlotte's lips remained in a thin line of disapproval.

At dinner that night gathered a table full of women, including Lady Sophia's friend, Lady Emmeline, who'd allowed herself to be "persuaded" to join them for the meal. The duke was absent, and Faith hadn't missed the fleeting glimpse of Lady Emmeline's disappointment before she'd settled down for a conversation with Lady Sophia.

Lady Duncan casually asked about the friends Faith visited, and before she knew it, she was discussing how she'd met Jane and Charlotte. She laughed as she told Lady Duncan their pet name for themselves.

"Excuse me, I didn't quite hear that, Miss Cooper," the duchess said, from her place at the head of the table.

Faith swallowed, realizing everyone was staring at her. "I'm sorry, Your Grace, I was simply telling Lady Duncan the amusing name my friends and I have for ourselves."

"And it is?"

"The Society of Ladies' Companions and Chaperones. There are so many different societies in London, we thought we . . . deserved . . . to be one. In jest, of course."

Lady Tunbridge arched a dark brow. "I would think you had more common sense, more—shame, shall we say."

"Shame?" Faith echoed, sitting up straighter. "Why should we be ashamed of necessary occupations?"

"I don't know how 'necessary' it is for Lady Duncan to have a companion, Miss Cooper, when she has us," the duchess said, casting wounded eyes upon her sister by marriage.

Lady Duncan sighed.

But Faith didn't want the woman to have to manufacture a tale to cover up the duke's manipulations. "Your Grace, whatever you believe of the need for my presence in this household, there are many other places where companions do the work the family can't—or won't. My friend Jane is the companion to an elderly, bedridden woman, whose family cannot be bothered to visit her more than once a month. Jane is the only friend this woman has left."

"Is she a *friend* if she's paid to be there?" Lady Tunbridge asked.

"Yes, she's a friend," Faith said coldly. "She's there to comfort the old woman in the middle of the night—and that is not the description of her position. She helps feed her, dress her, because no one is overseeing the maid, so she hurries, hurting the dear old lady. All that woman has is Jane between her and total isolation. I don't think there's any shame in that."

There was a moment's awkward silence.

And then Faith saw the duke standing just outside the dining room, his focus on her as potent as if he'd touched her. Her throat went dry, and she realized that because of her display of disrespect to his mother, the woman could very well insist she be dismissed. And then the duke might fight for her position, which would look terrible. All she had to do was stay quiet and out of the way— out of *everyone's* way.

The duke stepped back, enveloped in darkness once more.

Faith swallowed, mortification growing. To the duchess, she said, "Please forgive my outburst, Your Grace."

"You don't need to ask anyone's forgiveness,"

Lady Duncan said, slamming her hand down on the table. Her bracelets rattled together.

"Hear, hear!" said Lady Sophia, who smiled at her friend.

Lady Emmeline cast a quick glance at the duchess before letting her own smile grow.

"We did not mean to attack your situation, Miss Cooper," the duchess said stiffly, sending an unreadable glance at her daughter-in-law. "I was simply curious about your pet name."

"I—I thank you for your interest. My other friend, Miss Charlotte Atherstone, is not so fond of the name. She is a respected chaperone of good birth and very well connected, who has seen at least a dozen young ladies through successful seasons."

"I have heard of her," said the duchess. "Her talent and discretion are well known."

Faith nodded, and went back to her roast hare, eyes downcast. To her surprise, Lady Sophia reached beneath the table and squeezed her hand where it rested in her lap. She didn't risk smiling at the thoughtful young woman.

That evening, after enjoying needlework with Lady Duncan in the private drawing room, Faith escorted the woman to her bedroom, walked the few doors down to her own, and found herself standing on the rug before the hearth, wide awake.

The room was lovely, a coal fire glowing, the grate ticking softly. Although the bed was not turned down, Faith did not mind Ellen skipping that duty. In fact, she was nowhere to be found, but that was just fine. Faith had been given leave to treat Rothford Court as her home, so if she couldn't sleep, she would explore the library, something she was dying to do. She lit an oil lamp and carried it through the shrouded corridors, where other lamps already lit the way, making hers unnecessary.

Though the second floor of the library rose above her into darkness, there were lamps on several of the tables and gaslights on the walls near the massive bookshelves. With a sigh of happiness, she gave the globe a spin—

And heard a feminine gasp from below.

Startled, Faith bent, looked beneath the table, and saw her lamp gleam in a pair of frightened eyes. Faith let out her breath, holding back a nervous chuckle.

"Lady Frances, is that you?"

The girl crawled out of her hiding place, wearing a dressing gown over her nightdress. She crossed her arms over her chest and looked mutinous. "Go ahead and tattle. It won't matter."

"I don't plan to tattle. I, too, am seeking solace in the library. What is wrong with that?"

Frances looked uncertainly past Faith, as if she thought someone would jump out at them. "I'm supposed to be in bed."

"Me, too. I imagine we'll each find a book and take it back to our rooms. No one needs to know but us."

"I—very well, thank you," she added in too polite a voice.

She snatched the first book off the first shelf she could reach and fled. Faith stared after her, then, on a hunch, knelt down and looked beneath the table to find a collection of rock crystals piled neatly. So the girl hadn't just come for a book. But of course, that was none of her business.

"Hiding?"

Faith started at the deep male voice, dropping her head with a wince before slowly rising to her feet. Twice today the duke had overheard her speaking far above her station. She didn't want to come to his notice at all, didn't like being beholden to him.

But then she raised her gaze to his face, and once more, she felt the unsettled, nervous flutter in her stomach. She told herself it was because he now had power over her. His coat was gone, which seemed vaguely scandalous. His shirtsleeves looked so very white against the somber brown of his satin waistcoat.

"No," he said, smiling. "I know you're not hiding. I saw who ran out of here. I keep overhearing you with members of my household today."

She thought of the way she'd overstepped her bounds by talking back to his rude sister-in-law.

"Is Frances well?" he asked, looking thoughtful as he glanced at the door where she'd disappeared.

"I don't know," Faith answered. "She was quite upset thinking I might tell her mother—"

"As if you have anything you want to say to Lady Tunbridge."

Faith felt herself blush. "She's a little girl who feels safe in a library. I will certainly not ruin that for her. Will you?" she asked boldly.

"Of course not."

She took a deep breath. "As for her mother . . . I imagine you were quite shocked when you heard our discussion. I should not have—"

"Yes, you should have. She deserved your set down. I almost applauded, but I worried that upon discovering me, Lady Emmeline might chase me down the corridor."

Faith covered her mouth before a laugh could escape.

"Ah, you *do* have a sense of humor. I was beginning to wonder."

She tried to recapture her distance. "And I should let down my guard with you?"

His smile faded. "No. No, you should not do that."

He was studying her too closely, too thoroughly, and she was glad for her poorly styled hair and awful gowns. She didn't want him to *truly* see her, to think he could know things about her. They shouldn't be speaking at all.

But she couldn't make herself leave. "I like your library."

His smile returned, but faintly this time, his eyes still too intense. "I'm certain my ancestors appreciate that."

A silence too full of awareness rose between them—and she was also vastly aware of the chasm in consequence, in fortune, in everything that mattered in Society.

"Did you see the conservatory?"

She inhaled sharply. "You have one here in the city?"

"Of course. What self-respecting ducal mansion doesn't?" He walked to the far end of the library and threw open a set of double doors.

Faith moved forward as if in a dream, inhaling the rich scent of damp earth, then the sweet scents of exotic flowers. When she stepped across the threshold, the air grew moist and warm, and trees rose up above her as if to touch the sky through the panes of glass in their cast-iron frames. Gas-lamp globes seemed to hover in line along curving gravel pathways. Ferns swayed as they passed. Straight ahead rose a fountain that gently splashed like music, its basin a tiled pool with golden carp swimming amid conch shells.

As they stood there in peaceful silence, she felt strange being shoulder-to-shoulder with such a man, a duke. Yet he never made her feel inferior to him. She wondered if this, too, had to do with his military service, his grief at his mistakes, or if perhaps as a younger son, he'd never acquired the "airs of an heir." Thinking that almost made her laugh, and he glanced at her from beneath his light brown wavy hair, which seemed burnished in the low light.

"What is it?" he asked.

"Nothing, really, it's just . . . I would not have imagined myself like this just a few short weeks ago."

"Like what? Nothing much has changed for you. You still insist upon working, when I could—" He broke off.

"I assume you realized how that sounded and stopped yourself," she said coolly.

"Yes, though I did not mean as my mistress."

The word seemed to hover between them. She knew he thought her an innocent; and she shivered to wonder how he might treat her if he knew all her secrets.

"I'm sorry if I've offended you," he said in a low voice.

"You're forgiven."

"But I did hear you discussing your position and that of your friends at dinner. I was glad you made Marian realize what a fool she can be."

"I imagine she's been privileged her whole life, and doesn't know any different."

"There's a way to raise children where they understand their privilege and are humble, grateful, and glad to help others. She is the daughter of a duke, and our fathers had an understanding since her childhood that she would marry my brother Cecil, that she would be the duchess someday. He died an hour before our father."

"Her bitterness is quite sad."

"Thankfully, she is a decent mother. She loves Frances and occasionally indulges the girl as a parent should."

"But perhaps not in a library after bedtime. Lady Frances was quite worried about that."

He nodded, but had no response.

"Might we walk the paths?"

"Of course."

He put out his arm and she hesitated before saying, "I am in your employ, Your Grace, not a woman you are entertaining. But I thank you for your thoughtfulness."

He put his arm down awkwardly, and though she felt silly, somehow she just knew she shouldn't touch him, as if he were a match to her tinder. Side by side, they strolled the winding paths. Her skirts brushed against plants, causing a rustling sound that mingled with the water in the fountain.

"So, your brother had his bride chosen since birth," Faith said. "Was it the same for you?"

"No, not at all. My father was good to me, and one of the ways was that he let me have my head in my youth. It was generally accepted that when I was ready for a wife, he'd help me find one."

"But instead you went into the army. I know younger sons often do that."

"But he didn't want me to."

She glanced at him, but in profile, his expression was unreadable. "And yet you were able to go against him?"

"It wasn't easy, believe me. He didn't want to believe in my reasons."

"Your reasons? Oh, forgive me. You did not speak them quite deliberately."

He nodded. "They are not so very secret. My brothers resented their stepmother—my mother—and expressed their displeasure to me."

"But you were just a boy!"

"I tell you this not to make you pity me, for I think defending myself hardened me, even prepared me for the military. But by the time I was a young man of twenty-one, my brothers were openly telling me they would be cutting me out of my father's estate after his death. I began investing my allowance, but I knew it would never be enough. So I decided on the army, where a man could earn his living and his respectability."

"Your father was against such a sensible plan?"

"In his own way, he loved me, and didn't wish me harmed. Or he didn't believe I could make it," he added ruefully. "I finally told him about my brothers' threats, but he didn't believe me."

"I'm sorry," she said softly. "We all want our parents to believe in us."

He eyed her, but didn't question her, and she was relieved. She couldn't believe he was speaking of himself so personally—she wasn't about to do the same!

"So I began to spend wildly, and had the merchants send him all the bills. He changed his mind eventually. And soon I was a lieutenant in the Eighth Dragoon Guards."

She didn't want to talk about the army, didn't want to hear about him side-by-side with her brother, so she said, "And then you became the duke and returned home."

"And in the few months since my return, my mother has made it her mission to throw eligible young ladies before me. It's hard to evaluate a woman's merits when there are so many of them."

She smiled. "I imagine you fending them off, wading your way through them. But are you being a dutiful son and duke by at least considering marriage and your heir?"

They stopped at the end of a path, where closed doors led outside, and a bench rested nearby. She imagined the view of the external gardens would be beautiful from there.

"Yes," he said with an overly heavy sigh, "I am willing to wade through women for my mother."

She found herself facing him before they turned back the way they'd come. The fountain was a more distant sound from here, and the crunch of their feet on gravel had died away.

His voice a low rumble, he said, "I'm quite capable of discerning worthy feminine qualities all by myself."

She tried to make light of it. "Then what kind of woman are you looking for? I'll make sure to put them in your way—although the Lady Emmelines of the world don't have a problem doing this themselves."

He arched a brow. "She isn't very subtle. I can only see her as a little girl, Sophia's friend."

"She's not a little girl anymore."

"But I feel nothing when I look at her but a vague admiration for her prettiness, and a sense that there's little going on underneath."

"But she would look so lovely on your arm. She obviously has a skilled lady's maid." Faith touched her hair and winced.

To her surprise, the duke reached up to her hair. "Your style does make a person wonder whether it will all topple over."

She held her breath, shocked at the intimacy of him touching her hair, when she'd known other intimacies.

"Your Grace—" she began, in too breathless a voice.

"Surely there's a pin that needs adjusting. Ah, found one."

He pulled, and to her shock, her hair tumbled down past her shoulders.

Chapter 9

Adam watched the fall of Faith's hair as if it were dark water, and her shoulders like smooth stones to be tumbled over downstream.

He hadn't been thinking when he'd touched her hair. Every time he'd seen her all day, he'd wanted to fix it.

And now he'd revealed its glory, freed it from imprisonment to show him its sensual, dark loveliness. The moon shining through the glass up above made her black hair shine, framed the pale oval of her shocked face.

Her lips were parted, as if she meant to speak, but didn't know what to say. He felt the same way. Without knowing what he meant to do, he gently slid a long curl back behind her ear, and let his finger trace along the soft curve of her cheek and jaw.

She inhaled swiftly, then took a step back. "Good evening, Your Grace," she said, then turned and began to march quickly away.

"Wait, Miss Cooper!" He'd made a mistake—he couldn't let her go with this between them.

She didn't stop, so he caught up to her with swift strides. He wanted to take her arm, to force her to hear him, but touching her would be a bad idea. So instead he got in front of her and she was forced to stop, her expression closed and mutinous.

"I did not mean for this to happen," he insisted. "I want you to know I had no intentions of even touching you. But every time I see you, I wonder about your hair. Why do you even wear it styled so?"

She let out her breath, crossing her arms over her chest and speaking warily. "I wanted to do it myself, but didn't have the heart to forbid the maid Mrs. Morton assigned to me. She's still learning, and I intend to be patient with her."

"That is kind of you. But you should not suffer because of a maid's ignorance in my home."

"Don't make this more important than it is, sir. It will look bad for you—for both of us. You're taking this too personally."

"It *is* personal," he insisted between clenched teeth. "I cannot forget what I've done, what I've caused."

"If you feel so strongly, then remember that this sort of behavior is *hurting* me, risking damaging my reputation most of all."

"I never intended that."

"Then let us part reasonably, Your Grace. As

you predicted, I enjoy your aunt, and my duties are light and pleasant. Please bask in your being right and leave it at that."

She went through the doors to the library, and he stayed still for a moment, inwardly cursing himself for the mistake of allowing his attraction to her to overwhelm his good sense. It was much more difficult having her in his home than he'd imagined, and he knew it was due to his own weakness.

And suddenly, the house and his entire life seemed to close in on him. Gone were the times when every day was different, a matter of life and death, where only one's skill and intelligence kept one alive. His restlessness—and he had to face it, boredom—were making him take chances.

And who would suffer? Not him, but the one woman who needed his protection above all else.

Gritting his teeth, he moved back through the house. Though the old butler should have been asleep, Seabrook was awake and in the entrance hall, as if awaiting any orders from his master.

"Go to bed, Seabrook. Don't wait up for me."

"Shall I alert the stables, Your Grace?"

"No, I'll catch a hackney."

"But Your Grace, your greatcoat—"

Adam was already out the door. Yes, it was cold, but his coat was warm enough, and he didn't plan on being outside that long. He found a hack, and soon he was on his way to a dark side of London, where he hadn't been since before he'd joined the army.

He told himself he didn't know why he'd waited so long, but he knew. He'd been focusing on his title and his family, as well as the people who depended on him. It had been a little deflating to learn that his estate was so well run, the Lords so entrenched that Parliament paid little heed to him—that no one truly needed his intervention or guidance.

Until Faith. And look how he'd bungled that.

The hack let him off on a street where several of the gas lamps were strategically broken. But then he saw the half-closed door with the bright lamp overhead, a clear signal that gaming was going on. Shenstone had told him their old haunt was still active; Adam had insisted he wasn't interested.

Yet here he was, fleeing his own house, looking for something to do that didn't involve seducing an innocent.

He went through the half door and knocked on the inner. Someone peered at him through the eyehole.

" 'Tis Rothford," was all he said.

The door opened wide and a gracious "butler" guided him up the stairs into a room far more richly decorated, with handsome carpets, red and gilt paper on the walls, chandeliers over roulette and *rouge et noir* tables. Tobacco smoke drifted, the wait staff immediately came forward to offer him libation, and suddenly, it was as if he were still twenty years old, with the world fresh before him, trying to carve a place for himself against his brothers' and Society's expectations.

Why did it seem so . . . sad?

"Rothford!"

It was Shenstone, and somewhere deep inside, Adam had known his old compatriot would be there.

Shenstone clapped his back and grinned. "Couldn't stay away, could you?"

Adam didn't like to hear it said so honestly, but Shenstone was right, wasn't he?

And why shouldn't he be there? He had so much money he didn't know what to do with it, and obviously he had a need for female companionship, if he couldn't keep his hands off a woman under his protection.

And there were already women eyeing him, surely some of them the actresses he'd always preferred, good at hiding their true selves and playing whatever part they chose—being whoever he wanted them to be.

He tried to have a good time, and the gambling gave him a rush as he both won and lost. He flirted with women who knew what to expect, he drank until his new scruples cowered at the back of his skull.

But the thought of escorting one of those women to her home? He was uninterested, and couldn't even be surprised by it. Shenstone seemed to be studying him through the night, but Adam had no apologies to offer.

He wasn't the same man, who'd thought gambling and womanizing the height of excitement.

He'd seen so much more on the other side of the world. Shenstone would never understand even if Adam tried to explain. And he didn't want to hurt his old friend.

So in the early hours of the morning, he went home alone, feeling no better—in fact, feeling worse, ill-at-ease and confused.

And somewhere in that house was the one woman who seemed to make those feelings die down, who so fascinated him that all he could think about was her.

But he couldn't have her.

After spending the morning on Lady Duncan's correspondence, Faith was thrilled to retreat outside to the gardens surrounding Rothford Court. Lady Duncan sat in the shade, reading a book, while Faith weeded, talked to the gardener, and simply enjoyed the cool but lovely day. It was too early in the year for flowers outdoors, but oh, things were beginning to bud.

She let relaxation wash over her, and tried to forget her encounter in another garden with the Duke of Rothford. She had to trust in his self-control, because this position was perfect for her. She felt needed by Lady Duncan.

Why he'd touched her hair—why he'd changed things between them, she didn't want to know.

Lady Sophia joined them, along with her niece. Frances remained skittish on nearing Faith, as if waiting for Faith to reveal her night outing. Faith simply smiled at her and handed her a little shovel.

"Would you like to help weed?"

Frances spotted the gardener, then gave Faith a strange look, but at last, she let Faith show her the difference between weeds and spring greenery. Lady Sophia sat quietly and talked to her aunt.

After about twenty minutes of following Faith's example, Frances hesitantly said, "What's wrong with your gown?"

"Did I get dirt on it?" Faith asked with a laugh.

"No, it's wrinkled and looks too big on you."

Faith looked around dramatically and lowered her voice. "Please don't tell, but my maid is new to her position, and she's still learning. I don't want to hurt her feelings."

"My mother wouldn't stand for that."

"But your mother is a great lady. I am not."

"I asked Aunt Sophia, and she said we must not hurt the feelings of someone less fortunate than ourselves, that not everyone can afford fine new gowns."

Faith hid a smile. "That's very true. Surely in London or the countryside, you've seen many different kinds of women in many different gowns."

Frances nodded seriously. "Are your feelings hurt?"

"Not at all!" Faith said, smiling, even as she touched the girl's shoulder. "You are only asking honest questions."

"Is . . . is your maid inexperienced at styling hair, too?"

Faith laughed aloud, and finally, Frances gave her a timid smile in return.

After a while, she let the girl continue on without her, and went inside to fetch some lemonade and iced cakes to refresh the ladies. Frances had some, then was soon back on her knees in the dirt.

Faith winced and glanced at Lady Sophia. "Will her mother mind a little dirt?"

"She might, but I brought her to the gardens, so please do not worry about it. You two were having an intense conversation."

"Well . . . Lady Frances is worried about my unskilled maid." She gestured to her gown.

"And I understand her concern. Ellen has been with us for over three years. I never would have thought—"

"Please, Lady Sophia, do not worry about it. I am handling it, even though it might not look it."

"If you will not let me speak to her or Mrs. Morton, then let me offer another suggestion that will help. I want you to have some of my gowns."

Faith inhaled and frowned. "Oh, no, Lady Sophia, I could not possibly—"

"They are my older gowns, if that makes you feel better. My mother would probably resent me parting with newer ones."

She shared a smile with Lady Duncan, but Faith could not feel light.

"Lady Sophia, I am employed in your home. It would not be seemly to—"

"I want to." The young woman reached out and touched her hand. "And before you assume something negative, I have not been embarrassed, nor has anyone in the household mentioned it to me. I am simply so fortunate to have a wonderful brother who forces me to spend far more on myself than I normally would."

"Forces?" Faith said skeptically.

Lady Duncan chuckled. "As if I have to drag her to the dressmaker all the time."

Faith glanced at Lady Duncan. "Are you certain this would be proper to accept such a gift?"

"It would please me to see you in nicer clothes, Faith. You are a pretty young woman—you don't need to hide it."

Yes, I do, Faith thought, remembering the moonlit conservatory, and how her heart had pounded in her rib cage when the duke had simply touched her cheek. There was something wrong with her that she was so easily swayed by men.

Soon Frances's governess came to take her away for her lessons. Faith expected the other ladies to grow tired of the garden, but they didn't move. Lady Sophia seemed pensive, and Lady Duncan appeared to be waiting for whatever her niece needed to say.

When Lady Sophia said nothing, Lady Duncan at last lifted her monocle and looked through it at the young woman. "You did not seem pleased to see Mr. Percy yesterday."

Two splotches of red appeared on Lady Sophia's cheeks, but she said nothing.

"He is a young man very conscious of his place in Society," Lady Duncan continued gently. "You are a young woman who doesn't believe such things matter, because at your station, you've never had to face that dilemma."

"He is a gentleman, son of a gentleman," Lady Sophia burst out heatedly.

Faith was rather shocked at the emotion hiding beneath the woman's calm, friendly exterior.

Lady Sophia gave her an apologetic glance. "Do forgive me, but . . . I find his attitude and behavior so frustrating. I do not care that he is a vicar, but he certainly does."

"And he's right to care, my dear. He is not the sort of man your mother expects you to marry."

"I thought things would be different when Adam returned—he won't force me to marry against my wishes."

Faith was too curious about what the duke might do.

"No one will force you into anything," the elderly woman chided. "Even your mother. Your brother is concerned for your happiness, not what property a potential groom brings to the union. You are blessed in that regard, because most men feel otherwise."

"I know!" Lady Sophia said, slamming her fist down on her thigh. "And Mr. Percy is one of those! It is so infuriating!"

"You have discussed marriage?" Lady Duncan said, obviously surprised.

"He will not, of course. He is too proud for that. But he has made it clear that he feels himself beneath me, and will not pursue anything more than friendship. Are my wishes so unimportant?"

Lady Sophia turned imploring eyes on Faith, who was surprised to be included in this family conversation.

"Of course your wishes are important," Faith began cautiously, "but if he has strong opinions and beliefs, it might be difficult to alter them."

"But not impossible?" Lady Sophia said with hope.

Faith gave Lady Duncan an imploring glance, but her employer only gestured with her hand.

"I do not know, my lady," Faith finally said. "Are not men like us in many ways? Some men can be reasoned with and others will always hold firm to their first convictions."

Lady Sophia sat silently for several minutes, sipping her tea. "Very well, I will hope that Mr. Percy can be reasoned with."

"Do you plan to persuade the man to ask for your hand in marriage?" Lady Duncan asked, one eyebrow climbing toward her turban.

"No, not at all. But I will make him see that he cannot do without me."

"And how can you *make* that happen?" Faith asked, trying to hide her skepticism. "Because if he does not call on you . . ."

"Oh, he doesn't need to call upon me. We see

each other often enough when he is in town. And next time, he will see me showing my interest in another man. Perhaps jealousy will combat his ridiculous class-consciousness."

"And what about the man you falsely flatter?" Lady Duncan said, frowning. "You have not given that enough thought."

"Oh, don't worry, I will talk to Lord Shenstone about it. We understand each other well. He will go along with me in the ruse."

Faith did not think it all a good idea to court another man in public, especially not someone as jaded as Lord Shenstone seemed to be, but it was not her place to judge Lady Sophia. She'd never judge *anybody*.

She waited for Lady Duncan to object, but the older woman simply cocked her head and spoke mildly. "Give this deep thought, my dear. You don't want to do something that might hurt your family—or yourself."

"I certainly won't hurt anyone," Lady Sophia insisted. "And why would I hurt my brother, newly returned from a situation he won't even discuss with me?"

And it was obvious who was hurting in that sibling relationship.

The young woman again turned to Faith. "Your brother was in the army. Did he talk to you about it?"

Faith was surprised as sadness and frustration warred inside her. Lady Duncan's eyes went wide with sudden sympathy, even as Lady Sophia gasped.

"Oh, my dear Miss Cooper, I cannot believe I asked that of you. Do forgive me."

"Please, there's nothing to forgive. It was an honest question. But in truth, my brother and I weren't close, and his letters from India were infrequent at best. So no, he did not discuss anything important with me."

"But if he'd have come home to you, he might have."

"I don't believe so, but then again, my brother is nothing like yours. He did not care about my opinion. But I do know that some men will not bring up tragic memories for fear of hurting the ones they love."

"I know. I tell myself that, but . . . I believe he's hurting himself keeping it all bottled inside."

And there was nothing to say to that. Faith knew his secrets, knew his guilt, knew why he didn't speak of it. It was strange to know more about the man than his own sister.

She knew too much about the Duke of Rothford. She hoped it wouldn't put a strain on her relationship with the rest of his family.

Chapter 10

Two nights later, the duchess hosted her first dinner party since Faith's arrival, and Faith was forced to wear a gown of Lady Sophia's, since the young woman had already gone to the trouble of having several quickly altered by her dressmaker.

Faith stared at herself in the full-length mirror in her room and felt far too revealed. Oh, the top of the bodice was a decent height, and the peacock-blue damask was modest, but it had been more than a year since she'd allowed herself to be so . . . displayed. She'd gotten used to the layers of petticoats that hid her waist, the old-fashioned cut and bulk of extra material like armor. Lady Sophia's "old" gowns were simply from a season or two ago, and they hugged the newer, lighter corset she insisted Faith use. The young woman had been so delighted with the effect, even had her own lady's maid style Faith's hair as a learning moment for Ellen, but Faith could not rejoice.

She didn't want the duke to look at her, to wonder if she was displaying herself for him after the way he'd touched her. She'd been avoiding him, and she sensed with relief that he was doing the same.

At last, she could delay no longer and made her appearance in the drawing room to await their dinner guests. Lady Sophia clapped her hands together upon seeing Faith, who would have gladly shrunk back out the door at drawing notice.

"Oh, do come here, Miss Cooper!" Lady Sophia cried. "I knew that gown would look wonderful on you."

The duchess glanced at Faith briefly, then looked away again with her usual bland indifference. Faith couldn't even be offended; the woman treated everyone but her children the same way.

"You know Frances would love to see you arrayed so prettily," Lady Sophia continued. "You really should run up to the nursery."

"Excuse me?" Lady Tunbridge said coldly, eyeing Faith. "My daughter is not to be disturbed so late in the evening because of a *companion's* fancy. She needs to learn to treat servants with the polite and appropriate distance."

"Faith is not a servant, Marian," Lady Duncan stressed with exasperation. "And it wasn't her idea, was it?"

Faith wished she could step right back out of the room. She didn't like calling attention to herself. She hovered in the doorway, wondering how she could get out of the evening, almost wishing she were back at the Warburtons washing Adelia's underthings.

"Good evening, ladies," said the duke, right behind her.

She froze, glancing back over her shoulder. He was too close, so tall and broad, and she felt overly exposed with her fashionable gown. His arrogance might let him think she'd dressed up for *him*. If he looked over her shoulder, could he see down her—

She quickly stepped to the side to allow him entrance, and although he gave her a second glance, all he did was nod in passing and greet his mother with a kiss on the cheek.

Faith let out a shaky breath and wished for a corner to hide in. But the guests started arriving as if on cue, including Lord Shenstone. She saw Lady Sophia sizing him up, preparing to propose her scandalous attempt to make Mr. Percy jealous. The young woman was only distracted by the arrival of her friend, Lady Emmeline.

The dinner went well, and the men seated on either side of Faith treated her much more respectfully than at the last party she'd attended in her dowdy clothes. Though the duchess had made certain all knew she was Lady Duncan's companion, they still conversed with polite interest, and she tried to relax.

The duke glanced her way once or twice, but he seemed a master at portraying indifference. And perhaps it *was* indifference. She'd made it clear he was to keep away from her—maybe he was unused to such rejection and was now dismissive of her. It was as it should be. But her stomach was tight with nerves and even disappointment, which made her terribly disappointed in herself.

When the gentlemen joined the ladies in the drawing room after dinner, she was sitting near Lady Duncan and her friends, safely out of the way. She was able to watch Lady Sophia move easily through the men, bantering, laughing, and all of it without seeming like a flirt. She had a gift for putting people at ease that Faith admired. Lady Emmeline, aided by the duchess, remained within Rothford's circle, lovely in pink silk, looking upon him with an expression of happiness, if not outright worship.

But there was one gentleman, Lord Fillingham, who even Lady Sophia had a difficult time enjoying. He drank to excess, commented too loudly on subjects he should not, and began to pester the duke about how the army had improved his fencing.

"Shenstone says you quite defeat him every time," Lord Fillingham said, his dark hair falling over his forehead untidily. "I can understand that, of course, being that Shenstone does not have a high degree of skill."

Lord Shenstone was talking with Lady Sophia, but he heard this and looked over her head. "Fillingham, you and I have never had the pleasure of fencing," he said with faint sarcasm. "How disappointed I am that you are so quick to judge."

Lord Fillingham ignored him. "Come, Rothford, tell us of your prowess with the sword."

"I am a cavalryman, Fillingham," the duke said coolly. "I need not explain my skill. But perhaps it's time to call for your carriage."

People were looking at them both, whispering together in low voices.

"My carriage?" Lord Fillingham said, gesturing widely. "Why, the night is young, is it not? I think you want to distract all your guests from my challenge."

"There's a challenge in there somewhere?" Rothford asked, his lips quirked in a smile that never touched his eyes.

Faith saw Lady Duncan stand up, bracing herself on her cane as if to march toward her nephew's adversary. Faith hurried to her side.

"My lady, perhaps you should let the duke handle this," she said in a low voice.

"Yes," Lord Fillingham said, rounding on her, "let's let the duke handle this." Over his shoulder, he said, "I'm challenging you to practice your skills on me, Your Grace."

But he kept looking at Faith, which she found confusing and embarrassing.

"Then come to my fencing academy tomorrow. We have all the equipment we'll need, and all the space to exercise, will we not?"

"No, not tomorrow, tonight. Do you not agree

that it would liven up a dull dinner, Miss—what is your name again?"

She took a deep breath. "Miss Cooper."

"Of the barrel-making Coopers?" he asked, laughing at his own joke.

She heard Lady Duncan draw in an angry breath, but Faith put a hand on her arm.

"My ancestors probably did make barrels, my lord. And they bettered themselves to become gentlemen. So I have deep pride in my name."

And suddenly the duke was there, standing between her and Lord Fillingham as if the man had threatened her with bodily injury instead of attempting an insult.

"Very well, I accept the challenge," he said, mixing both affability and steel beneath his words. "Let's roll back the carpets and delight our audience."

She opened her mouth to stop him, but suddenly realized she had no authority to do so and should certainly not call any more attention to the fact that he'd been offended on her behalf. It was a minor slight—he should have ignored it. Now he had the members of his family frowning their bewilderment at him, and Lady Sophia glanced at Faith in confusion.

The other male guests started talking in happy tones as they stripped off their coats to move furniture and roll back carpets. The duke returned from somewhere with a set of blades, which he held out to Lord Fillingham.

"Your choice, sir, even though you challenged me."

"And I'll take you up on that, Rothford." He chose one and slashed it through the air, making Lord Shenstone step back. "Ah, the safety tip already buttoned on. You're taking no chances."

"There are ladies present, after all," the duke replied blandly. "The sight of your blood might bother them."

Lord Fillingham just laughed. "Who wishes to be my second?"

"This isn't a duel," Lord Shenstone said, frowning. He glanced at the duke. "Are you certain this is a good idea? He might have overimbibed."

"He hasn't," the duke answered, even as he stripped off his coat, encouraging the titters of the women. "I remember him drunk. No, he's been hinting at this ever since I returned, and tonight he crossed a line. If he wants to be so publicly put down, I'll gratify him."

The duke gave her one brief glance that she felt clear to her toes. He wouldn't have agreed to the challenge but for the silly slight against her, she was certain. What was he thinking to call attention to her like that?

"Oh, this will be fun," Lady Duncan said, rubbing her hands together gleefully.

Faith almost gaped at her. "Fun? Someone could be hurt."

"Pshaw, my nephew won't allow that to happen."

Surely Lady Duncan knew what he was capable of, but Faith felt a little sick inside. She stayed beside the elderly woman, who could barely stand still, she was so excited.

And then the two men stepped out into the center of the floor and faced each other. Lord Fillingham grinned, and even the duke offered a faint, confident smile. Then they both raised their swords and stepped back.

"Shouldn't they be wearing padding of some kind?" Faith murmured.

"The tips are covered—do you see that?"

Faith didn't care—the edges of the rapiers were sharp, weren't they? But she couldn't say another thing. Otherwise she'd sound far too nervous on the duke's behalf.

And it was soon obvious there was no need. He met Lord Fillingham's sword with confidence, parrying each thrust, even jumping a low swing once, to the oohs of the onlookers. The steel clashed and rang out, and soon he was driving Lord Fillingham back across the room, until the man was bent backward over the grand piano.

And then the duke stepped back and waited for his opponent to right himself. That seemed to make Lord Fillingham angry, for he ran and slashed, and Rothford neatly stepped aside, then caught him by the arm when he would have fallen into the audience.

Rothford held his arm from behind and said something quietly into his ear.

Lord Fillingham nodded, and when the duke released him, he kept his sword low and bowed stiltedly. "You have won, Your Grace. I cannot deny your prowess with the blade."

The duke nodded, then put his hand out for the sword. Lord Fillingham offered it to him hilt first. As the duke took the swords out of the room, Lord Fillingham forced a grin and stared about him.

"We put on a good show, did we not? Come, lads, let's set the duchess's drawing room back to rights."

He led the men in replacing the carpet and furniture, but the other guests did not stay long. By twos and fours they left, giving Lord Fillingham pitying looks, off to spread the news of the latest little scandal. Faith watched as the duke spoke to several guests, including Lady Emmeline, who breathlessly praised his skill and swore she'd never seen two men in combat.

"We weren't in combat," he said shortly. "True combat is far more uncivilized, desperate, and bloody."

One of the last to leave the room was Lady Duncan, who seemed to want to offer consolation to her nephew, though she didn't understand his grim mood.

"You did nothing wrong, Adam," she assured him. "Put on a good show when that lout wouldn't take no for an answer."

The duke glanced at Faith and away, and she

knew in her bones he put on that "show" because of her.

She was escorting Lady Duncan upstairs when the woman said, "Oh, drat, I left my needlework in the drawing room. Will you fetch it and leave it on the table outside my room? I fear I will be falling into bed before you can return. Such excitement!"

By the time Faith walked back into the drawing room, only Rothford was there, leaning against the mantel, a drink in one hand as he stared at the coal grate.

He looked up and met her gaze. "Forget something?"

She nodded and searched several sofas and chairs until she spotted it, then held the needlework up.

He took a healthy swallow of his drink, looking back into the hearth. And for some reason, she couldn't make herself leave.

"Your Grace . . . are you well?"

He nodded, glanced up again, then for the first time that evening, perused her gown in a leisurely but bold manner. She inhaled at the sudden heat that seemed to make her corset too tight.

"I couldn't say it earlier, but you look lovely in that gown."

"It is a gift from your sister. I promise, it was not my choice, but she insisted—"

"And she was right to insist. You needed garments, and the improvement is striking."

She lifted her chin. "I do not want to look striking."

"I know. But you were striking even in ill-fitting gowns."

He said that wearily, without passion. She almost couldn't take offense—almost.

She looked at the open door, then stepped closer to him, saying softly, "Don't talk like that."

He ground his teeth for a moment. "You are right, I know."

She turned toward the door.

"Why was my sister spending an inordinate amount of time with Shenstone? He is not for her."

Faith hesitated, unwilling to break a confidence. "She knows. But I think she plans to make her own decision."

He sighed, then took another drink, though he didn't appear drunk.

"I am glad you care for your sister," she began slowly. "If you don't mind my interference—"

He chuckled without true amusement.

She frowned at him. "You would do well to confide things in her. She's hurt you will not discuss your time in the army."

"Would *you* discuss it, if you were me?"

"Maybe I would. It might help to confide in someone."

"I already have."

She stiffened. "If you mean me, it's not the same thing."

"And my aunt."

"Then maybe Lady Sophia is feeling left out of your confidences, and you're the only brother she has left."

He nodded. "I take your meaning. I will consider it. Good night."

And when she realized she wanted to stay, to comfort him, that made her turn and flee. Upstairs, she lay Lady Duncan's needlework on the table as instructed, then hurried into her own room and leaned back against the door.

To her surprise, Ellen rose from the chair before the hearth.

Faith jerked in response, then gave a sigh. "Oh, Ellen." She'd never had her own lady's maid before, and the girl's unexpected presence continued to startle her.

"You need help to get out of that gown."

"I do. I appreciate your remembering, because I didn't."

When even her corset strings were loosened and at last she could take a deep breath, she dismissed Ellen to her own bed with gratitude, then finished disrobing and donned her nightdress. By the light of a single lamp, she silently took down her hair and brushed it out, stroke after stroke, staring at herself in the mirror.

What kind of woman was she becoming? This man who'd forced her to take employment in his home, who blamed himself for her brother's death, who'd altered every path of hers these last few years—she could not stop thinking about him.

She thought of him as a man—she wanted him to touch her, she wanted to feel his lips against her mouth, against her breast.

With a groan, she buried her face in her trembling hands. She was wanton—she'd never wanted to face that about herself. She'd thought herself a spinster forever when she'd let Timothy Gilpin take her maidenhead. She was lying to herself even then.

When the duke had practically defended her against a minor insult, she'd watched enthralled at the graceful movement of his body, the muscles that flexed beneath his shirtsleeves. He'd been unable to control his temper, had perhaps reverted to the wildness of his youth.

Maybe that wildness called to her, because in her own way, she'd been wild. She should go now, simply leave and be done with him and with her own passion.

But she couldn't. She was her mother's only support.

And perhaps that was too convenient a reason, she thought bitterly, tiredly.

Chapter 11

Adam didn't take his breakfast in the breakfast parlor, but instead retreated to his study, with the mullioned windows overlooking the garden. He wanted only coffee to help clear his aching head. He'd drunk too much after everyone had gone to bed. His memories were hazy—oh, he knew he'd fought Fillingham, like a fool. He'd had no problem resisting the taunts until the man had insulted Faith.

Adam winced and rubbed a hand across his tired eyes. Who had noticed *that* mistake? Surely Faith. He remembered talking to her afterward, had seen her concern and wished he hadn't. It had taken everything in him not to go to her, to tell her he'd never permit anyone to hurt her again.

But *that* would hurt her, he knew. He'd caused her enough pain. He'd told her she looked lovely; maybe even his admiration was pain to her.

There was a faint knock at the door.

"Come in."

Seabrook entered, holding something in his hand. "This was delivered to the servants' entrance for you, Your Grace."

Adam frowned. "The servants' entrance? That's unusual."

Seabrook handed it over with a bow, then left the study. Adam frowned at the plain, rough paper, sealed with a formless blob of wax. He broke it open, and the childish scrawl made him blink in surprise.

Faith is lovely. Wherever she goes, you can't stop looking at her. But I'm watching you.

Surprised and confused, he read it again, and anger joined the mix of his emotions. What the hell was this? Someone was spying on him, trying to intimidate him.

Someone had noticed his interest. Had they been looking for a return to his old ways?

He fisted his hand on the paper, wishing he could crush it into a ball. But what would that do?

He rang the bell for Seabrook and then asked him to send for Cook, a large, husky man who obviously enjoyed his food.

Cook bowed. "Your Grace."

"Thank you for coming. Do you know who left this note?" he asked, holding it up.

"A scruffy young boy, sir. I thought it was strange and tried to question him, but he ran off."

"Thank you. If this happens again, please keep the boy with you and send for me. You may go."

Seabrook lingered after Cook left, a faint frown the only thing showing his concern. "Your Grace, might I help in some way?"

"No, but I appreciate the offer."

Seabrook left Adam alone with his thoughts. He wasn't going to tell Faith, of course. She'd resign her position, even if it meant living on the streets.

And what was there to tell? Someone who knew him wanted to rattle his chains. But it was a good reminder to avoid being seen too much in public treating Faith as anything other than his aunt's companion. He thought he'd been doing a decent job of showing his disinterest, but maybe not. Though the note had come after his mother's dinner party, he knew everyone there and couldn't believe it was one of them. Could a more distant acquaintance have seen him talk to Faith in Hyde Park? Or when he'd met up with the ladies' shopping trip on Regent Street? Or when he'd gotten her alone in a corridor at the Randolphs' dinner party to convince her to work for him? There were too many instances of questionable behavior on his part.

But who the hell cared if he flirted with someone in his employ? Many peers did worse than that and suffered no ill consequences. The women always suffered, of course, and he would not let such notoriety befall Faith. He would have to be much more careful the next time they were in public together.

That same morning, Faith was in the entrance hall, adjusting her shawl and tying her bonnet ribbons, when Lady Sophia came down the broad staircase.

"Miss Cooper, are you going somewhere?"

"I'm running several errands for your aunt. Could I do something for you?"

"No, no, but that's sweet of you to offer." She reached the marble floor and paused. "Would you mind if I accompany you?"

Faith blinked at her, then smiled. "Of course not. I would enjoy the company. But honestly, if you need me to pick up something for you, it's not inconvenient."

"And you're sweet to offer. Let me fetch my shawl and I'll be right back." Halfway up the stairs, she turned around. "Did you send for the carriage?"

"No, I was going to walk or hire a hackney."

"Nonsense, you can use a carriage anytime you'd like." To the young footman who stood at attention, she said, "Hales, please have Tallis bring a carriage around."

"Yes, my lady."

Not a half hour later, they were riding in the carriage, when Lady Sophia put her arm through Faith's.

"We don't need to be so formal, do we? Please call me Sophia, and I will call you Faith."

Faith smiled. "I'd like that."

Sophia was so easy to be with, so friendly and intelligent. But she wasn't sure one could be friends with a relation of one's employer—the duke's sister. But obviously Sophia was trying, and Faith appreciated that.

Sophia's smile faded into an expression of earnestness. "I actually had a reason to accompany you. I wanted to speak in private. I—I came back to the drawing room last night and overheard you and my brother discussing me."

Faith stiffened. When had she come in on their damning conversation? Hopefully not too early, when he'd been saying her looks were "striking." But Sophia did not seem upset or wary.

"I—I was trying to help," Faith said at last. "I know you want him to freely discuss his troubles with you. It's not my place, I know, but . . . it came up."

"Yes, you deflected him away from my plans with Lord Shenstone. I appreciate that. You encouraged him to talk to me. But . . . it's very obvious you and he have had discussions about the war, and I was confused."

Faith didn't know what to say, how to defend herself. Did Sophia think Faith was . . . pursuing the duke? "My lady—"

"Wait, let me finish. And it's Sophia, remember?" she said, a faint smile returning.

Faith tried to relax.

"It struck me as odd, because he has not known you long. But then I thought about the war, and suddenly your name struck a chord. I went back to his letters, and there I found mention of a Sergeant Cooper. Your brother?"

Faith nodded warily.

"So our brothers served together," Sophia said with satisfaction, as if a riddle had finally been solved. "You told us that your brother died in the war. Did you . . . come to find Adam?"

"No! Sophia, no. My brother was not much for letters, and I didn't even know he'd served with the duke. His Grace . . . found me."

Sophia looked startled.

"He just wanted to help," Faith hurried to say. "He felt badly about Mathias's death. I told him I didn't need his help, but he persuaded your aunt to become involved, and I accepted her offer of a position without realizing . . ." She let that sentence fade away. Was she trying to prove her own good intentions by casting doubt on the duke's?

Sophia shook her head. "Oh, he can be so frustrating, always thinking he knows best. I don't remember it so much when he was younger, before he left England. Let me tell you, he's *not* going to manipulate me into the marriage he thinks is correct."

"Has he tried?"

"Well . . . no, but he's been vocal when he sees me with someone of whom he disapproves."

"You mean Mr. Percy."

Sophia narrowed her eyes. "There's been nothing for him to truly disapprove of, since Mr. Percy always keeps far too respectable a distance between us." She said the latter with some bitterness. "But I don't mean to bring all this up again, except to say that Lord Shenstone has agreed to pretend to court me whenever Mr. Percy is near."

Faith frowned. "You must know his lordship better than I do, to trust him so."

"Well, he's not exactly every maiden's dream husband, but he's titled, and I do not think he'd take advantage of his friend's sister's dilemma. Did I say that right?" And she laughed.

Faith smiled in return, relieved that Sophia was not angry with the subterfuge of how she'd won her position. Together, they alighted from the carriage at a stationer's, then proceeded to the bookstore and the dressmaker's, where Lady Duncan had an altered gown to be retrieved.

And though Sophia chatted happily, waving at friends, introducing Faith everywhere without revealing her position in the household, Faith should have been pleased and content. But . . . she kept feeling as if she needed to look over her shoulder. This was the second time she'd felt watched—or was it followed? But she could never see anyone suspicious, just other shoppers enjoying the day.

Maybe people they'd left behind were simply curious about who she was, and how she knew Sophia, and were studying her as she left. Surely that was it, she told herself, and tried to relax as they completed their errands.

Adam was determined not to let a cowardly message bother him. He was going to be very careful to treat Faith as the companion of his aunt that she was. He would not think of touching her smooth skin again; he would not remember staring into her silver-gray eyes as if they contained the secrets of the world; he would not imagine her parted lips on his, the taste of her in his mouth . . .

God, he had to stop thinking about her.

But when they attended another dinner party the next night, he found himself on edge, his gaze raking the drawing room over and over again, looking for strangers, or someone who couldn't meet his eyes. Faith sat properly with Aunt Theodosia, and he tried not to see her gown, which bared her shoulders and the tops of her breasts. She wisely never looked at him. His sister, on the other hand, kept giving him curious glances.

He'd known the guests all his life, but besides Shenstone, none had been close friends in his youth. Who knew what kind of people they were, voyeurs at heart, or those who just enjoyed a good scandal?

And then he saw Lady Emmeline heading toward him with purpose.

He turned about and quickly asked his sister to dance. It was a waltz, and she flowed smoothly about the floor as he dodged other couples.

"I had this dance saved for Lord Shenstone,"

Sophia said, although she didn't look all that angry.

"He won't mind waiting."

In fact he could see Shenstone frowning at them. He whirled his sister past and let her skirts sweep his friend's feet, and then grinned.

"That was cruel," Sophia said.

But he could tell by her quivering lips that she was amused.

"So tell me about Lady Emmeline."

"You are interested?" she asked, her gaze flying up to his, her countenance lit with happiness.

"No. I remember her too well as a child, so that's how she's stayed in my memory."

"Oh." Her shoulders sagged a bit.

"You wanted me to court her?"

"Well, not if *you* don't want to. But of course, she has hope that you might feel some affection for her."

"I can tell," he said dryly. "I will do my best not to lead her on, but if she doesn't start taking my hints, I might have to be more direct."

She sighed. "Would you like me to—"

"No, I can handle it. I just needed confirmation that I wasn't seeing what wasn't there."

"You weren't."

After another circle of the floor, he asked, "So is there something I should know about you and Shenstone?"

She didn't quite meet his eyes. "No, we're simply friends. He knows I like to dance, so he asks me."

"He is not exactly your innocent country gentleman."

"I know that," she said, her smile impish. "After all, he's your friend, and I grew up hearing stories I wasn't supposed to hear."

He gave her an exaggerated wince. "I've changed—matured, even."

"I can tell."

The final chord had barely run through the drawing room when Shenstone appeared at their side.

"Lady Sophia, shall we dance?"

She gave a brilliant smile and a curtsy as he put her hand into Shenstone's.

"Thank you, my lord, I would enjoy that."

"And then come talk to me, Shenstone," Adam said.

"Do you want to dance with me, too?" Shenstone asked with a smirk.

Adam shook his head and walked away. Before he'd taken two steps, Emmeline appeared in front of him.

"Your Grace, is that Sophia and Lord Shenstone?" she asked, as if she couldn't see.

"It is."

"How lucky that they are doing the quadrille together. It is one of my favorite dances."

Adam hid a sigh and bowed his head. "Will you do me the honor?"

Her laugh was light and musical. "Oh, the honor would be mine, Your Grace."

Emmeline was a lovely dance partner, very graceful, but she wasn't whom he wanted to dance with. He looked for Faith, and found her still sitting with the old ladies, the chaperones, the companions, and it made him want to grind his teeth.

He couldn't ask her to dance, let alone touch her in any way.

He didn't trust himself—and someone was watching.

"Oh, the heat is quite overpowering, isn't it?" Emmeline asked, fluttering her lashes. "Perhaps I need a breath of fresh air."

The terrace loomed almost forbiddingly past the open French doors. If he were alone, it would have seemed private, refreshing, and peaceful.

"Why don't you sit, and I'll fetch you some lemonade."

"Lemonade?" she said blankly. "I am not a child, Your Grace."

"Do forgive me. Here is a chair. I'll be back in but a moment."

He did return, too, and though she might have been foiled, she accepted the champagne with a graceful smile. He was soon able to disengage and find the men's card room, where the smoke nearly overwhelmed him.

He spotted Shenstone almost immediately, throwing down his cards in disgust as his opponents laughed. Adam beckoned him with a jerk of his head, and Shenstone arrived bearing two glasses of brandy.

Adam sipped his gratefully. "I have a favor to ask of you."

"You want to know the newest gaming hell?"

"No."

"Too bad." Shenstone eyed him. "You look . . . irritated."

"I am. You know Sophia's friend, Lady Emmeline?"

For a moment, he thought Shenstone looked wary, but Adam told himself he was mistaken.

"She is far too interested in me to be making sound decisions tonight. And she didn't want lemonade, but champagne. I need to get just a moment of fresh air before the heat and the odor do me in. If you see her trying to follow me, could you stop her? A bottle of my best port will be waiting at your town house if you do."

Shenstone didn't even hesitate, only said smoothly: "I'll do it—for the bottle of port."

"I thought you'd see it my way."

"Are you heading there now?"

"I am."

"Then, after you."

Adam frowned at his friend, hearing a faint coolness beneath his words, but Shenstone just smiled at him and gestured toward the corridor.

Chapter 12

Faith sat in her safe corner, listening peacefully as Lady Duncan and her friends chatted away about grandchildren, charities, and the foibles of whomever happened to dance past them.

She was finally relaxing, telling herself that nothing would go wrong. Earlier, the Chamberlin ladies had expressed various reactions to Sophia's old gown, in which Faith felt positively bare. But Sophia had laughed and told her to forget her fears, for she looked very respectable next to some young ladies.

"Miss Cooper, would you care to dance?"

She stiffened, recognizing the voice immediately. Timothy Gilpin stood above her, his pale complexion damp in the heat of the crowded drawing room. Though he attempted to look pleasant, he only managed uneasy.

Lady Duncan elbowed her. "Go!" she whispered excitedly.

As if she'd been waiting for Faith to be so blessed.

Faith rose to her feet and put her hand in his. "Thank you, Mr. Gilpin."

The country dance allowed brief conversations here and there, and when they came together, she said, "You didn't even want to be seen with me last time we met. And now we're dancing?"

"My wife is in attendance," he said between smiling lips, "and this makes me look like I care about the poor wallflowers. Although in that gown, I'm not sure you'll remain with the wallflowers long."

Faith felt heat rise in her face, and she wished she could tug on the top of the bodice. "Glad I could help you do a good deed in her eyes," she said dryly.

They separated in the dance, and she turned to find herself bowing to the duke. Her eyes widened—she'd been so focused on the man from her past, she hadn't even seen the man in her present.

"Your Grace," she murmured, not meeting his eyes.

"Miss Cooper."

Soon enough the dance took her back to Timothy. "So why is it so important to look good to your wife?"

He hesitated. "We never kept secrets from each other, did we?"

"I didn't. But apparently you've kept our acquaintance a secret from your wife."

He frowned, then forced another smile. "Marriage is not . . . what I imagined. But you seem to have done well for yourself, living in a duke's home. That is recent, is it not?"

Warily, she said, "I just began to work for his aunt. Having to support myself—that is 'doing well' for myself?"

His gaze dropped to the gown again. "This makes me think you're doing well. And I've been watching you tonight—you look happy."

"Lady Duncan is a thoughtful, gracious woman, easy to be near. The family is generous with their cast-off garments," she added pointedly. "I am content."

"I'm glad someone is," he said sarcastically.

As children they'd meant so much to each other, she thought sadly. She hated to see him almost despondent. "Do you have children, Timothy?"

"No."

"I hope you are soon blessed, because surely, they will brighten your life and your marriage. I would give anything to have what you . . ." She let that thought fade away. Obviously, she still spoke too freely around Timothy.

As the dance took her away from him, he was staring at her intently, and it was almost a relief to turn away—until she saw Rothford, and this time they had to link hands. His skin was warm and firm, calluses on the palms and fingertips representing the hard physical work he'd done in the army. He glanced past her, and she knew he was evaluating Timothy. When he didn't question her, she was tiredly grateful.

When the dance was over, Timothy escorted her back to the wallflower row, and she watched him walk away and approach his wife. She remembered the woman as being newly settled near their village, but once Timothy had shown interest, Faith herself had backed away from any awkward friendship. And her own circumstances soon changed so drastically she hadn't been fit for proper socializing.

Sophia sank down beside her, breathless after her own dance. "I saw you with that gentleman—how wonderful!"

"It was kind of him, yes. And you were dancing with Lord Shenstone."

Sophia leaned closer. "All subterfuge, I promise. I saw Mr. Percy watching us, and I could swear that whenever I began to turn away, his smile died."

"Perhaps he doesn't think Lord Shenstone has the proper . . . reputation for you."

"Hopefully, he will soon realize that *no one* is proper for me but him."

"Are you certain of that?" Faith asked cautiously.

"I am." Sophia's smile was replaced by a look of earnestness. "Last summer we spent many happy hours walking in the country together, attending the same parties, and in general exchanging long conversations. I thought . . . I thought he was ready to ask for my hand. And when he didn't, I was quite distraught, even angry. And he knew it. I even subtly asked him what he wanted, and he was very earnest when he explained how little he had to offer a young lady, especially the daughter of a duke. He's made the decision, and apparently, I have no say."

"He sounds like a proper, thoughtful man."

"Too proper. What care I that he has little money or influence? I have enough for several lifetimes over."

"Perhaps he is too proud for that."

"He would rather us both be miserable, as long as he has his pride?" Sophia asked bitterly. Then she cleared her throat and forced a smile. "Enough of that. I will get what I want in the end. Did you see Shenstone and Emmeline dancing the last dance?"

"I did."

"Did you see how it happened?" When Faith gave her a bemused look, Sophia went on. "I saw my brother head for the terrace alone, pulling a cheroot out of his pocket. And then I saw Emmeline bearing down on him as if she'd follow, little realizing what might happen if people saw them. My brother would not be happy to cause a scandal with her. Much as I love her dearly, he only thinks of her as a sister, or so he told me tonight. I watched in mounting worry as Emmeline was about to follow him out the door, when suddenly Lord Shenstone was there, asking her to dance. I thought she might have hesitated, but he obviously didn't allow her to refuse, for soon they were waltzing."

"Very handy for your brother to have Lord Shenstone around," Faith mused.

Sophia sighed. "I do wish he'd find a young lady and settle down. It would have been lovely were it my dearest friend. Mama is growing preoccupied with this, convinced whatever malaise has Adam in its grip will fade if he's happily married."

Malaise?

Faith could only nod, having nothing to say. It wasn't her place.

Sophia was asked to dance again, and Faith felt restless, watching all the dancing. She offered to fetch Lady Duncan a drink, then set off around the edges of the drawing room. People watched her casually, but it wasn't the same as that prickly, self-aware feeling she'd had when she was shopping with Sophia. She entered the refreshments room and there was a huge table overflowing with treats, and a side table with a punch bowl and glasses of champagne.

She filled two glasses with punch, then turned and almost collided with Rothford, who'd come in behind her.

"Oh!" She caught her glasses in time, but several drops landed on his satin tailcoat. "Oh, dear, here is a napkin."

Smiling, he took it from her hands and dabbed his forearm. "It is nothing. I'm wearing black."

Someone moved past them to take a plate along the buffet table, and Faith awkwardly topped off her two glasses.

"Are you enjoying your evening?" he asked politely.

She stared up at him, and for a moment, she imagined how she'd really feel being swept about in a waltz in his strong arms. She forced a smile. "I am, thank you."

"I saw you dancing and was glad for it. I do believe this is the second event I saw you talking with that man. Do you know him?"

Was he jealous? No, surely he was only curious. For a moment, she wanted to hide everything to do with her past, but it was too easy to discover this particular truth.

"He is Timothy Gilpin, heir to a barony near my village. We grew up together."

He arched a brow. "How interesting. Was he a friend of your brother's?"

"He was a friend of mine, too," she answered truthfully.

She glanced at the doorway to the drawing room. Were they standing here too long? But no one seemed to be taking notice of them.

"A friend?" he echoed.

She smiled, but was not going to explain everything. "We did childish things together—rowed on the pond, collected rocks, chased geese."

"You had no feminine companionship?"

"I did, but the girls were mostly content with their sewing and painting. I liked the outdoors and running about."

His smile deepened. "I can see you doing that, running free and happy under the sun."

They stared into each other's eyes a bit too long, until she forced herself to look back at the two glasses in her hands.

"Was this before or after your father died?" he asked.

"Before. He died when I was sixteen, and it was then that I learned our lands were not earning enough to support us. We weren't able to socialize with neighbors much after that. Mathias was determined not to sell off our land, so he joined the army to help support us."

His expression grave, he said, "I'm sorry to bring up such a painful past. I wanted to know about you. There was no young man who wished to marry you?" He glanced out the drawing room door, as if he could see Timothy.

"Your Grace, I am without dowry, without beauty. Those things matter, and you cannot deny it."

He seemed about to say something, but stopped himself. But she couldn't help wondering if he'd meant to deny her assessment of her features. No, surely she was foolish thinking that.

"I'm sorry," he said simply. "I'm certain you would prefer to be married with children."

"Certainly, but not married to a man I couldn't love."

"And that was Mr. Gilpin?"

She glanced away, trying not to blush with guilt. "No, we never loved each other."

"But this supposed good friend of yours could not find a way to help you when your brother died?"

"It was not his place, sir, surely you see how improper that would have been. And he was betrothed by that point."

"And that was when you took the position with the Warburtons."

"No, not for another year and a half. We managed to get by by selling some of our personal items." It was getting harder and harder to meet his focused gaze. That sale had only lasted them six months, and then she'd been forced to try something drastic.

"Well hello!" said the overly bright voice of Lady Emmeline.

Her eyes glittered upon the two of them, and Faith thought they lingered on her a bit too long.

"Good evening, my lady." Faith turned to the duke, trying for a reasonable excuse. "I'm so sorry I spilled my drink upon your sleeve, Your Grace."

"It was nothing, Miss Cooper."

"Your Grace," Lady Emmeline said, her back to Faith, "perhaps you could hold my plate and help me choose the best things to eat."

Faith left them to the serious deliberations and

returned to Lady Duncan. The elderly woman didn't even know she'd been gone long, just took the drink and went back to explaining how she'd survived a storm at sea on one of her trips to Egypt.

But Faith found herself watching through the double doors, where she could just see the duke and Lady Emmeline standing together talking. It felt a little strange that although she'd felt alone when talking with him, anyone who looked had an easy view.

In fact, she could see Lord Shenstone watching Rothford and Lady Emmeline, his face impassive.

Two days later, Wednesday morning, as Adam's valet was helping him dress, he thought back to his conversation with Faith at the dinner party. He hadn't been able to get it out of his mind. Every time he saw her hurrying through the corridors, barely making eye contact and giving him a polite smile, he'd gone back to that conversation again. Though she'd been open about the problems of her adolescent years, something had seemed . . . off. She'd been vague and uneasy when conversing about the time between Cooper's death and taking a position with the Warburtons. Of course, her personal life was her own, but . . . was she embarrassed about something?

Or was he simply so curious, he'd stopped pretending he could ever treat Faith with the right detachment?

Just as he was tucking his shirt into his trousers, someone knocked on the door with an urgent beat. The valet, a quiet man who seemed intimidated about serving a duke, opened it and stepped back.

Seabrook was there, breathing deeply.

"Seabrook?" Adam said, going to the old man. "Are you well?"

"You received another letter at the servants' entrance, Your Grace. Cook tried to stop the boy—and it was a different boy, by the way—but he failed." Seabrook actually put a hand on the wall to steady himself.

Adam didn't waste any time on the letter, but ran past him, calling over his shoulder. "Did he head for the street?"

"Yes, sir. Dirty tan trousers, black patched coat, cap."

Adam raced down the corridor—two maids flattened themselves against the wall—and took the stairs that outlined the entrance hall. A footman gaped at him.

"Open the door, Hales!" he called, before reaching the landing.

Hales hurried to do so, and Adam barely slowed his speed as he crossed the threshold. He ran down the pavement, through the gate, and found dozens of people moving past in both directions, dressed in all manner of styles.

But nowhere could he see a little boy.

He swore silently to himself and nodded curtly at a man who tipped his hat to him. The woman on his arm stared wide-eyed at Adam, and he realized he'd come out in only his boots, trousers, and shirtsleeves. He turned around and walked sedately back inside.

More servants were gathered in the hall to stare at him, joined by Aunt Theodosia and Faith.

"What is it, boy?" his aunt asked, as if he were eight and caught where he shouldn't be.

"I tried to catch a messenger," he said, not pausing as he ascended the stairs again.

"A messenger?" she called up to him, sounding disbelieving.

He didn't look back. Seabrook was waiting in his bedroom, the valet gone.

"I didn't catch him," Adam said.

Without a word, the old man handed over the note, on the same rough paper.

"Thank you, Seabrook. You may go."

Feeling tense, Adam broke open the seal and read:

She's still there, in your home. You don't know anything about her. Your obsession is showing.

He sank down in a chair near the hearth and read it again. What the hell did this person hope to accomplish? The last message was about him keeping away from Faith, but this one seemed more personal—

As if the anonymous writer knew something about Faith that he didn't.

He pulled out the first letter from his drawer and compared them: the same paper, the same scrawled, almost illegible hand. He couldn't even tell whether it was a man or a woman.

And then he had a thought—was this an actual threat toward Faith?

Once again, a letter had come after an event with dozens of people. He hadn't danced with Faith to call attention to her, but they had talked almost privately together in the parlor.

If the letter writer thought he'd release Faith from his service, send her away, then that person was a fool. It was only making him more curious, more determined to stick close to her and make sure she wasn't targeted just because she knew him.

But if it was truly about Faith, he had to know. He would contact Raikes again and send him north to her village, to find out anything in her background that could harm her.

Chapter 13

After luncheon, Faith was about to leave for her weekly trip to see the Society of Ladies' Companions and Chaperones, when she heard Frances's raised voice.

"But Miss Hervey promised me I could go out!"

Faith had never heard the young girl raise her voice. She walked forward slowly to find the duchess seated in her morning room, frowning at her granddaughter.

"Now, Frances, Miss Hervey is ill today, and the cool breeze will make her worse. Do return to the nursery and occupy yourself with your schoolwork."

"But today is our outing! Mother already left so I can't go with her and—" She broke off, took a deep, shaky breath, and hung her head in dejection.

"Excuse me, Your Grace," Faith said cautiously.

The woman looked up and frowned. "Yes, Miss Cooper?"

"It is my afternoon off. Lady Frances could accompany me on a walk to the park. It would be no trouble. As long as you think her mother wouldn't mind."

The duchess didn't even hesitate. "Excellent idea. Frances, you are lucky Miss Cooper offered. You will follow her direction in all things, of course."

Frances gave Faith a slow growing smile. "Of course, Miss Cooper. Thank you so much."

Faith was glad Frances had finally gotten over her shyness where she was concerned. She held out a gloved hand, and the girl took it. Soon they were walking out the front door.

"Where shall we go, Miss Cooper?"

"I have some friends to meet in Hyde Park."

The girl was quiet for several minutes, until at last she said, "Why don't you have a husband, Miss Cooper?"

Faith had known little girls have questions, but that was a discerning one. "I never met a man to love."

"Mother says sometimes if we have a fondness for a man, it's a good place to begin."

"That's true, but that fondness should be quite strong, don't you think?"

"And you never felt that?"

"It is a shame, but no." How to tell a young girl that marriage was based on so much more than love?

"It must have been your dowry," Frances said, nodding thoughtfully.

Faith blinked at her but didn't know what to say.

"It cannot have been you, because you're very nice, and you're pretty."

"Why . . . thank you, Lady Frances."

They walked along companionably until they entered the gates of the park.

"What shall we do?" Frances asked. "Hunt for frogs?"

"One of my favorite things ever, when I was your age. But first, I must say hello to the friends I came here to meet."

Jane and Charlotte were waiting on their usual bench, both full of smiles as they were introduced to Lady Frances.

"I know you all will talk," the little girl said solemnly. "I need to look for frogs on the Serpentine. Might I go, Miss Cooper?"

"Always stay where I can see you, Lady Frances."

When the little girl was a distance away, Charlotte said, "And now you are a governess? You seem to take on more positions everywhere you go."

Faith winced. "Lady Frances's governess was ill today, and she wished to go outside. I didn't think you'd mind."

"Oh, we don't," Jane said, watching the girl squat near the bank of the small lake. Wistfully, she said, "I would love to see young children more."

They were all spinsters, and for a moment, the air about them was solemn with unfulfilled dreams. But they were also practical women, Faith knew, who did not dwell on what they could not have.

"Faith," Charlotte said, "I saw you at the Lady Ludlow's dinner party the other night, but you did not see me."

Faith turned to her, wide-eyed. "But . . . though there were many people, how could I have missed you? Oh, please forgive me, Charlotte."

"You did not look yourself—I almost didn't recognize you."

She looked down at Faith's shawl, which covered another elegant gown.

Faith sighed. "Lady Sophia insisted I wear her cast-off garments. I do not quite feel myself in them."

"You look lovely," Jane said brightly.

Charlotte gave her an irritated glance, and Jane bit her lip.

"Well, it certainly isn't as wrinkled as her last gown," Jane insisted, "but your hair . . . dear Faith . . ."

"I know, I know. I think the bonnet is barely holding it in place. My maid, Ellen . . . she is trying, but . . . she is a sullen, strange creature, and I wish to give her the benefit of the doubt."

"You looked better at the dinner party," Charlotte said impassively.

"Lady Sophia insisted her maid work with me, to show Ellen. I do not think the instructions have yet taken." She touched Charlotte's gloved hand.

"Please tell me you forgive me for not greeting you at the dinner party."

"I forgive you, but there is something you are too close to see—I watched the Duke of Rothford that night."

Faith swallowed, trying to look serious rather than worried.

"I have heard . . . stories of his youth. Much as he's been a soldier for many years, it seems his wisdom is still lacking—or else he has missed our fair sex far too much. He kept you in the refreshments room for far too long, talking."

Faith winced. "I know, but it's hard to escape without being rude. He's a nice man."

"He has designs on you," Charlotte said boldly.

Jane gasped. "Oh, Charlotte, that cannot be!"

Faith leaned toward her friend. "Any man might sin within his heart. It's how he acts that matters. He is an honorable man, Charlotte. He cares about the good opinions of his mother and aunt and sister."

"Does he?"

When Adam returned from his business meeting, he felt satisfied that he would soon find out the truth about Faith, and know that this anonymous blackguard was fomenting trouble for trouble's sake. He found his mother, aunt, sister, and sister-in-law in the family drawing room, awaiting their callers.

He frowned. "Where is Miss Cooper?"

"This is her afternoon off," Aunt Theodosia said, spectacles perched on her nose as she looked up from her needlework. "She took Lady Frances to the park with her."

"I beg your pardon?" Marian cried, standing up at the piano bench. "You did not tell me this. Why is she not with her governess?"

"Because her governess is ill," Adam's mother said languidly, even as she smiled at her son. "The child was quite happy to be out of doors. Did I do wrong, Adam?"

"Of course not, Mother," he said. He'd worried that this blackguard was subtly threatening Faith—but he'd thought he had time to ensure her safety, to talk to the staff about tightening the security of Rothford Court, to make sure she never went out alone. He was a fool.

Marian drew herself up. "I will have to speak to Miss Cooper about the familiarities she takes upon herself."

"Oh, Marian, do sit down," Aunt Theodosia said with exasperation. "I don't see you taking your daughter for a walk when she wants one."

"Of course I do!"

Adam headed for the entrance hall. "I'll leave you ladies to your callers."

He didn't bother sending for his horse, knowing that would take time he didn't have. Instead, he marched quickly toward Hyde Park. He didn't mean to frown, but at least a dozen people practically jumped out of his way.

He knew right where to find Faith, and when he saw her with her friends in the distance, relief moved through him and he slowed down. He could never imagine her hurt, not ever again. He realized she was becoming more and more important to him.

He might have tried to stay out of sight, but the chaperone, already frowning at Faith, spotted him with her sharp eyesight, and drew herself up aloofly. She must have said something to Faith, who whirled about until she saw him, then her blush was clearly visible.

As he approached, he bowed his head. "Good afternoon, ladies."

Faith's younger friend was wide-eyed as she gazed up at him, but not the elder.

Faith looked between him and her friends with embarrassment. "Your Grace, allow me to introduce Miss Charlotte Atherstone and Miss Jane Ogden. Ladies, His Grace, the Duke of Rothford."

Both women came to their feet and curtsied. Miss Ogden touched Miss Atherstone's arm as if she were slightly unbalanced, and then he noticed she held one leg stiffly.

"A pleasure to meet friends of Miss Cooper's," Adam said.

"Your Grace," Faith said, "is something amiss?"

"It seems my mother should have consulted Lady Tunbridge before allowing Frances to leave the house."

"Oh, dear, she was upset?"

"Mildly."

"Then I shall take the child home at once."

"Where is she?" he asked, frowning. Damn, was he going to have to worry about every woman in his household until he solved this mystery?

"Down by the Serpentine," she answered, then spread her hands, "catching frogs."

"Ah, a favorite pastime. You enjoy your conversation a while longer, and I'll see what my niece is up to."

He walked away, then smiled when Frances looked up from the embankment and shouted, "Uncle Adam! Come look what I found!"

He made all the appropriate remarks about the frogs' colors and jumping abilities, but he kept glancing at the ladies on the bench—her Society for Ladies' Companions and Chaperones, if he remembered correctly. He would have liked to call them that to see their reaction, except that would have been betraying a confidence.

The older woman didn't trust him—that was easy to see. She was watching him even now, saying something serious to Faith.

Warning her about him?

Six years ago, he'd been the kind of young man every chaperone warned their charge about—bold, reckless, wild, uncaring about a woman's reputation. He'd taken pride in it. But now he didn't want Faith to believe the worst of him, wished she could know he'd do anything to keep her safe.

He looked around. Was someone watching them even now?

And then Frances plopped hands-first into the edge of the Serpentine, wetting herself up to the elbows. She glanced wide-eyed at him, then burst into laughter, and he couldn't help grinning.

He didn't know if that made him the stuff of good fatherhood, but he wanted to give it a try someday soon.

An heir and all that, he told himself, not looking at Faith.

He helped Frances to her feet and brought her back to Faith, who was already standing.

"Oh, dear, the frogs pulled you in, did they?" she asked.

Frances giggled, and Adam couldn't help smiling from her to Faith. Until he saw her "chaperones" frowning at him.

"We should go," Faith said.

If it were any other time, he would tell her to stay while he took Frances home, but she couldn't be alone anymore.

"I will be happy to escort Frances, Your Grace. Please do not trouble yourself."

"I'll walk with you, Miss Cooper. I have business at home." He nodded to her friends. "Ladies."

She waved but it was halfhearted, and he wondered again what they'd been saying to her. He didn't like anyone making her unhappy. But of course, he regularly did a bang-up job of that himself.

"I'm sorry to have made Lady Tunbridge cross," Faith said, then gestured toward Frances, who was joyfully wringing out her sleeves as she walked ahead of them. "And this won't help."

"I was watching her for the water mishap. She was perfectly clean and dry until I arrived." He glanced over his shoulder, where her two friends had already leaned their heads together to talk. "Why do I have the feeling I have not made a good impression on them?"

"You are paying too much attention to me," she said softly. "People are watching."

He stiffened, almost catching her arm to stop her, but remembering himself in time. "What do you mean people are watching?"

"Your Grace, I am but a companion in your household. I know you feel responsible for me because of my brother, but you've done what you wished, and you need to let it go. People are noticing the inappropriateness of your . . . attention to me."

If only she knew the depth of that. And he wanted to make her happy, to step back as she wanted, but now he couldn't. And he couldn't tell her why, not the real truth.

When he didn't speak, only frowned and continued to walk with his hands behind his back, she stole a glance at him.

"Sir? Do we have an understanding?"

He sighed. "I don't know if we do. I cannot forget that you are in this situation because of me. I'll do what I must to help and protect you, but I'll try to be more subtle about it."

She pressed her lips together and narrowed her eyes. "I cannot change your mind?"

"No, you cannot." He wanted to tell her she'd have to travel with a footman at all times now, but suspected that would sound better coming from his aunt—not a cowardly thought at all, he told himself.

Trying to lighten the mood, he said, "Though this is none of my business, I did like the look of your hair at the Ludlow dinner party the other night. Why the extremes?"

She rolled her eyes. "Sir, my hair is not your concern."

"It is when my servant is styling it."

"I've told you already, Ellen is new to this. I know she is a servant, but I wish to have a decent relationship with her. Things are slowly improving."

"A decent relationship with your maid?" he asked blankly.

"You are a man; perhaps it does not even make sense to you, but I like to be on easy terms with everyone around me."

"And this maid does not treat you well?"

"Please do not put words into my mouth. We will be fine."

He frowned, but Faith held up a hand just as Frances hung back when they approached the gate at Rothford Court.

Frances looked up at him solemnly. "Uncle Adam, maybe my mother will not mind my wet sleeves so much if I am with you."

"That makes perfect sense." He reached for her hand and gave it a squeeze, even though his own gloves grew damp.

Faith gave him a reluctant smile, and he knew she was still perturbed at him. He couldn't stop thinking about the maid, and why her behavior both bothered him and raised his curiosity. And suddenly it started him on a different thought, that perhaps this blackguard had connections to someone inside the house. But surely not a maid.

Once they were inside, where there were already several lady callers, Marian didn't put up much of a fuss about Frances's wet sleeves, and the girl happily went up to the nursery. Faith retired to her own room, it still being her afternoon off, and Adam was lucky enough to catch his aunt returning to the drawing room.

He pulled her aside and spoke softly. "Aunt, I need you to do something for me without asking me questions."

She lifted her monocle and stared at him. "This is highly peculiar."

"I do not wish the ladies of the household to run errands or go on walks without a footman. As a duke, I have a high profile in London, and perhaps my past deeds have not endeared me to the public."

"Nonsense, you were a young man, never imagining you'd inherit the dukedom."

"Regardless, I would feel better if the ladies had a degree of protection on the streets."

"Well . . . that makes sense, my dear boy, but I have the feeling there is more you're not saying."

He leaned down to kiss her cheek. "I always have things I don't say. I'm a scoundrel, remember?"

Chapter 14

Three days later, on their next shopping outing, Faith was surprised when Lady Duncan insisted Sophia and Faith take along a footman. Well, perhaps "surprised" was the wrong word—nothing the old woman did could be surprising anymore. Against all accepted etiquette, she liked to place calls upon eligible young men, to better acquaint herself with which man might suit which debutante—to Sophia's mortification. Not that it was all for Sophia; she offered matchmaking advice to all the young ladies, when she paid calls on *them*. Faith was relieved that Lady Duncan didn't ask her to come along on those fact-finding missions—it would have been terribly awkward. No young gentleman was looking to marry her. It made her feel a bit old.

And then she'd catch the duke looking at her, his gaze, usually so respectful, hinting at a smolder that made her feel hot and cold and yearning.

What was wrong with her? A man's admiration was one thing, but she should not respond to it with such eager feelings, feelings that she had to work so hard to suppress.

She tried to tell herself that admiration for her person was fine—and even flattering—as long as he didn't act upon it. But she still shivered when she remembered the dark, moonlit conservatory, and how the simple touch of his hand upon her cheek had seemed as intimate and forbidden as the act of sex itself.

Which was ridiculous, of course.

All these thoughts ran through her foolish brain as she walked beside Lady Sophia, the footman trailing behind.

"Faith, I heard an interesting piece of news from my lady's maid today. She claims that my brother had private words with your maid and the housekeeper, and that poor Ellen was actually shaking with distress when the interview was over."

Faith winced. "I asked your brother to let me handle Ellen."

"You two actually discussed the maid?" Sophia said, eyebrow arched in almost the same way her brother's did.

"Well . . . even he seemed to notice my hair styling. He probably doesn't want me to represent his household poorly."

"That doesn't make sense. But being lately of the army, he does have a sense of military authority with the servants, as if they're all his soldiers.

Anyway, you should not fret. I just wanted you to know that I'm certain Ellen will be much better now."

And scared to death, and thinking that Faith tattled on her. Faith wasn't happy.

Suddenly Sophia took her arm and gave a little squeeze. "Look, it's Mr. Percy, just crossing the street ahead of us. How do I get his attention without appearing foolish?"

Faith hid a smile. "We can just keep walking toward him. He will have to acknowledge us. Unless he's upset at your accepting Lord Shenstone's courtship."

Sophia gave a little gasp. "That would mean my plan is working."

And then Mr. Percy saw them, and Faith had the pleasure of watching his gaze both brighten and soften when looking upon the beautiful Sophia. Sophia blushed becomingly, and Faith found herself hoping that the young woman could have this relationship, if it made her happy. And she had to admire her for going after what she wanted.

For just a moment, she thought she saw a touch of sadness in the young vicar's eyes, but he banished it.

"Mr. Percy, just the person I wanted to see," Sophia said boldly.

Mr. Percy bowed to Faith, then took Sophia's outstretched hand and briefly held it in his own. "I am always happy to be of help, my lady."

"Could we discuss the Female Aid Society? I

am active with the charity here in London, but I was wondering how it can be broadened in the countryside."

He looked pleased at her concern, and the two of them turned to begin walking down the street. Faith dropped back behind to give them some privacy.

Soon she spotted a gentleman she knew, but she could not brighten like Sophia did for Mr. Percy. Timothy Gilpin was alone as he moved forward, and there was a languidness about him that confused her. And then she wondered if he'd been drinking at such an early hour of the day. When he saw Faith, there was no look of pleasure for her. She bitterly wished their time as children could be remembered fondly, but her foolish intimate afternoon with him had clouded everything good they'd once shared—at least in his mind.

Sophia and Percy turned into a bookshop, and Hales, the footman, hesitated near Faith.

"Do follow your mistress, Hales. She might have packages for you to carry. There is a friend of mine approaching. We won't go far."

The footman hesitated, then dutifully followed the other couple. By this time, Timothy had seen her and approached. Though his feet came to a stop, his upper body seemed to keep moving forward until he pulled back.

"Good morning, Mr. Gilpin," she said hesitantly.

"Faith."

His disrespect surprised her.

He glanced into the bookshop. "You move in high circles now, don't you?"

There was a faintly belligerent, almost menacing quality to his voice, and for the first time, she felt almost . . . unsafe. In broad daylight on Regent Street.

"We've discussed my situation before," she said quietly.

"I guess all along you wanted better than what you had, than what a simple gentleman from the country could give you."

Her lips briefly parted in shock. She was forced to move closer to preserve their privacy, when she wanted nothing more than to escape him.

"Timothy, there was never any talk of an attachment between us. You were engaged when we parted, not I. But we were on friendly terms. What happened?"

"You know what happened," he sneered, his words faintly slurred.

She spread both hands, her reticule bumping against her hip. "But I don't. I know you're unhappy now, but that's no reason to mistake what happened in the past."

And then he put his hand on her arm, and his grip was not gentle. She did not want to be seen pulling away, but her fear was rising steadily.

"Timothy, release me," she said, a cool command. "Our footman is just inside the door."

"Threatening me now with the power of your duke?"

"No, trying to remind you that you're a gentleman. You do not wish people to see you behaving otherwise."

He inhaled deeply, then released her. "You are correct. It was . . . thoughtless of me."

That wasn't exactly an apology. "Timothy, I know you are unhappy, but only you can make things better for yourself."

He sighed. "I don't need to be preached to. I have that on a daily basis."

And then he turned away, and his first step was practically a stagger, until he righted himself and carefully put one foot in front of the other.

Faith rubbed her arms, feeling chilled. What was wrong with Timothy? He was actually making it sound like she'd *rejected* him! It had to be the alcohol he'd imbibed making him say such foolish things, making him change the past to suit whatever was going on in the present. Was he trying to pretend his marriage was her fault?

Sophia and Mr. Percy emerged from the bookshop. She carried a paper-wrapped package, and her face positively glowed with happiness.

"Faith, I was going to insist you come in the shop with us, but then I saw that you had company. I hope it went well."

But there was a seriousness hidden within her cheerful voice that said she had noticed the tension between her and Timothy even from inside the shop.

"All is well, my lady," Faith said.

Mr. Percy cleared his throat. "Then I will leave

you two ladies to your shopping. Thank you, my lady, for consulting me on the Female Aid Society. There is much good to be done there, and it cheers me to see your interest."

When he walked away, Sophia didn't bother to conceal the adoration. The footman almost seemed to blush as he moved past her to take up his place behind.

"He is such a good man," Sophia said reverently.

"So it has seemed in our brief acquaintance."

Sophia took her arm. "I refuse to give up hope, especially when he speaks to me so gently."

"Perhaps . . . that is not fair of him, if he's determined not to court you?"

"Oh, no, it says to me that his feelings are more powerful than he can contain. I am truly flattered."

Faith hid a sigh and hoped that her friend wasn't setting herself up for disappointment.

Back at Rothford Court, Faith returned her bonnet and shawl to her room and found Ellen hanging a newly pressed gown in the wardrobe.

"Ellen, may I speak with you?"

The pale girl nodded and stepped toward her, shoulders back like a soldier.

Faith sighed. "Please do not tell me that His Grace talked to like you were one of his men."

Ellen tilted her chin but said nothing.

"I heard today that he spoke with you, and I want you to know that I asked him not to."

Ellen shot her a brief, bewildered look. "He's the duke, miss. Why should he not say whatever he wants to me?"

"I know he's the duke, but . . . I thought you and I were slowly reaching an understanding. I did not complain to anyone in authority about you."

Ellen shrugged, and Faith wasn't certain the girl believed her.

"That is all, Ellen, and thank you."

The girl slunk away, and Faith desperately wished she could march down to the duke's study and tell him exactly what she thought of his high-handed behavior. But it wouldn't do to seek him out. And he wouldn't care anyway, for he always believed he was right. She couldn't imagine what it was like to be a man, let alone a peer, and know you could do or say anything you wished.

Two nights later, Adam was escorting the entire household on a visit to the pleasure gardens at Vauxhall, on the southern bank of the Thames. Even little Frances was in attendance, because Sophia insisted that it was the last night that Mademoiselle Caroline, the "Greatest Female Equestrian in Europe" (so said the newspapers), would be performing.

"Every young girl should see a famous equestrian, as well as the fireworks," Sophia said, as they one by one left the barge Adam had hired to take them to Vauxhall pier at dusk.

The women all wore or carried masks on sticks, many with feathers, and Adam thought they looked like a flock of colorful birds. He wore his own plain mask tied across his upper face. As they entered the grounds, he was glad to see Faith lower hers, to see the expression of wonder on her face as she saw the gas-lamp globes high in every tree, lighting the way down the Grand Walk. Near the Grove, where the orchestra already played in its Gothic temple, four colonnades housed the supper boxes where they would dine later. But first the Rotunda, to see the horsemanship show.

As they were awaiting entrance, crowds all about them, both high and low born, Sophia said to him, "I hope you do not mind if Emmeline joins us."

He forced a smile. "Of course not. She is here with her family?"

"Yes, but she made sure she took a supper box near ours."

Faith looked away, but not before he saw the smile she tried to hide. Even his aunt's companion recognized his reluctance, but not his sister.

But then, he'd felt a connection with Faith almost from the first, an understanding he'd never felt with any other woman. It caused him to think of her as more than his aunt's companion—he thought of her too much.

As for Emmeline, he'd been grateful to Shenstone for guiding her away at the last dinner party, and he'd sent along his best port as promised. He'd invited his friend to attend tonight, and perhaps more arrangements could be made between them. Shenstone didn't seem to mind being seen on the arm of a popular, beautiful young lady.

But Emmeline found their party just as they'd barely set foot on the grounds, and her family agreed that she could accompany them. They all followed the crowds that meandered through the grounds, along paths that led to gloomy grottos and shadowy temples. Frances giggled with wonder, especially when she saw the gaslit pond with a gigantic Neptune and eight sea-horses rising out of it. Then Emmeline got too close pointing out fish to Frances, and Adam had to grab her arm just before she toppled in. She looked at him like he'd rescued her from a charging elephant in the Punjab.

He was infinitely glad when the equestrian show began, and he could keep Frances between himself and Emmeline. But Frances proved far too curious about the shadowy grounds of Vauxhall rather than whether a lady equestrian could dance on an unsaddled horse and jump over boards. She kept asking Adam question after question, and he was relieved when it was time to head to their supper box, decorated at the rear with a curious painting of fairies in a forest. At least that distracted Frances for a while, until they were served their shaved ham, tiny chickens, and assorted biscuits and cheese cakes. He gave her a few shillings for the fruit girl when she might next make an appearance.

And through it all, he watched the crowds. There were so many people, he couldn't imagine a threat to Faith manifesting itself here, with so many witnesses. But he wouldn't let his guard down.

"Frances?" Lady Marian said sharply.

Adam looked down the table toward his sister-in-law.

She rose to her feet, napkin falling to the floor of the supper box. "Frances!" Now her voice was louder, and a touch wild.

Adam looked under the table and to the supper boxes on either side of them. "She's not here?"

"No, and I didn't see her leave."

"Did anyone see the fruit girl go by?" Adam asked. "Frances had money for it."

"You gave her coins to spend?" Marian demanded. "Without consulting me?"

"Marian, don't be foolish," Lady Duncan said. "He was treating the girl. I'm certain she's nearby."

"But she kept talking about Neptune in the pond," Faith reminded them all. "Do you think she would have gone back for a second look?"

There was a frozen moment before Faith grabbed her mask and marched to the stairs at the rear and headed down without asking anyone's permission.

"We'll go, too!" said Sophia.

She and Emmeline got between him and

Faith, who definitely shouldn't be wandering the grounds alone. All three young women disappeared down the stairs.

"Aunt Theodosia, remain here in case the child returns," he ordered.

His aunt saluted him.

His mother looked concerned. "What should I do, Adam? My poor grandchild . . ."

"You and Marian walk together among the supper boxes and see if any of the guests have seen her. I'll search the grounds."

"Perhaps you'll need to search for our young ladies, too," Aunt Theodosia said.

He knew she was trying for levity to lighten the tension, but he couldn't smile for her benefit. Not only was a ten-year-old girl alone amidst the rowdy patrons, Faith was making herself a target. Not that she knew it, of course. It would be so much easier if he could warn her of the possible threat, but he knew she'd leave London to protect the household—and then there'd be nobody to protect her.

Adam walked briskly down the gravel paths, following the Grand Walk, the South Walk, and then the Hermit's Walk, figuring that the lit transparency of a hermit might intrigue a little girl.

And it had. He found her right up front, trying to peer around the image and see how it was lit from behind.

"Frances," he called.

More than one person got out of his way, several ladies curtsying. He realized he'd forgotten to don his own mask, and did so at once. It covered the upper half of his face, plain black, no frills or feathers like some of the dandies trying to impress their women.

Frances didn't try to run away, only gave him a brilliant smile. "Uncle Adam, I thought I was going to find a real hermit, and instead it's just a picture of an old man all lit up."

"Maybe there's a real hermit, but hermits don't like crowds. A transparency makes sense." He put a hand on her shoulder until she looked up at him again. "You gave us all a fright, Frances, your mother especially."

She winced. "I didn't mean to run off, but I tried to find the fruit girl, and there were so many people I got carried away."

"I specifically said the fruit girl would come to us, did I not?"

She lowered her gaze. "You might have . . ."

"There is no 'might' about it. You must return to the supper box and face the consequences of your behavior."

She heaved a dramatic sigh and let him take her hand. By the time they returned to the box, Marian and his mother had also returned, and to his surprise, Marian took one look at Frances and burst into tears. She was such a cool, repressed woman, it was easy to forget that she seemed to love her daughter above all.

"Where did you go, young lady?" Marian demanded, a bit too shrilly.

Aunt Theodosia took her arm. "Marian, she's here and safe. Do calm yourself before you have an attack."

"How can I?" She rounded on Adam. "This is all your fault—giving a curious child coins and encouraging her to wander."

It was partly his fault, and he bowed to her. "You are right, Marian. I should have consulted you."

"Mother, it is certainly not Uncle Adam's fault!" Frances cried.

As she was defending him, he realized all three younger women were still missing.

"You are a good girl to defend your uncle," Marian said, "but do not think I don't realize you willfully disobeyed me. If you wanted to see the Hermit, we would have seen him before the fireworks. Now we will remain here."

"Oh, Mother!" Frances cried, flinging herself dramatically into a chair.

"Has anyone seen the three young ladies of our party?" Adam asked, frowning.

There was a brief silence before his mother said, "But you followed Sophia."

"Too late to see where she went in the crowd. I'll find them."

He wasn't all that worried about Sophia and Emmeline. They did not have an anonymous blackguard hinting at threats. But Faith . . .

Back out into the crowd he went, where every masked person seemed suspicious. Mouths open in laughter were false beneath peacock-feathered eyes. Groups of men with leering gazes made him think of predatory jungle cats. His younger self would have been one of those men. Faith may have had her mask, but if anyone was following her, he'd know who she was.

He did see Sophia and Emmeline from a distance, but didn't chase them down. If they returned to the box, then people would know Faith was out here alone.

Adam didn't see her on any of the open walks through the Grove, so he headed deeper into the gardens, where shadows blocked many of the gas globes high up in the trees, and people were now deliberately trying to hide their assignations. The ponds still drew too many revelers, but there were several ancient "ruins" farther away from the main pleasure garden walkways. Perhaps Faith thought a little girl might like to explore.

But big girls explored, too, and he caught a glimpse of Faith from behind, disappearing into the gloom of a Roman temple. Though he ducked behind a tree and watched to see if someone approached, no one seemed to be following, and the lamps didn't extend down this path. He turned and followed her up the faux-marble stairs.

She gave a gasp and whirled around, the sequined mask pressed hard to her face as if for protection. The satin of her gown glistened by distant light, and suddenly she looked like the fairy in their supper box painting, distant, ethereal, lovely.

"Faith, it's me." He lowered his mask.

She lowered hers as her shoulders briefly slumped. "Your Grace, you startled me."

"Of course you're startled. You're off in a remote place alone, putting yourself in danger."

"Never mind that, we have to think about Frances. She must be so frightened. Heavens, *I* can find reason to feel frightened with so many strangers about. Has anyone seen her? Oh, could she have wandered to the Thames?"

Her voice was growing more fearful, her tone higher in panic.

He took her by the shoulders and gave her a little shake. "Faith, calm yourself."

"But Frances—"

"I found her and escorted her back to her mother."

"Oh, Adam!" she cried.

And then she fell into his arms. It was what he'd dreamed of on sleepless nights, holding her, feeling the press of her breasts to his chest, the flare of her hips in his hands. He forgot all about where they were, why they were alone together. He forgot the risk of his dishonor and her ruin. There was still a corrupt beast inside him, waiting for this chance. All that mattered was that they were alone, and she was with him, and he wished he never had to let her go.

Wasn't this how people felt when they wanted

to marry? Now that was a shocking thought, but he couldn't be surprised.

She lifted her head and looked up at him, and the faint moonlight or a distant globe just touched her face, made the sheen of her eyes seem to glow, glistened on her parted lips.

And then he kissed her.

Chapter 15

Faith had thought the duke's appearance out of the darkness was startling, but nothing surprised her more than looking into his eyes, gleaming out of the dark shadows of his face, and realizing she'd thrown herself against him, so boldly wanton without even questioning it.

Her behavior had the usual male response—he leaned down, blotting out the world beyond, even her very conscience, and kissed her.

And suddenly she wasn't Miss Cooper, spinster lady's companion, anymore. She knew what to do to excite passion, how best to increase her own pleasure. She didn't think, or she would have been lost in recrimination and regret.

She simply existed, here in Adam's arms, languid with the knowledge of sensual pleasure. When he kissed her gently, it wasn't enough to combat the urgent need that had been building inside her. She'd been dreaming of him, even that simple touch on her cheek, imagining his hands on her body, him filling her. She opened her mouth, boldly suckling on his lip, burning for him.

At last his tongue swept into her mouth and she met it with her own, dueled and rasped and tasted. She clutched his shoulders, pressed herself hard against him, even rolled her hips into his, inciting his shudder.

"Faith," he said against her mouth.

"Touch me, Adam. Oh please, touch me," she added on a moan.

His hands slid up and down her back, then settled on her backside and pulled her even harder against him, controlling their thrusts until she was panting against his mouth. Her own hands roamed his shoulders and arms, feeling the muscles of a man who'd done more these last six years than frequent gambling dens or ballrooms.

She gasped when he broke their kiss and pressed his mouth to her forehead, her cheek, her jaw. She arched backward, letting him sweep aside the shawl from her shoulders, revealing the gown's bodice she'd been hiding. It showed too much, and though she'd regretted it earlier in the evening, such concerns were long gone. She moaned as he traced his open mouth down her neck, licked at the hollow in her throat, traced a path to the valley between her breasts. Barely able to think, she was caught in a haze of heat and passion and desperation.

Then his hand came up and caught her breast,

pushing it higher, so that his mouth could skim the high curve.

She felt . . . lost, overcome—and suddenly very frightened. It was as if another woman had emerged from inside her, and all along she'd barely been held back.

Faith broke away from the kiss, unable to catch her breath, her breasts rising and falling in the moonlight, Adam watching her.

"Your Grace, I—I—" What could she say, how could she explain what kind of woman she was, without risking her position, her livelihood, her very soul, if she didn't stop herself from wanting what she should not have?

"That kiss—" he began, then his words faded as he stared at her mouth.

She realized his breathing was labored, too, that he was just as affected. But what did that matter? He was a *man*, and could do as he wished. And now he knew what kind of woman she was, that she was sinful, that she was no innocent—at least at kissing, she reminded herself. There were many women who kissed, but went no farther.

But inside her disquieted mind, she could lie to herself no longer, could not ignore that she was already long ago ruined, by her own decision. At the depths of her poverty, she'd given in and taken a protector. She'd thought for certain that the degradation of being a man's mistress would have wiped such carnal needs out of her, but apparently not.

"I—I should not—we should not have—" And then words failed her.

"I kissed you," he said hoarsely, quietly. "It wasn't your fault."

"I didn't push you away."

He arched a brow. "Maybe I'm irresistible."

"Don't!" she cried, then covered her mouth and looked around as if they might be seen. "Don't tease me or make light of what we did. Don't return to that young man you must have been, who didn't take such things seriously. That's not you anymore."

He tensed, lowering his head and looking at her with flashing eyes.

"You know—you know I have kissed before," she said. "I like it . . . too much. We cannot do that again—we *must* not! I am in your employ. I'll lose everything if we're caught."

"I won't let that happen."

"No?" she said bitterly, backing away from him. "You are not God or a king. You can protect yourself, but not me."

"I'll *always* protect you, Faith."

He said it with a sincerity that was almost frightening.

"Ohh," she groaned in anguish, turning away from him before looking back. "Don't do this. You don't owe me any more on my brother's behalf. And—and stay here. Let me return alone."

"Find Sophia and Emmeline. If they're still out there, they don't know about Frances, so you can't confess the knowledge. Just go back to the box with them. You'll be safe."

"Adam, I'm safe from everything but you."

That hurt Adam more than he'd thought possible. She was right—and she was wrong, but he couldn't explain. After lifting up her mask to cover her face, she turned and vanished into the shadows, her gown one last glimmer as if in a dream.

He stood frozen, feeling anguished and confused—and aroused. So very aroused that even now his body hummed with it, his need a source of guilt and also freedom.

Because she felt it, too. God, she felt it, too, and acted upon it. Her mouth was a revelation, her experience, her demand, her passion. Shockingly bold and sensual. Yes, she'd kissed him without reserve, but he wasn't certain how much farther she'd ever experienced desire. She wasn't one of the rich widows or actresses of his youth, although being near her, kissing her, reminded him of those days, the thrill of forbidden desire.

She was a mystery, a fascinating mystery he had to unravel.

And protect.

He ran then, mask back in place. Near the edge of the elm trees, he spotted her catching up to Sophia and Emmeline near the supper boxes, and in a moment, he could go back.

"Rothford?"

He knew Shenstone's voice, even though the man wore a striped mask over most of his face.

"Shenstone."

"You've been running?" his friend asked.

His voice sounded . . . odd.

"Frances was missing, but I found her. Then I had to find the ladies looking for her."

He found himself wishing Shenstone would remove the mask. His body seemed stiff with tension. Had Shenstone seen Faith run from him?

"I'm glad the girl is fine. I have to meet with friends." Shenstone nodded his good-bye and turned away.

Adam stared after him, thinking that these last few days, he'd seen little of his friend. "Care for a fencing rematch this week?" he called.

Shenstone acted as if he hadn't heard. But later, during the fireworks, Adam watched his friend return, but not to apologize or even speak to him. He stayed with the ladies, Sophia and Emmeline, making them laugh, letting them hold his arms as they craned their necks to see the brilliant fireworks exploding overhead.

Adam didn't know what was going on, but he almost thought Shenstone was working his wiles on Sophia—under Adam's nose.

Faith spent the next two days forcing herself to be pleasant and normal, writing speeches with Lady Duncan, who was too polite to ask her what was wrong, if she sensed anything at all. Faith had trouble focusing on the book she was reading aloud to the lady, kept losing her train of thought about the speeches.

And at night she lay achingly awake, desperate for more of Adam's caresses, staring at the play of shadows across her ceiling and wondering why God had cursed her to so enjoy the touch of a man not her husband.

She wasn't naïve—of course young ladies swooned at stolen kisses from their suitors. But Faith knew what happened next, had lain beneath a man, felt his body moving over her, inside her, knew what ruin it led to—and she'd kissed Adam anyway.

She couldn't even call him by his title anymore—she'd touched him too intimately, ached to do more. In her lonely bed, she dreamed he was there with her, touching her, and once she awoke from sleep, her hand settled on her breast. She'd cried then for what her year as a mistress had done to her, revealing her nature.

She couldn't blame Adam, though he'd initiated the kiss. He was a man, and she'd thrown herself into his arms. He probably sensed what she didn't want to confront in herself. He'd kissed her—and she could have broken away, demand he stop. Instead, she'd met his advances with bold, demanding ones of her own. What must he think of her? She'd barely been able to face him these last two days, had actually hidden when she could, if there was a chance he would pass by. In the evening, when they'd been with his family, she hadn't risked meeting his gaze, had pretended that her needlework was all encompassing.

At last, her outrage and despair settled into resignation and acceptance. It was her nature to be wildly passionate. Surely there were other women who had to suppress such sins. She would bear it because she needed this position. And she would keep ever aware for a chance at other employment, even if the situation wasn't as good.

It was all she could do, because thoughts of Adam filled her days and nights. If only she could hate him, but she . . . liked him, even admired him. He was so good and protective toward his family, and he'd changed his scoundrel ways.

But these feelings had to stop.

Adam's investigator had left his card the day before, when Adam was away, indicating he would return on the morrow. Adam had been tempted to go to his offices, but that would look incredibly suspicious. Of course dukes were known to hire investigators—but dukes couldn't seem desperate about it. So he was pacing his study Wednesday morning when Raikes was shown in.

"Your Grace," he said respectfully as he took his seat across from Adam's desk, "I have more details to fill in the picture of Miss Cooper, but first the maid. My associate here looked into her background, and it was not difficult to find. She is the bastard daughter of a gentleman who refused to support her and her mother."

Adam frowned. "That is a man of the vilest nature. Do I know him?"

"He is Mr. Darby, with an estate in Sussex, but he is usually in Town for the Season. I would think you two do not socialize in the same circle." The last was added dryly.

"I don't recognize the name, but I will not forget it. So our maid might have very conflicted feelings on being forced to work for her livelihood."

"She might, sir. Do you suspect her of something?"

Adam had not confided the truth of the blackguard's letters, and he didn't intend to. "I don't know. I will keep her background in mind. If her work does not improve, I might be forced to release her. What about Miss Cooper? I asked you to look into where she lived before she was employed by the Warburtons."

Raikes confirmed and fleshed out the details that Faith had already told him about her quiet country life, her friendship with the baron's son, her father's death, her brother's enlistment. "For six months afterward, she and her mother remained together, and neighbors realized their situation was reduced, that they had to release their few servants, that they began to sell family items." He frowned. "Then one day, Miss Cooper was simply . . . gone."

"Gone?"

"She didn't live in the village and no one knew what became of her. Since Mrs. Cooper continued to be able to afford her cottage, everyone suspected that Miss Cooper had taken employment as a governess or perhaps something as lowly as a shop clerk, and therefore her mother would not speak of it. You gave me the time frame she began her work with the Warburtons, and I was able to confirm that. But for a year, she is unaccounted for."

What had happened to her? Was it something so serious she could be threatened with it?

"Thank you, Raikes. I need you to return and find out where she went. Someone has to know something. Search the surrounding villages. If she didn't have much money, she couldn't have gone that far. You don't have to find her childhood friend, Timothy Gilpin—he's already here. I'll deal with him. But I do have another assignment for your associate. I need him to look into Miss Charlotte Atherstone and Miss Jane Ogden, chaperone and lady's companion. They both work in Society, although Miss Ogden's employer appears to be a bedridden widow. They are friends of Miss Cooper who will meet her today in Hyde Park, as they do every Wednesday afternoon. It will be easy enough for you to follow her there and see them for yourself, even follow them home to discover their employers."

"Very good, Your Grace," Raikes said. "Will that be all?"

"Send your bill to my steward, including an estimate of the expenses you'll need for a return trip north. And thank you for your discretion."

When Raikes had gone, Adam had second thoughts about assigning him to two innocent spinsters, but he could not forget that Miss Atherstone had been very disapproving of him. And Faith had only known them the few months she'd been in town. Adam wasn't about to ignore anything that could help him find answers.

For months, finding and helping Faith had made him feel like he had a purpose, the chance to make a difference in a person's life, rather than governing from on high in the House of Lords. He thought it would end with helping Faith take a better position, but now, with the blackguard's letters, his interest in the chase made him feel like a soldier again, made him feel alive.

Or maybe it was Faith herself who made each day fresh and new. Since their kiss at Vauxhall Gardens, she'd been avoiding him. But that kiss had been haunting his dreams, the feel of her body still in his arms. If anyone else had told him such tales, he would have advised finding a mistress. Instead he was focused on the mysteries that swirled around Faith Cooper.

The next morning, Adam was in the entrance hall, about to leave for his club, when Seabrook hastened down the long corridor that led to the servants' wing.

"Your Grace!" Seabrook went past Adam and opened the front door. "A boy with another note. Black pants, tattered red sweater." He craned his neck toward the street. "I do believe he's right there, pretending nonchalance."

Adam ignored the greatcoat one of the footmen held out and hurried down the front stairs. He was through the main gate, and still the boy didn't look behind him, just whistled, hands in his pockets like he belonged on the fashionable street.

Adam put a hand on his shoulder. "Don't struggle," he said in a low voice.

The boy jerked and stiffened, his body poised for flight.

Adam gripped him harder. "You were just at my home, and I need answers as to who sent you there."

"Don't know what ye're talkin' 'bout, guv'nor. I ain't done nothin' wrong."

"And I'm not saying you did," Adam said, turning him around and taking off the boy's cap so they could look into each other's eyes.

The boy's were wide with defiance and a trace of fear beneath a mop of dirty blond hair. "I'll scream," he said, chin raised.

"And I'll call a constable and claim you stole my watch. Who will they believe?"

The boy swallowed and nodded. He couldn't be more than eight.

"Whot do ye want?" he said defensively.

"You brought a note to my house."

"That's not a crime! 'Tis a service, it is!"

"Who did you deliver it for?"

"Don't know his name, o' course. 'E gave me a quid and I thought me heart would burst."

"So it was a man? What did he look like?"

"'e was just a toff in a top 'at, didn't notice no 'air color. I only saw 'is coin."

Adam let him go, knowing it was useless. The boy didn't run, just sauntered away, and Adam couldn't help smiling at his attitude. His smile faded as he remembered where the boy, and so many others like him, was going.

When Adam returned to the entrance hall, Seabrook awaited him.

"You caught him, Your Grace," the old man said with satisfaction as he handed over the note.

"I did, but it didn't do much good. He knew nothing."

"Sir," Seabrook began with an unusual hesitation, "your aunt is awaiting you in your study."

Adam arched an eyebrow.

"Would you prefer that I hold on to the note for you?"

Adam smiled. "No, but thank you, Seabrook."

He pocketed the note, then entered his study. Aunt Theodosia had made herself comfortable in the chair across from his desk, and now she was watching him expectantly through her monocle.

"Good morning, Aunt."

"It is a fine morning for me, but I think not for

you, since you felt the need to chase a street urchin for all the world to see. Out with it, young man."

He sat down behind his desk, linked his hands together and smiled. "Aunt Theodosia, I am not Frances's age."

"No, you're a big boy who's lately been having a problem. Footmen for security when we're merely shopping? The way you hover around us when we attend evening affairs? And you make Miss Cooper positively nervous with your hovering, by the way."

He kept his expression impassive.

Her determination faded into true concern. "Something's wrong, Adam, and I need to know."

He sighed, and at last put the new note on the desk. "This is the third anonymous note I've received."

She drew herself up. "Blackmail?"

"No, that's what's strange. A different boy has delivered each one, and this is the first boy I've caught. A man paid him to deliver it. That was all he knew, and I believe him."

"What are the notes about?"

He handed over the first two, knowing they'd incriminate him. He watched her read, having already memorized them:

Faith is lovely. Wherever she goes, you can't stop looking at her. But I'm watching you.

　She's still there, in your home. You don't know anything about her. Your obsession is showing.

He broke the seal on the newest one.

You risk much to have her—she's not worth it. I know what she is, what she's done.

He inhaled sharply. This was the first note to openly say there was a secret in Faith's past.

"You read too slowly," Aunt Theodosia said. "Hand it over."

He did and sat back to study her face. She revealed nothing except a frown of concentration. At last she pushed the notes into the center of his desk, then sat back herself.

"For what it's worth," he began, "I have not 'had' Faith."

"No, but you look at her."

He didn't answer.

"And she looks at you."

He frowned.

"And now someone else has noticed." She sighed. "I trust that you and she will do what's best for both of you."

"You trust me to do what's best for her?" he asked.

"I do. You've changed, Adam."

He looked away. "Sometimes I don't feel that way."

"Trust yourself." She looked down at the notes again. "Does Faith know about these?"

"No. How can I tell her? She'll run, and then I won't be able to protect her at all."

Aunt Theodosia nodded. "She probably would. The girl is loyal, and would never want to risk people getting hurt because of her."

"None of the notes have threatened anyone physically. But this is the first note that openly says she has a secret, the kind that would be scandalous if it came out. Do you think it could be true?"

She shrugged. "We all have secrets."

"I'm having her investigated. Quietly. I can't help her if I don't know what it is."

"Understandable," she said with a nod. "Do you suspect anyone?"

He jumped to his feet, startling his aunt. "That's just it—I am clueless, and I'm starting to see suspects everywhere, even my closest friend."

"Shenstone?" his aunt asked sharply. "Why would he even care about Faith? He would encourage you to renew your old scandalous ways."

"I would have thought so, but he's been cool toward me lately, and I don't know why. But for his behavior, I would have discussed this with him. Now I can't risk it. There is Gilpin, of course, Faith's childhood friend who seems very angry every time I see him. I did a little research—he has an unhappy marriage."

"And he overimbibes, which can addle the mind. Who else?"

"I'm sure she can't be a suspect in this, but I've looked into Faith's maid, Ellen. She is the bastard of a gentleman who will not acknowledge or support her."

His aunt's eyebrows climbed under her turban.

"That explains much. But why would she want to get rid of Faith? We'd just assign her to something else."

He nodded.

"And Faith believes their relationship—along with Ellen's skills—is improving."

"I'm even having Faith's two friends investigated."

"You mean the Society of Ladies' Companions and Chaperones? I cannot believe it of them—not of two women who could use such a name to make light of themselves."

He shrugged. "Can you think of anyone else?"

"The Warburtons? Could they have discovered something about Faith?"

"All they'd have to do is spread a rumor of the truth—Faith would be disgraced, and that would be it. These threats, or whatever they are, are coming to me. My conduct is being scrutinized, as well. Am I supposed to believe I should release Faith, and nothing more will be said?" Suddenly angry, he swept the notes to the floor. "Someone is enjoying having power over me—this isn't just about Faith."

"I do believe you're correct, Adam. So what do you plan to do next?"

"Await word from my investigator about Faith's past. Once I know what I'm dealing with, I can make plans." Not that he had any idea what those plans would be, when so far, he hadn't been able to find the blackguard.

"And you don't want to ask Faith for the truth?"

"If she's taken great pains to hide something in her past, I don't believe she'd reveal it willingly—and certainly not to me. And I don't want you talking to her, not yet at least."

"Oh very well, even though I am quite good at getting others to reveal what they don't mean to."

She arched her own brow at him, mimicking him, he knew.

"There was no persuasion to get me to talk—you spied on me."

"Hmph." Then she mused, "It seems too obvious that it is Mr. Gilpin, but he bears watching. I don't like how he treats Faith."

"Has he attempted to visit her?"

"No, but we've both seen him approach her at parties, and she's disturbed afterward." She gave a crooked smile. "At least now I know why we've been assigned a footman for security. Marian is not pleased."

"Why does that not surprise me?" He stood up and came around the desk, offering her an arm. She ignored it and used her cane as she slowly came to her feet.

"Keep your eyes open, Aunt Theodosia. It feels good to have someone else watching out for Faith."

"Even though the most I can do is wait until this villain is close enough and hit him with my cane?"

He smiled, but knew it was forced. When his aunt left his study, he paced to the window and found Faith where she often was—in the garden, helping the gardeners with preparations for spring.

She was as innocent as a flower—and he had to keep her that way. Safe, protected, so she could flourish.

Chapter 16

Adam was nursing his third brandy over the billiard table that night, and his shots were beginning to go wild. His sister entered the billiard room, shut the door, and leaned back against it, expression determined.

"Am I not allowed to leave?" he asked dryly.

"What has been your problem today, Adam Chamberlin? You sulked in your study, you barely said anything to anyone at dinner, and now you're sulking in the billiard room."

"I do not sulk," he said, leaning one hip against the table.

"Very well, 'brood.' Why are you brooding? I keep telling you it will do you good to talk to someone." She came closer and put a hand on her arm. "Talk to me, Adam. Who else loves and understands you like I do?"

He couldn't tell her about the blackguard's letters. But he didn't seem to have the will to resist her entreaties anymore.

So, with as little emotion as possible, he told her about the men who'd died because of an idea he'd instigated and convinced his regiment to carry out. How he and his friends Blackthorne and Knightsbridge had been determined to help the families left behind.

Her eyes had grown damp while he talked, but now brightened. "Faith! It's Faith you've been helping."

He nodded, then leaned down to eye a shot and almost staggered sideways.

"Oh, Adam, I'm so glad! She deserves your help. I've met the Warburtons socially, and I must say, they are misers who hire as few servants as possible and work them as hard as they can. Did you notice Faith's hands without gloves when she first came to us? She must have been doing laundry, or cleaning—not that she'd speak of it. Oh, Adam, thank you for at last confiding in me. I'm so proud of you!"

He hadn't done much to be proud of until the army. And all the good was overshadowed by the death of his men.

But talking to Sophia had somehow clarified things for him. He felt a renewed sense of purpose, a hope for the future that had been lacking for so long. How had he not seen the truth over these last few weeks?

He had to talk to Faith.

Faith had just gone up to her bedroom that night when there was a knock at her door. She opened it to find Ellen standing there, fingers twisting nervously.

"Miss Cooper, His Grace would like to speak with you."

Perplexed, she glanced at the clock on the mantel. It was after ten, and he'd been uncommunicative with his family that evening. Now he wanted to talk to *her*? It had taken her a week to finally stop flinching when she heard his voice, to suppress the memories of his kiss, of the way he'd made her body come to life. She didn't want to see him alone.

"He's waiting in his study."

And then Ellen turned and marched away.

Faith was tempted to call her back, to give her regrets, to complain of a headache. *Coward.*

Taking a deep breath, she closed the door behind her and descended through the mansion. Gas lamps illuminated the corridors, but there was an unusual hush of silence. At the study door, she paused, took a deep breath, and then knocked.

"Come in."

His voice was low and intimate, and it made her remember being in the dark shadows of a ruined temple. She shoved the memory away, put a polite smile on her face for her employer and entered, deliberately leaving the door wide open.

He lounged behind his desk, arms wide on the

armrests, a snifter in one hand. He smiled at her, and she had the strangest sensation of a jungle cat happy to see its prey. She really hadn't looked at him for days, and now he quite stole her breath with his handsomeness and the way he exuded sensuality with those half-lidded eyes.

"Close the door please," he said.

Her smile faded, her chin raised, but she obeyed him, then remained near the door. "May I help you, Your Grace?"

"You called me Adam last week."

She blinked at him. "We aren't discussing last week and the mistakes we made, in case you have forgotten."

"I have not forgotten. In fact, I remember *everything* too well."

Her mouth went dry. He rose languidly and came around the desk. She took a step backward toward the door, but all he did was perch on the edge of the desk, one ankle crossed over the other, arms folded over his chest. It made him look broad and masculine, and reminded her of being held against that body.

"In fact," he continued, "I have thought of nothing else."

She tilted her chin, archly shaking her head at the same time. "I, on the other hand, have forgotten that insanity."

"I don't think you have."

He straightened and began to walk toward her. Two emotions warred within her, the desire that had swept her away that night at Vauxhall, and the fear that she couldn't stop him, whatever he wanted to do.

He must have seen something in her eyes, because he halted several feet away, and his gaze gentled.

"I won't hurt you, Faith," he murmured in a low rumble.

"This hurts me. Please don't ask me to be alone with you again."

"Even if I do this?"

To her shock, he reached for her hand and held it between his own.

"Faith, will you do me the honor of becoming my wife?"

She snorted a laugh of disbelief and pulled her hand away. He didn't smile, only looked at her intently.

"Your Grace, *Your Grace*," she repeated, to remind him of his title, "you have been drinking."

"But I haven't been drinking much. Trust me, this isn't even mildly inebriated for me. I'm being perfectly serious. I want to marry you."

"Stop teasing me!" she said, hands on her hips as she leaned toward him. "I'm not to be toyed with when you're bored or guilty."

"I'm not bored and this is not because of guilt," he said, all patience and sincerity.

"Then stop pretending you need to go to ridiculous lengths to help me. You've done enough. One kiss doesn't make you responsible for me for life."

"Maybe not, but one kiss showed me that I've never felt this attracted to a woman before."

She gaped at him.

"I can't stop thinking about that kiss."

"That is *lust*," she said. "Go find yourself the kind of woman who wants that from you." It made her a little sick saying that, knowing once she'd had to be that kind of woman. But not anymore, and certainly not with him.

"I don't want that kind of relationship. I want a wife I like and desire, and together we'll have children—a family."

A twinge of pain made her speak sharply. "You don't mention love, but you do mention an heir. Do you see me as someone meek, who will give you what you want?"

"Meek?" he said, smiling at last. "That is not the adjective for you. As for love, I do not want to lie to you. But we are so attracted to each other that love will come with time."

"You are too certain of yourself, too arrogant. Do you have an answer for everything?"

Now he grinned, putting his hands on his hips. "Try me."

"You are a duke. I am a commoner. You are expected to marry well and bring a beautiful, well-dowered, noble wife to the union. Your mother doesn't even like me now, let alone as a prospective bride."

"I don't care about any of that."

"I do!" And deep down, she cared about how

she could possibly keep her secret, and what would happen if—when—it came out. Everyone would be trying to dig into her past, wondering how she was worth landing a duke. And then she'd bring terrible shame and ridicule down on his whole family. She would never do that.

Even though the thought of being in his arms each night, safe and cared for, was suddenly overwhelming.

"I won't marry you, Your Grace."

She turned to reach for the doorknob, and suddenly he was there, his body pressing hers firmly into the door. She gasped, overwhelmed by the power of him, the way his hardness fit to her softness, the way she wanted him to touch her more.

"You can't force me, Rothford," she whispered raggedly. "My body might react to you, but I'm not ruled by my emotions—unlike you."

He put his mouth against her neck and inhaled deeply. "God, you smell good."

His lips skimmed along the curve of her neck and behind her ear. She gasped as he nuzzled her there, then nibbled at her earlobe.

"You can't force me," she whispered again, eyes squeezed shut.

He straightened away from her and spoke quietly. "No, I would never do that."

She looked over her shoulder first, to see his solemn expression. Slowly, she turned around until her back was against the door. "I can go?"

"Of course you can go. But I'm not withdrawing my offer for you."

"This is ridiculous," she said, trembling. "And you cannot tell anyone about this. I won't be the cause of tension and anger within your family."

"I won't say anything because I won't have to. I'll simply make you see that I'm right."

She felt for the knob behind her, opened it, then slipped out the narrow opening. She practically ran to her bedroom, knew she must have looked panicked if anyone saw her. But they didn't, not at this time of the evening, with the family retired and the servants already abed. In her own room, she closed the door and locked it.

As if that would stop him should he choose to come in.

But her denial had been enough to stop him, hadn't it?

Feeling dazed, she walked across the room and sank down in a chair before the hearth. A coal fire burned in the grate to combat the early-spring chill, but still she rubbed her arms and sat unseeing.

The Duke of Rothford had asked for her hand in marriage.

It seemed ridiculous and outrageous—but it was true.

She wasn't in love with him; he wasn't in love with her. But they were attracted to each other, and that was far more than many marriages had.

Yet the prospective bride wasn't usually a former mistress.

She winced. How would she convince him that she couldn't marry him without telling him the truth?

Chapter 17

Adam sank back in his big leather chair and linked his hands behind his head. He wasn't at all surprised that Faith had refused his offer of marriage. She was a proud woman and thought he only pitied her. It would be a bit of a challenge, coming up with a way to win her over—without telling her that someone appeared to know something in her past. He would make sure she'd never even need to think about it again.

He had to convince her that the proposal was about her, and how he respected and desired her, how well they suited. Yet, he also couldn't let his family know about his secret wooing. The challenge amused and inspired him.

Over the next few days, he made certain he was at every meal she was, being the genial head of the household. At breakfast that first morning after his proposal, he thought for certain she'd be full of blushes and unable to meet his gaze. But the opposite happened. She was cool and polite, deferential as always, looking him in the eye as if to say, *I have forgotten about last night, and soon you will, too.*

But he wouldn't forget. Marriage to her would not only make them both happy, but would convince the anonymous blackguard that threats were useless, that Adam would never give up Faith.

Besides meals, he appeared at calling hours to be with his mother and aunt, greeting visitors, so he could look everyone over and see who might look too interested, perhaps even guilty.

Occasionally, when he thought he could get away with it, he snuck a note into a book Faith was reading, or into her sewing basket. They were notes to confirm that he was thinking about her, that he wouldn't forget what he'd asked. He never signed them, of course, and if they were found, Faith could claim them from an anonymous suitor. But he liked to see her blush when she found the notes and quickly hid them.

Once in the evening, his sister played while he sang, something he hadn't done since his youth. His mother and aunt looked pleased at the love song, Marian bored, and Faith buried her face in her needlework. But he knew she was listening.

When they attended Society functions, he was forced to step back from his courtship. He wanted to take her into his arms, to show the world she was his, especially that Gilpin fellow, who drank too much and glared whenever he saw her.

They attended the Wallingford ball several hours' carriage ride west of London, on a massive estate that bordered the Thames. It was a crush of people, the first truly warm day of spring making it unbearably hot. The odors of people, perfume, candles, and gas lamps were overwhelming. But the dancing went on anyway, forcing the crowds to press back toward the wall, several rows deep. Adam saw Faith shoved into a corner, the perspiration that dotted her face, the misery she couldn't quite hide. As a companion, she never had a moment's escape from the fringes of the ballroom.

And then suddenly he saw her begin to creep along the rear of the crowd, toward the French doors that led to the terrace. Adam did the same from his side of the room, nodding absently when people greeted him, making sure all knew he didn't have time to stop. Then he went down a corridor that led to the men's card room, but turned off it for another exit to the grounds that sloped down to the river. He knew the layout of the mansion well, from long-ago house parties.

He felt almost like he was back in combat, his movements quiet as he kept to the shadows. He followed the edge of the terrace, able to see couples strolling along its torchlit perimeter. He slipped into the trees at the far end, and at last was able to see Faith standing above the wide sweep of marble stairs that led down into the gravel paths of the gardens.

Come to me.

He willed those words over and over again, and with only a glance over her shoulder, she hurried down the stairs. Other couples strolled the paths, of course, so it was tricky to find the right moment.

And at last she was momentarily out of sight of anyone else, and he emerged through the trees, took hold of her hand, and pulled her after him.

"Adam!" she hissed, stumbling as she was forced to follow him into the dark.

He pulled her close to whisper in her ear, "I know where I'm going. Be patient." He tugged, and when she still balked, he said, "Do you want me to carry you?"

He couldn't see her face, but imagined her frowning. In only a few minutes, they emerged onto the lawn outside the main gardens. The ground angled toward the Thames, and he could see boats, the lanterns hung on their prows bobbing like fireflies in the water. With the house ablaze behind them, they had some meager light. Through the open windows and doors they could hear the music—a waltz. He'd always wanted to dance with her.

He pulled her into his arms. "A well-bred girl such as yourself surely knows how to dance."

"Adam! I cannot dance with you!" Her words were soft and furtive, and she kept looking back at the house.

"No one can see us, and if they do, we're so far away they won't know who we are. Dance with me, Faith. I've wanted to dance with you at every event we attended."

"We participated in the same quadrille once," she reminded him.

"And we barely touched hands. I want you in my arms. One dance, Faith."

She hesitated for a long moment, then said with great reluctance, "One dance."

It was a glorious dance. He swept her away, with no other couples to interfere in their progress. The feel of her supple back was magic beneath his palm. Her hand in his was how it was meant to be. She danced beautifully, following his lead as they circled about. He pulled her closer and closer, letting his thigh slide between hers as they took the turns. Her head dropped back and they held each other's gazes.

And suddenly he realized she'd be his if someone saw them. He was so close to having her as his wife, it made him a little reckless. But then he knew he couldn't do that to her, give her a public scandal.

But perhaps there was another way to do it . . .

Faith's cares and fears fell away at the magic of dancing in Adam's arms. He was strong and graceful, supportive and powerful. His hands guided her with the same feeling as a caress. With every whirl of the dance, the light from the house played on different sides of his face, lightening and darkening. And he was smiling through it all, with almost . . . tenderness.

But she couldn't believe that—didn't *want* to believe that.

"Don't pull away," he said softly.

"I'm not."

"But your expression is."

She didn't know what to say, and instead closed her eyes and simply . . . existed within her body, in the sensations he aroused, the rhythms of the music. All the reasons she shouldn't be there faded away.

And then the music ended, and he caught her up against him, both breathing faster. She stared into his eyes that glittered like starlight.

He let her go and bowed. "Thank you for the dance."

She hesitated, but somehow the magic wouldn't leave, and she sank into a deep curtsy. "I've never . . . danced like that before," she admitted, rising back up.

"Never? You are a gentleman's daughter. Surely they had country assemblies in your village?"

"They did, but . . . the waltz was scandalous in our remote north. Though I practiced it, I've never danced it with anyone other than my dancing instructor. And you are . . ."

"Far superior in both technique and grace?"

She bit her lip to hide her smile. "Taller."

He winced. "A man has to do much to earn your praise. Won't a marriage proposal do?"

Her smile faded, and she was surprised by the feeling of grief that welled up inside her, grief for all the things she'd never have, a husband, children. "Oh, Adam, don't ruin this special dance."

His eyes grew shuttered. "If you think happiness means ruination."

She lifted up her skirts and ran, back through the trees bordering the gardens, hesitating near the path to make sure she was alone, then reappearing, trying to walk sedately toward the terrace.

It was hard to feel sedate when her heart was thumping madly, when she had just experienced the most romantic moment of her life. No man had ever treated her the way Adam had, and she experienced a moment of longing and regret.

Did she actually *want* to marry him, even though she knew she wouldn't?

She might care for him, but that only emphasized her need to refuse.

When they returned to London the next day, Adam was filled with purpose. He now knew Faith would never willingly marry him, so he had to bring it about. He'd promised he wouldn't force her, and truly, he wouldn't. The final decision would still be up to her. He would just make it harder for her to refuse.

Only his family could be the ones to find them together, would make certain the scandal wouldn't go beyond Rothford Court. Maybe not even all of his family needed to be involved, he mused. His aunt and his sister would be the most likely to be sympathetic, but insistent that Faith and he needed to marry.

But try as he might, he couldn't come up with a way to get Faith alone with him, and still manage to have his family find them. He needed an accomplice, and who better than Sophia, full of dreams of romance and happily-ever-afters? She admired Faith and understood his connection to her.

After they arrived home that afternoon, he found his sister helping her maid unpack. The maid bobbed a curtsy and left upon seeing him, and Adam strolled into the room and closed the door behind him.

Sophia, standing over her trunk, gave him an amused glance. "This is an unusual visit. I assume you need my help in a private matter?"

He smiled. "I've been asking Faith to marry me for a week, and she keeps refusing."

Sophia froze, then her mouth slowly sagged open.

"That's a better reaction than Faith's," he said wryly. "She snorted and laughed in my face."

Sophia winced. "Oh, Adam, I'm sorry. But I imagine she thought you were joking."

"Maybe for a moment, but then she realized the truth. I've never met anyone who made me imagine a future together before her."

Her expression softened. "That's quite romantic, dear brother."

"She doesn't think so. She thinks I'm doing it out of guilt or boredom—her words."

"Are you? The guilt, anyway?"

He paused. "We met under those circumstances, and certainly, I will never forget what I cost her, but I enjoy her, I'm attracted to her, and I believe we suit."

"But, Adam, do you love her?"

"I don't know what it's supposed to feel like, so I won't lie and say I do. She says we have no love, although she cannot deny there's an attraction."

Sophia pinkened. "Well, that might be more than I need to hear."

His amusement faded. "I fear her concerns about our differences in consequence will make her leave Aunt Theodosia's employ. She might end up with another Warburton family again, all in the name of pride."

"You honestly think it's pride?"

"I do. Pride and maybe fear, because after all, it's not every day one becomes a duchess."

"If you want my advice, all you can do is be patient."

"I've been patient, I've been romantic. I've slipped her notes, I've sung to her, I've danced with her under the moonlight."

Her eyes widened. "Last night? That was quite daring. What if you'd been caught?"

He arched a brow.

"Oh, then she'd have had to marry you."

"I didn't dance with her for that reason, but it gave me an idea. Perhaps you and Aunt Theodosia could catch us alone? That way any scandal wouldn't spread beyond family. I don't want Faith embarrassed. I just want to be her husband."

"I don't know, Adam. It's rather deceitful."

"Do you have another suggestion? She's going to risk going out on her own again, just because she thinks she's beneath me. I don't care about a dowry or anything like that. She's a gentleman's daughter, not a fruit girl, for God's sake. Sophia, I need your help."

Taking a deep breath, she lifted her chin. "All right, I'll do it. I like Faith, and I think she'd be good for you. And I'd love another niece or nephew. Do you have a plan?"

He took her hand and squeezed it in gratitude. "Tell me what you think."

The next evening, the duchess and Lady Tunbridge were at a dinner, but Lady Duncan decided to rest before her meeting the next day. Together they'd prepared a speech, and Faith knew she'd be smashing. Adam had gone out, thank God, so she didn't have to avoid his intense gazes. Consequently, she was alone in the family drawing room with only Sophia for company. The two women read books in peaceful companionship, even though Faith thought Sophia had been acting rather . . . excitable during the day. Even the fact that Mr. Percy visited during morning calls had not seemed to settle her down. Maybe that was part of the problem, excitement that he'd missed her and come to visit her—on the pretense of paying his respects to the duchess, of course.

Sophia suddenly closed her book with a snap. "Oh, dear, I totally forgot to write a letter that needs to be posted in the morning. Have a good evening, Faith!"

Faith barely had a moment to say good night before Sophia was gone. Faith sighed and shook her head, returning to the exciting part of her book, Jane Austen's *Persuasion*, where the heroine, Anne, was just about to read the romantic note from her long lost love, Captain Wentworth. They'd been separated for eight long years, had missed out on joy together.

She refused to think of her own situation in that light. She might be denying Adam, but it was for a far better reason than Anne had. Anne had been persuaded by a friend that it was an inferior match, that his prospects were poor. Faith knew it was her own prospects that were poor, so she was doing the right thing. She would never regret her decision like Anne did.

Though, inside, she felt like weeping much of the time. What was wrong with her?

The door opened.

"Did you forget—" She broke off, seeing Adam enter and then deliberately close the door behind him.

He was wearing shirtsleeves without cravat or waistcoat, unbuttoned at the throat. It was so casual, so intimate, that it sent a hum of nervousness through her.

Slowly, she set down her book. "Your Grace, may I help you?"

"I couldn't stop thinking about our dance two nights ago."

She felt her cheeks redden as she rose to her feet. "Please, I don't wish to discuss it."

"I want to be able to dance with you like that openly, for all the world to see."

"You mean for all the world to snicker behind their fans," she pointed out sarcastically.

"They would never snicker at a duchess. That's what you don't understand. There is power in such a position—prestige. People will want your favor. Yes, they'll be shocked at first, but it's not as if dukes haven't married commoners before."

"Your Grace—"

"Dance with me." He took her hands and led her away from the sofa. "I'm not asking anything else."

"Oh, you're not?" she answered wryly.

"We're alone—you can dance with me."

"There's no music," she said reluctantly.

He brought her into the proper waltz position. "We don't need music," he said against her temple.

And then he took her for the first curve around the sofa. She had no choice but to follow or be dragged, for he was that strong. His shirt was so fine that she felt she was touching his bare shoulder. Soon, it became almost enjoyable to dodge furniture, to stop and swirl far too close to the fire screen. She actually laughed aloud as he whirled her in a tight circle, and she spun so much she came up against his body, her head bent to his chest.

"Faith," he whispered against her hair.

The ache of regret and sorrow never truly left her, and now it seemed to strangle her words as she said huskily, "I have to go, you know that. Charlotte knows of a position for me. I was waiting until after tomorrow's speech to explain it to your aunt."

He cupped her face in his warm hands until she was forced to look at him.

"What will I do without you?" he asked.

Staring into those vivid blue eyes, she was compelled to reach up, to touch his face, the leanness of his cheek, the soft warmth of his lips.

"This is good-bye," she whispered, coming up on her toes to softly kiss him.

The touch of their mouths was like an electric spark between them. They hesitated, lost, and then with a moan she opened to him, and they came together with all the heat and overwhelming passion that flared and encompassed them.

She would never have this again, she knew. For the rest of her life, these would be the memories that would sustain her, that would let her know that once a man cared just for her, and not what she could do for him.

Her hands slid around his waist, and then up beneath his loose shirt, feeling the warm hard muscles of his back.

"Oh my!" came a cry.

Faith and Adam broke apart, and she turned toward the door, hand covering her wet mouth in shock.

Sophia and Lady Duncan stood in the doorway, both gaping.

It was Lady Duncan who collected herself first. "Get out of the doorway, Sophia, we must close it before—"

Sophia seemed to shake herself as she moved aside, risking another wide-eyed glance at her brother. "Before . . . what?"

"Your mother sees!"

Sophia gasped. "But she's not supposed to—"

"What is going on?" said the duchess in an annoyed voice. She pushed past Lady Duncan. "After that dreadful dinner, I do believe I need a glass of . . ."

And then she saw them. Faith hadn't been able to move, just stood too close to Adam, hugging herself, knowing it was too late to run, to explain, to do anything. Then Lady Tunbridge threaded between them, and her face paled with distaste.

Instead of gaping, the duchess stiffened right up and spoke between compressed lips. "Adam, what is the meaning of this?"

Faith wanted to cover her face, but there was no hiding. This was all her fault. Once again, she'd proved weak where a man was concerned.

But no, even at the height of this humiliation, it wasn't just any man who drew her—it was Adam.

He sighed. "I'm sorry you all had to see this."

Lady Tunbridge and the duchess looked at Faith as if she were lower than a worm.

"To think that my Frances has lived in the same home as . . . as . . ." Lady Tunbridge couldn't seem to find a word to describe her.

"That's enough," Adam said coldly. "None of this is Faith's fault."

Lady Tunbridge continued as if she hadn't heard him. "When this gets out, we will all be the center of scandal."

Adam took almost a menacing step toward her. "This is not getting out. And if it does, I'll know that a member of my *family* spread the gossip."

"You don't have to worry about me," Faith finally said in a trembling voice. "I believe I have another position to go to."

"As if you should be in respectable people's homes," Lady Tunbridge sniffed.

Faith blinked hard to fight against the stinging.

"That's enough, Marian," Lady Duncan said coldly. "You forget yourself. There were two people alone in this room, not just one."

"You're not going anywhere," Adam said to Faith. "I am not risking your reputation like this."

"What reputation?" Faith demanded. "I have none, Adam, none worth worrying about."

"*What* did you call my son?" the duchess demanded.

Faith winced. "Your Grace—"

"She can call me Adam, because soon she'll be my wife."

That brought everyone to a silent standstill.

Oh no, Faith thought, *I've given Adam even more reason to behave nobly, to press for marriage.*

"Adam!" his mother said faintly, leaning hard against the piano. "You will not marry a—a—"

"No, he will not be marrying me," Faith interrupted.

In a kindly voice, Lady Duncan said her name, but Faith refused to listen.

"I am not the sort of woman who can be a duchess—we all know that."

"Faith, that's not true," Sophia said plaintively.

Faith looked at the young woman who'd become her friend, and smiled sadly. "You are being kind, Sophia, but it's the truth. I've only been on the fringes of your world, and I can't come farther." She rounded on Adam. "I won't marry you."

And then she couldn't look at so many judging faces anymore, and ran from the room.

Chapter 18

Adam stormed past his family, but he didn't follow Faith. He knew she was upset and needed a chance to calm down.

He'd been a fool, never imagining how ugly it could get, how she'd blame herself. He'd just wanted what he wanted—he wanted her.

He'd caught Sophia's wide-eyed look of guilt—another innocent he'd traumatized.

In his study, he paced, reminding himself that this was the worst of it, that he was still doing the right thing. He and Faith belonged together; she deserved the life he'd had a hand in taking away from her. He wanted to give her everything.

It wasn't guilt, he told himself, but justice and maybe even love.

When someone knocked, he didn't answer, but then his aunt came right in.

"I don't need this now, Aunt Theodosia," he

said, holding up a hand. "I've made a mistake, but I will rectify it."

"Apparently not the way Faith wants you to."

He grimaced. "I will convince her that she's wrong. I don't give a damn where she comes from or what she's worth. She'll be my wife."

"Is protecting her all this is about?" she asked in a softer voice.

With sarcasm, he said, "Did it look like I was protecting her?"

Lady Duncan sighed. "She is my employee. Apparently, *I* have not protected her."

"Aunt Theodosia, stop. I am not some overly aggressive master using a woman for my own ends. I want to marry her—frankly, I've wanted that for weeks, only she thought we shouldn't marry."

She blinked at him. "Oh. Strangely, that makes me feel better. Nevertheless, I am going to talk to the girl."

"I don't know if that's a good idea."

"I'm not asking your opinion." She sniffed mildly.

Faith sat on the window seat and hugged herself as if she'd never be warm again. She didn't know what to do first—pack? Not that she had any place to go yet; Charlotte only mentioned an elderly relative of her employer who might be looking for a companion.

But she couldn't leave what had just happened

to face an uncertain future. In her mind flashed all their faces again: Adam looking startled, Sophia pale, Lady Duncan surprised. But it was the duchess and Lady Tunbridge whose expressions reminded Faith of all she'd be facing should this scandal come out. They'd shun her, and so would everyone else she knew. It would be like living in Lord Reyburn's village all over again. Few people had spoken to her except to take her coin in stores. She'd been alone—although she preferred it that way, she'd always told herself, considering what she was doing there.

A knock sounded at the door, making her flinch.

"I am indisposed," she said loudly from across the room.

The door began to open anyway.

"Adam, I don't wish to—"

And then she saw the bright red turban of Lady Duncan, and she fell silent. Tears stung her eyes, and she turned away, knowing how much she'd disappointed the woman who'd taken a chance on hiring her.

"L-Lady Duncan," she began, only to hear her voice tremble with suppressed emotion.

The elderly woman limped to her and sat down, putting an arm around her. And that kindness made Faith cry in earnest.

Lady Duncan handed her a handkerchief. "Now, there, dear, please cease this crying. It's not necessary, you know. I do not think badly of you."

"We shouldn't have—I shouldn't have—" A sob interrupted.

"Do you not think I was young once? You would blush in horror if I told you how my first marriage came about. I was a feisty young woman, little caring what the rules were."

Faith blew her nose and stared at her with watery eyes. "That's—that's kind of you to say, my lady, but it doesn't change anything. I have . . . embarrassed you, humiliated the duchess, and—and set such a terrible example for Lady Sophia, who even now is trying to find a way to win Mr. P-Percy. What if she t-tries . . ." Her voice rose and faded into a squeak.

"Mr. Percy is quite the strong young man and can take care of himself. And I wish right this moment that you would stop acting as if everything that happened tonight was your fault. You have a partner in this, young lady, and just because he's a duke, doesn't mean he can get away with everything."

Faith slumped. "Regardless, I will not let him be affected, ma'am."

"Well, he is affected if you're with child."

Faith flinched. "We have never done more than kiss, my lady, I promise you. There is no chance of any . . . consequences."

"Well, that's one complication we don't have to worry about. No rushed wedding."

"No wedding at all!" Faith said, jumping to her feet. "Whatever Adam—His Grace—says, he would regret it someday. I already regret all of this. He is meant for someone like Lady Emmeline"—*someone innocent and pure*—"not a commoner like me, with no bloodline, no money, no beauty."

"Faith—"

"I will never be a part of this family, Lady Duncan, can you not see that?"

"If Adam wants you to be a part of his family, then you can be. Only he matters in your marriage, not his mother, not that silly Marian. It's not as if Marian ever looked past her poor husband's future title to love the man beneath."

"I don't care what Adam wants."

"Don't you? Do you care how dishonorable it will look, if he does not marry the girl he compromised?"

"C-compromised? He didn't—we didn't—"

"You were caught alone together, and you weren't seated on opposite ends of the sofa, my dear. I honestly don't believe someone in the family will leak the truth, but there are servants, and they do gossip."

She thought of Adam, so nobly offering to marry her, suffering shame in public when that didn't happen.

But he wouldn't suffer at all if he knew the truth.

"I must talk to him," she said at last, wiping her eyes, resolve making her feel almost numb.

"Good. Do that. Between you both, you will solve your problems."

Just not the way you think, Faith thought bitterly. She started to hand back the sodden handkerchief, thought better of it, and set it aside.

"Go to him, dear. I'm sure he's waiting for you. Try his study."

The house was silent and ghostly as she moved down through it, oppressive as if generations were looking down from every painting to judge her. Rationally, she knew Lady Duncan was right—Faith was not the first person to do something scandalous in this house. But it felt personal and humiliating to her, and that's all she could focus on.

A faint light showed from beneath the study door, and she knocked before she could change her mind.

"Come in."

She heard the curiosity in his voice and opened the door.

"Faith," he said with warm concern, coming around the desk.

She put up a hand before he could touch her. "Don't. I'll melt into a pitiable heap with your comfort. We cannot pretend this didn't happen, and I don't want you to suffer for what we did."

He groaned. "What the hell do I care what other fools think? I only care about you."

"Then if you truly care about me, you'll listen and understand. I'm already ruined, Adam, and not because of you. I made choices years ago, and I've had to live with the consequences ever since.

And one of the consequences is that I cannot marry."

"Faith—"

"No, just listen," she begged, hugging herself. "Once you hear what I've done, you'll understand why marriage is impossible. You need to understand that you won't suffer any dishonor because of me. How can there be dishonor when you've only kissed a woman who's already been a man's mistress?"

"Faith—" he implored, then broke off.

Something in his face changed—she could see him pale, saw the anguish he didn't bother to hide. It ripped her heart out to hurt him like this. He whispered her name, but she held up a hand.

"Hear me out," she demanded, barely able to look at him. "If—if I become your mistress, then you will just be doing what other men already do. You won't suffer on my account."

She finally took a breath, waiting for his shock and revulsion or maybe intrigue. She felt as if she'd received a blow to the stomach, as if she might never breathe normally again.

But his expression was gentle. "I don't want you to give yourself to me in that way. And I don't care what happened in your past."

Her mouth dropped open and she took a step away. "How can you not care? Surely you don't understand. My past could affect your sister, your niece."

"That's rubbish," he said firmly.

They stared at each other, and though she saw compassion in his gaze, it didn't matter.

"Adam—"

"I don't care about what other people might say—I care about you. My sister would feel the same way."

"But . . . if it comes out, your family will be humiliated."

He came closer, and she flinched when he held her upper arms.

"So there'll be gossip for a time. My mother lived down bringing no dowry to her marriage—so will you. My aunt had several public affairs when she was widowed, and much gossip ensued. We all survived. And we're happy. You and I will be happy, too."

"As your mistress."

"No, as my wife."

"You don't understand, Adam. You don't know the whole story." She didn't want to speak of the ugliness, but he had to be convinced that marriage to her would never work.

He drew her forward to a little sofa beneath the window and made her sit beside him. "Then tell me, Faith, for surely I deserve to know, since it's because of me you were desperate. But it won't change anything."

She took a deep breath. "I was the mistress of a married man. His wife had been in a coma for many years, but she was alive, Adam."

"And did you go offer yourself to him on a whim?"

She flinched. "Of course not. I went to ask for a letter of reference so I could look for a position."

His eyes narrowed. "It was cruel of him not to give you one."

"He's not the only one. I asked Timothy Gilpin if I could ask his father for a letter, and he refused."

"Another sterling example of manhood," Adam said darkly.

Faith waved a hand in dismissal. "He's a coward. He was engaged and worried his fiancée would think—oh, what does it matter? I could have refused Lord Reyburn, but I didn't."

"You had no one else to ask for a letter, did you?"

She ignored that. "He allowed me the use of a cottage and spending money."

"Did he treat you well?"

"I—yes, yes he did. He was a kind gentleman. We probably played chess and talked more than we . . ." She flushed and looked away. It was upsetting and strange to discuss past sexual relations with another man. "Then he became ill and I nursed him for three months until his death."

He took her hand. "That was very kind of you."

"He was kind to me. And then his son granted me a letter of reference for what I'd done."

"And that's how you came to work for the Warburtons."

She nodded. "So you see, none of this is a secret. It could come out at any time."

"The things I did in India aren't a secret," he countered. "They could come out at any time."

"It's not the same thing!"

"No, mine are worse. You are only guilty of trying to survive, Faith."

"You did the same."

He ignored that. "I admire you tremendously."

She searched his face, and all she saw was kindness and support and caring. "But—"

He touched a finger to her lips. "Marry me, Faith. If you care what people think, then imagine what they'll say when I pursue you like a besotted fool."

She bit her lip, shocked that he'd almost made her smile. "But . . . Adam, this will cause you more heartache than you can imagine. Someday you'll truly regret it."

"I won't. So what is your answer?"

She sighed, feeling too tired to fight anymore. "All right, I'll marry you."

He grinned his charming grin, but that didn't shake her feeling of eventual disaster. She was giving in, not happily agreeing, and that wasn't the right motivation to marry. He hadn't said he loved her, she didn't know if she loved him. And she was afraid she was agreeing because she had nowhere else to go, and another scandal would be her utter ruin. Not a good way to begin a life together, she thought.

"Adam, I want you to understand that I will not forget about my passion to help young ladies. I might not be able to be a chaperone, but I want to help, and for women to feel like they can come to me for advice someday."

"It sounds like a worthwhile calling," he said seriously. "I support anything you'd like to do."

She blinked in surprise. Would he really be such a "perfect" husband? She sighed. "I should move out, Adam. Now that we're engaged—"

"No."

She shot him a surprised look at the uncompromising firmness of his voice. "Adam, you know it's not proper for your fiancée to live in the same home with you."

"We have dozens of chaperones. Frankly, I don't care what people think. For once, I'll rely on the fact that I'm a duke. You're staying here, safe and protected."

"Protected?"

"I don't want people like the Warburtons to decide to use you."

She wasn't sure what he was implying, but she let it go. When he leaned in to kiss her, she turned so that his lips touched her cheek.

He straightened, unperturbed. "Let me tell my family. I don't want them to ever hurt you again like they did tonight."

"Adam, please don't blame them for their understandable shock and anger. Promise me."

"Very well, but only for you. My betrothed."

She stared at him. "I . . . it already feels strange."

"Not to me. You've made me happy."

"I hope so, Adam," she said softly. "I hope so."

Adam was able to hold his smile until the door closed behind her, and his last glimpse had been her bowed shoulders. She'd had to bear so much. He sank into his chair and ran both hands down his face.

He felt ill, physically ill.

One reckless, arrogant decision he'd help make in India had changed so many people's lives. Good men had died, and one woman had sacrificed her innocence to survive. He'd done this to her as if he'd sold her himself. He felt dazed with grief and confusion, almost as much as when those men had died and the overwhelming knowledge of his part in it had first become apparent.

First thing in the morning, he would call off Raikes, cancel his fact-finding search about Faith before he learned the truth. He didn't want anyone else to be able to hurt his future wife.

She was so strong, and he admired her so much. She deserved better than someone as flawed as he was, but he was too selfish to give her up.

When Faith didn't come down to breakfast, and Frances remained in the day nursery, Adam stood at the head of the table in the breakfast parlor and faced his family. They'd obviously been talking nonstop until his arrival, and now they looked at him in silent suspense.

"Faith has agreed to be my wife," he announced bluntly.

"No!" cried his mother, aghast.

Marian gasped, her expression one of outrage. Sophia and Aunt Theodosia exchanged relieved glances.

"It took some persuasion after the way some of you behaved last night," he continued.

"The way *we* behaved!" the duchess countered hotly. "She is a commoner, Adam! 'Miss Cooper'—do you not hear the laboring class in her name alone? Someone in the not-too-distant past made *barrels*!"

"I don't care about her ancestors," he said, striving for patience. "I care about her, and how I've treated her."

"But the scandal!" Marian interjected.

He ignored her. "Mother, do you not remember how people reacted when Father married you?"

She visibly flinched.

"You had little dowry to speak of—and Faith is the same."

"Though it is unkind of you to remind me," she said in a calmer voice, "surely you have not forgotten that our happiness did not last long."

"I hope that I have learned from those mistakes." He knew a moment of uncertainty. Did he really know how to make a woman happy—a woman he was *forcing* into marriage? "There was pressure from Father's family, and I do not expect any of that kind of pressure on Faith. Do we have an understanding?"

No one said anything for a moment, and then Aunt Theodosia rose and limped toward him.

"Bend down, young man, so I can give you a kiss of congratulations."

He did. "Thank you, Aunt."

Sophia hugged him and whispered, "I'm so glad it worked out!"

He wasn't quite sure it *would* work out, but he wasn't about to say that.

Faith came down late to breakfast, as Adam had requested, so she tried to tell herself she wasn't a coward. He wanted to send a tray to her room, but she'd refused. *That* would have been truly cowardly.

The footmen had been starting to clear the sideboard, but immediately backed away with a bow. Did they already know?

She wasn't all that hungry, but took some toast and hot chocolate. Just as she sat down, the duchess entered.

Faith stood back up. "Your Grace," she murmured, bowing her head.

"Miss Cooper." Her voice was laced with scorn. She gestured to the footmen, who scurried from the room and closed the doors behind them.

Faith stood awkwardly, unsure what to do.

"What can I give you to call this foolishness off?"

Faith stared at her. The duchess was trying to

bribe her? "Ma'am, I begged not to marry him. But how would it look if I ran away? It would look like I'd let him be dishonored."

"How noble of you," she said sarcastically.

"Whatever you may think, I care about him. I've made a commitment, and I will not disappoint him."

"Of course you will—how can you not?"

"Mama!" Sophia exclaimed from the doorway. "If you cannot be polite, then you should leave."

The duchess swept out on a cloud of indignation, and Faith sank back into her chair, the toast no longer appetizing.

Sophia pulled up a chair. "I'm so happy you agreed to marry my brother!"

Faith gave her a faint smile. "Then you are the only one."

"There's Aunt Theodosia—and Adam. Adam is very happy, too."

She had nothing to say about that, asking instead, "But what about your friend Lady Emmeline? Will she not be terribly disappointed?"

Sophia sighed. "She will be, yes, but I never saw the match myself. I would never have said that to anyone, because it wasn't my business. Just like it wasn't my business to say that I could see there was something between you and Adam from the moment you arrived."

Secrets, Faith thought. "I don't know about that."

"He told me about your brother's death and how he felt responsible."

Faith glanced at her in surprise. "Really? He didn't tell me he'd discussed it with you."

"Are you upset?"

"Of course not. You're his sister, and he should be able to talk to you."

"Faith, just remember, sometimes good things happen for a reason." She squeezed her arm. "So when is the wedding?"

"I don't know. We haven't even discussed it."

Sophia laughed. "Oh, don't mind me. I have wedding on the brain. I am pleasantly envious of you."

"Please don't be. You, too, will have your happy ending."

"I will," Sophia said with determination.

The rest of the day passed strangely, what with Adam giving her the present of a beautiful ring, and then talking marriage settlements. She tried to say she didn't want anything, but he said how would it look for his duchess and children not to be taken care of should something happen to him?

His duchess. It seemed overwhelming and hard to believe—and that would make his mother the dowager duchess, and Faith wasn't all that certain she'd be happy about that, what with her emphasis on her still youthful looks.

But the saddest thing was that Frances seemed to be avoiding her. Faith could only hope that the little girl would get used to the change. If her mother would allow it . . .

By the end of the week, Faith had gladly permitted Adam's mother to take over the wedding arrangements. She was relieved that her future mother-in-law was even interested. The duchess and Sophia suggested the color of the wedding dress—pale pink—the dress Sophia would wear as her bridesmaid, the actual date of the wedding, and when the invitations would go out. And her new wardrobe—it took every bit of firmness Faith had to insist that she didn't need a full trousseau, that Sophia's generous gift of clothing was more than enough. She thought she might have earned a measure of respect from the duchess with that one. Lady Duncan kept asking her privately if she had her own opinions, but honestly, she didn't. She was simply trying to use the time with the duchess to form some kind of . . . acquaintance, if not a feeling of friendship or family.

And in the evening, she felt Adam watching her, and it made her flustered and nervous. They hadn't even kissed since the engagement—she'd avoided any moments alone—because she could not stop wondering what he expected from an experienced woman on their wedding night.

Chapter 19

Late Wednesday afternoon, Faith was surprised to hear that she had callers. The wedding invitations had gone out, of course, and there were many curious people coming by every day. Most people were polite to her face, and she guessed that since they'd never bothered to notice her as a lady's companion, they had to satisfy their curiosity.

But callers specifically asking for her? She hurried down from her bedroom, entered the public drawing room—and gave her first broad smile in she didn't know how long.

"Charlotte! Jane!" she cried, hurrying to them.

They were standing awkwardly near one of the many sofas scattered throughout the room. Jane kept glancing at the frescoes on the ceiling with guilt, as if she wasn't supposed to notice the splendid artwork.

She held Jane's hand first, then reached for

Charlotte, who looked at her as if she expected her to be different.

"I'm so glad you came!" Faith said. "I've missed you terribly."

"When you didn't come last week, we were concerned," Charlotte said coolly.

"I should have sent a note. I am terribly sorry."

"And then we received our very own invitations to your wedding!" Jane said excitedly, then settled down after a glance from Charlotte.

"I hope you will attend," Faith said. "I was going to visit you both and ask if you'd be two of my bridesmaids."

Jane gasped aloud. "But . . . you will not mind my limp?"

"Of course she wouldn't mind your limp," Charlotte said, then frowned. "While that is thoughtful, bridesmaids should be of your own age and station."

"You are of my station," Faith said softly. "Would you consider it? The duchess has picked out lovely dresses."

"You've bought us dresses?" Jane squealed.

Lady Tunbridge was in a far corner speaking to an elderly couple, and now she looked up with a frown. Faith found herself not so intimidated by her anymore, so she simply smiled and turned back to her friends.

"Please tell me you'll stand up with me," Faith said in a softer voice. "I am feeling rather unworthy of all that is happening for a ducal wedding."

"Do not ever think that!" Jane exclaimed, reaching to squeeze her hand.

Faith smiled. "Thank you for saying that, but how can I help it? I did not set out to make this happen," she assured them, glancing at Charlotte.

Charlotte sighed. "I did wonder at his attentions to you at the beginning. I am glad to see they were honorable."

And then Charlotte looked past Faith, and Faith turned around to see Adam coming into the room, larger than life, shrugging his greatcoat from his broad shoulders. He was as handsome as a fairy-tale prince, and everything felt even more unreal.

He came forward and bowed to each of them. "Ladies, it is so good to see you again. Will you be attending our wedding?"

"We have both received permission, yes," Charlotte said.

"Good. If necessary, I would have had a word with your employers myself."

Faith was surprised when Charlotte actually blushed.

"They've agreed to be in the wedding," Faith said, feeling her first true moment of happiness in a long time.

Adam put his arm around her waist and she found herself hot and embarrassed.

"I'm glad you'll be a part of our big day," Adam told the women.

And then he discussed some of the details,

which Faith was surprised he remembered. She watched him put her friends at ease, even soothe Charlotte's ruffled feathers. He truly had a gift with people.

Seabrook announced Lady Emmeline's arrival. Sophia, who'd just entered the room, went right to her friend, but Faith felt as if the woman cast a dagger her way just with her eyes.

Adam looked down at Faith and said regretfully. "I must greet her."

"Of course."

When he'd crossed the room, Jane whispered, "Why is that woman staring at us?"

"That is Lady Emmeline Keane," Charlotte said. "I do believe there was talk that she was destined to be the next Rothford duchess."

"The duke never believed that," Faith said, then winced. "Do forgive me. That sounds defensive. Of course Lady Emmeline can feel disappointed."

Whatever Adam said, Lady Emmeline nodded once or twice, not crying certainly, but her dejection was plain.

"Come sit with us, dear," Charlotte said, pulling her to a sofa. "Tell us more about the wedding."

Two nights later, just before the engagement party given by the duchess, Ellen was helping Faith into the first new gown she'd had in honor of the wedding. Ellen, who before the engagement had been more pleasant, had recently returned to her dour self.

At last Ellen stepped back, and Faith looked in the mirror. "Very nice, Ellen," she said, of the simple arrangement. "Lady Sophia offered me the services of her maid, but it's obvious I made the right choice."

Ellen blinked at her. "But, Miss Cooper, I assumed, once you're duchess, that you would make other arrangements. I am certainly inexperienced compared to some."

Faith turned from the mirror and smiled at her maid. "No, you and I have grown to suit each other. If you don't mind, I would like you to stay with me."

Ellen's slowly growing smile turned her plain face luminous. "Thank you so much, miss!"

As they continued to smile at each other, a knock vibrated the door. Ellen opened it to find Frances standing there, looking over her shoulder and twisting her fingers together.

Faith grinned. "Frances, please come in!"

Ellen departed and Frances closed the door behind her.

"I—I came to see your gown," Frances said with hesitation.

Faith stood up and twirled, the six flounces on her magenta skirt rippling. The bodice was cut straight across her shoulders, and Ellen had pinned a simple flower wreath in her hair.

"You look beautiful," Frances breathed.

Nothing could have made Faith feel happier.

"I am so glad you approve." She paused. "I have missed seeing you this week."

Frances screwed her face up. "I wanted to see you, too, to tell you I'm glad you'll be my aunt, but my mother . . . she makes things difficult."

Faith approached and gave her a hug. "I'm so sorry for that. I never want to make things worse for you. You do what you need to, to keep your mother happy, and I'll know that we're friends, even if we can't see each other much yet. I'm confident that will change soon."

Frances smiled up at her. "I hope so!"

Faith walked downstairs feeling a small return of the optimism that had faded fast after Charlotte and Jane's visit.

Adam was waiting for her outside the public drawing room, and he drew her down the corridor to the private one. "You look utterly ravishing."

"Thank you," she said, casting down her gaze. It was hard to look at him and not be dazzled. She was soon to marry this man. It all seemed frightening and unreal most of the time.

"Did you finally take my advice about Ellen?"

"No, tonight I informed her she'd be the lady's maid to a duchess, and I couldn't have made her happier."

To her surprise, he frowned as if this was serious. "Adam?"

"No, it's nothing. Now tell me whatever you've done to bewitch my mother. I need to know for future reference."

She gave him a reluctant smile. "I simply let her do whatever she wanted."

"I don't think she'd ever find a more accommodating daughter-in-law."

And without any warning, he leaned down to kiss her, capturing her mouth before she had a chance to deflect, as she'd been doing the last week. And suddenly she couldn't remember why she'd been deflecting. They kissed with passion and urgency and anticipation, and for a moment, it was so easy for her to forget all her concerns.

At last Adam was the one to pull back, but only enough to press his forehead to hers as he caught his breath. "I had almost forgotten how wonderful this is between us."

She stared into his blue eyes, so close to her own. Would it *stay* wonderful?

He straightened and held out his arm. "Come, it's time to meet the public."

She shuddered. "Not something I'm looking forward to. Our callers this week already ran the gamut of every reaction to our engagement. I can only imagine tonight will be even more magnified."

"Then let them see our happiness and be envious."

She gave him a nervous smile and let him lead her to the drawing room. The next hour did see every emotion: censure, laughter, jealousy, curiosity. Faith learned to ignore the negative and appreciate the rare positive reactions, the people who thought Adam had never looked happier, or who thought the Rothfords needed some livening up.

Her biggest concern—that Timothy would attend even though he hadn't been invited—gradually faded. Lady Emmeline had to be there, of course, and it was strange to watch Adam's friend Lord Shenstone remaining at her side, consoling her even as he sent angry glares Adam's way. Faith asked if Adam knew what was wrong with his friend, but all he did was shake his head, mouth grim. Faith prayed she would not be the cause of their friendship disintegrating.

Sophia was still going on with the fiction of being pursued by Lord Shenstone, so she, too, was forced to be a part of their unhappy threesome. More than once, Faith saw Mr. Percy looking on just as unhappily, and finally she went over to talk to the man.

He bowed. "Miss Cooper, you look very happy tonight."

"Surely you're being kind, sir. I feel far too nervous to look happy. It is rather overwhelming to be a part of such an important family."

He nodded gravely, and she hoped he was thinking of what it would be like were it him.

"But I find that most everyone has been welcoming to me," she continued, "and the change, although drastic, is not as important as the relationships I've formed."

He gave her a sideways glance of amusement. "You are not very subtle, Miss Cooper."

She sighed and smiled. "No, I've never been accused of that. And I know your attachments are none of my business. But . . . you and I are not that different."

"We are very different, Miss Cooper. Your husband will be a duke. Lady Sophia deserves and needs a husband of high rank, too."

And then he bowed and left her, and she felt like an interfering fool. Who did she think she was to give advice—the duchess?

As the musicians readied the waltz, Adam found his betrothed and took her away from his sister. He leaned down to say softly, "At last you and I will dance in public."

He found he liked Faith's blushes, especially when they were about him. More and more all he could think about was how near her room was to his each night. But he knew she'd have a poor reaction to even the hint of another scandal, so he stayed away.

But here, in front of all of Society, he was able to hold her close, feel the tremble of her nervousness by his hand on her back, and his other hand encompassing her own. He whirled her into the dance, and saw the moment she realized people were standing back to watch them.

"Adam," she began tentatively.

"Don't pay any attention to them. Just look at me and remember we will show them how happy two unlikely lovers can be."

She nodded, but there was no true happiness

in her eyes, and he knew he'd have to work hard to see it grow there. He was ready for the challenge.

As they waltzed, he hoped he'd shown the anonymous blackguard that he didn't care about rumors or empty threats. It had been three weeks since he'd received a note. He hadn't sent Faith away—he was marrying her and wouldn't be dissuaded.

Anyone at their engagement party could be the one holding a grudge against him, powerful enough to make the person discover Faith's past and try to use it against Adam. And of course, there was Gilpin, who wasn't in attendance, but was one of the suspects who was angrier with Faith than Adam. It was frustrating to have this hanging over his head, with nothing concrete to take to the Metropolitan Police.

And then there was Shenstone. Adam wished he understood what was going on with his friend, if Shenstone really could be so upset with him that he'd threaten an innocent woman. Such a "prank" might be something Shenstone would do once on a drunken whim, but could he really have continued? And why—because he was upset Adam didn't contact him immediately on arriving in England? Upset they were no longer drunken compatriots at every gaming hell in London night after night? Adam was trying to forge a better life for himself, and instead of supporting him, Shenstone was flirting with Sophia to annoy Adam—

and maybe trying to sabotage his marriage with threats.

He gritted his teeth as he watched Shenstone say something to Sophia—and her look of misery. What the hell was he trying to do?

"You don't look happy," Faith said as the dance ended. "I don't even think you were aware you were dancing with me."

He blinked down at her in surprise. "You're right," he said softly, drawing her aside. "I keep seeing Shenstone and Sophia, and I'm not happy about it."

"Have you talked to him?"

"No, not in depth anyway."

"Maybe you should. Look, he's heading into the corridor right now. You can catch him."

He smiled and leaned down to kiss her cheek. "Thank you for your understanding."

"He's standing up for you at the wedding, isn't he?"

Adam hesitated.

"You didn't ask him yet?" she said in astonishment. "Oh, I promise not to tattle to your mother."

He gave a reluctant laugh. "Then I'd better rectify that."

Adam moved through the crowd as quickly as he was able, nodding politely to guests but making it apparent he couldn't talk. In the corridor, he saw Shenstone just entering the card room and called his name, half expecting to be ignored again.

But Shenstone came back out and waited for him.

"Can we talk?"

"You don't have much time to talk lately, Rothford," he said coolly.

"I do now." He led him downstairs to his study and shut the door.

"You know," Shenstone said in a strangely conversational tone, "you're about to be married. Most men in your situation need some last exciting . . . experiencès before the big commitment. Do you remember that actress who would never even make time for you? I understand she's free now and—"

"Why do you keep bringing up my past?" Adam asked sharply. "I know we're at different points in our lives, but surely we can find something else to talk about."

Shenstone shrugged. "Maybe I've got nothing else to talk about. I'm still the same as I always was, remember?"

"No, I don't think so. You're angrier and bitter."

The last of Shenstone's smile faded. "And you're dull."

"But apparently, my sister is not."

"We amuse each other. Is something wrong with that?"

"She's too innocent for you—and I want her to remain that way."

"So you think I'd harm your sister's reputation, like you seem to have done to Miss Cooper?"

Adam inhaled swiftly, then let it go. "I am marrying her."

"And she looks just jubilant about it. And let's not forget Lady Emmeline, who thought she'd be the one to marry you."

"I cannot be responsible for what Lady Emmeline thought while I was gone all those years," Adam said tightly. "As for Miss Cooper, that's none of your business."

"And my relationship with Sophia is none of *your* business."

"As her brother, it most certainly is."

"She's of age and can choose whom she wants."

"Are you seriously going to pursue her?" Adam demanded.

Shenstone lounged back against Adam's desk. "I didn't say that."

With a groan, Adam ran a hand through his hair. He should confront Shenstone about the threatening letters, but didn't know if that would be showing his cards too soon. And wouldn't the man just lie, if he was capable of such threats? "I don't understand why we are having such difficulties between us. I thought you would stand up for me at my wedding."

Shenstone snorted. "You haven't asked, have you?"

"You haven't seemed like you would accept the honor."

He narrowed his eyes, then said softly, "I won't."

He walked past Adam, deliberately brushing

his shoulder, and closed the door behind him. Hands on his hips, Adam stared out into the torchlit gardens surrounding the mansion. Perhaps he should have brought up the letters, but something inside kept him from doing so.

Was he supposed to believe one of his oldest friends was angry enough to research Faith's past and threaten him with anonymous letters? But he couldn't risk doing nothing, so he would contact his investigator and have a man follow Shenstone, too. How long could this possibly go on?

Chapter 20

The next morning, Adam decided to visit Raikes's office rather than await a messenger back and forth between them. He looked out the window to the entrance hall to judge the weather—and saw a ragged little boy coming through the gate. It was both a kick in the stomach and a surge of alertness that an approaching battle always brought. He ran back through the house to the servants' stair and headed down to the kitchen on the ground floor, startling Cook just as a knock sounded at the servants' entrance.

"Just take the note," Adam said quietly, as all the pages, scullery maids, and kitchen maids goggled at him. "I'm going to follow him."

"But Your Grace, should not one of the footmen do it for you?"

"No, I need to take care of this myself."

Cook nodded, cleared his throat, and everyone got out of sight of the door. Not half a minute later, Cook called, "He scampered off, Your Grace!"

Seabrook took the note as he reached the kitchen with his slower pace. Adam went through the outside door and saw the boy still running toward the far corner of the house. Once he took the turn, Adam started after him, running at a slow pace. He saw faces pressed to the ground floor windows as he passed, and knew he was giving his servants a fine midmorning joke.

Once on the street, he felt a little more confident in following the boy through the crowds. That is, until they headed east, where the city streets got more and more crowded. At last, Adam just gave up, realizing he couldn't possibly run all the way to the East End, if that's where the boy was headed. He'd been hoping that if a gentleman had paid him, the boy would return to give a report, but apparently not. There'd been no waiting hackney to convey him either. He was heading directly east—back home, poor lad.

Adam caught a hackney home, and Seabrook met him in his study to hand over the note, bow, and depart. The note looked exactly the same, and Adam glared at it before breaking the seal.

So much for believing the blackguard had given up.

With a heavy sigh, he read:

You'll be sorry when everyone finds out your new duchess is a whore.

He slammed the note down hard. So was the threat to reveal the truth? What the hell did this person want from him? Just to make him crazy with frustration? To make him break off the engagement? Every step of the way, Adam had done exactly what he himself wanted to do, while taking security precautions for Faith, and nothing had happened except these damned notes.

But was this a threat to reveal Faith's background, if she became his wife? That would hurt her, but certainly she'd be better able to withstand the storm as his duchess, rather than a woman alone in the world. He thought again about informing her, but he was taking care of things. She'd only worry—or flee. And he didn't want either of those things. He wouldn't tell his aunt until after the wedding—no need to upset the old girl.

As he'd planned, Adam went to Raikes's office and had him begin to watch Shenstone, even though it made him sick. He heard a report that Miss Ogden and Miss Atherstone had unblemished records, while Gilpin was never out of sight of the investigator, if he wasn't in his own home. But of course, that didn't mean he couldn't have hired a man to find a boy . . . so what did having suspects followed even prove? But he had to do *something*, and perhaps someone would make a mistake.

But he was going to marry Faith, and nothing would stop him.

The night before the wedding, Faith retired early to her bedroom. She was already in her nightdress and dressing gown, seated at her dressing table, her hair down to be brushed, when she heard a knock at the door.

"Come in, Ellen," she called.

Adam stepped into the room and closed the door.

She froze with her hairbrush at the crown of her head.

He smiled. "Don't let me disturb you. Just think, after tomorrow, I'll be able to watch you every night."

She slowly lowered the brush, then licked her suddenly dry lips. "But we aren't married yet."

His smile grew crooked. "I know. I had some news to impart, and some of it is not what I'd hoped for. I had sent a footman and maid to escort your mother to the wedding."

She took in a deep, startled breath. "I posted the invitation, but she never responded."

"I'm sorry to say that she turned down the opportunity to attend."

She let her breath out in a long sigh. "I cannot pretend to be sad. Though your motive was to be kind, next time, please consult me first."

He came over to stand behind her, and their eyes met in the mirror. "I assumed you wanted her to attend, since you sent an invitation."

"The correct reason was that I did not want to explain things to your mother."

"Aah, forgive me."

"Adam, are you always going to do this, not discuss things with me?"

"I was hoping to surprise you."

She softened. "I know, and I should take that into account. It's just . . . my mother did not approve of what I had to do to support her—although she took my money regularly enough. But I have not seen her in over two years."

"Do you correspond?"

"I send her regular letters, and once in a while she responds. But I'm a sinner in her eyes, and I'm not certain marrying a duke will change that."

"I'm sorry," he said simply.

She turned around on the bench and touched his arm, rising to her feet. "You've said that enough. We're past it. Thank you for thinking of me. Did your mother tell you who else had agreed to attend? Your two fellow soldiers from the Eighth Dragoons and their wives—Viscount Blackthorne and the Earl of Knightsbridge. Is there anything I should know before we meet?"

But they were standing close together, and his eyes were watching her mouth, and she found her thoughts getting far too distracted.

"Adam?" she whispered.

His gaze flicked to her face as if surprised she'd spoken.

She bit her lip to hide a smile, and couldn't help feeling pleased that although she was worried about their marriage, she had no need to worry about the strength of the attraction between them.

He cleared his throat. "I'm glad they've come. I'll ask them both to stand up with me at the ceremony."

"You didn't send them private notes in advance?" she asked, shocked that he'd let such an important wedding detail go until the last minute.

He seemed baffled. "Why should I? I know they'll accept."

"But . . ." And then she let it go. Men simply thought differently from women.

"Our wedding is rather normal compared to Blackthorne's. He married our commander's daughter by proxy. I attended the ceremony in India, although the bride was in England."

She stared at him in surprise. "Of course they'd met."

"No, not until we returned last autumn."

"That's incredibly brave and trusting," she said, positive something dire must have occurred to make that happen. "I understand the earl recently married, as well."

"I was able to attend that wedding, too. Just so you're aware, the bride has been blind since childhood."

Now her mouth really did drop open. "You have the most fascinating friends, Adam. I'm looking forward to meeting them."

His gaze dropped to her mouth again, and then lower, where she was without the protection of corset and layers of petticoats.

"Do you know what I'm looking forward to?" he asked softly.

"A good wedding breakfast?" she teased, though her heart seemed to be beating in her ears, and she couldn't take a deep enough breath.

He pulled her into his arms and kissed her hungrily for what seemed like endless minutes of mutual passion. His hands skimmed down her back and captured her backside. Her nightclothes were so thin it was as if he touched her bare flesh, and she moaned.

How far would he go—how far would she let him? She'd spent their several-week engagement avoiding this contact, knowing that if she let him touch her, she might burst into flames. It felt that way now, like she was so hot she could strip off her clothes.

"I've been aching for you," he said against her temple. "I want to touch you, to show you how you make me feel."

Passion, desire—those feelings were permissible in a marriage, but they weren't love. How could Faith let herself love him, when she could be the cause of the social ruin of his whole family?

He stiffened. "You're drifting away from me, I can feel it."

"I'm sorry. I'm just so . . . . frightened."

He cupped her face to look into her eyes. "Of me?"

"No, you've been good to me. I'm afraid I won't be a good wife for you, that my past—"

"Stop it," he said firmly. "Don't speak of it again."

"But it happened, Adam, and we can't wish it away."

"I'm not wishing anything away. Everything you've experienced has made you the person you are. But it's the *past*, and we are going forward into the future, the married future where I make you blissfully happy, day and night. Your doubts make me think you don't trust me."

"Oh, Adam, you've been honorable to me." She saw the flash of pain in his eyes, knew he was thinking about his own mistakes. It was her turn to say, "*Everything* is in the past. Let us both promise that we'll forget it." And then she kissed him softly, awash with tender feelings for him because the sorrow that had first brought them together had turned into a mutual regard. Was it love? Or was she too afraid to admit that? "Sleep well, Adam."

He sighed. "I must leave?"

"You must leave." And for just a moment, she had a terrible thought. She wasn't a virgin—what if he insisted on staying?

But he never said that, only kissed her brow and left.

And she hated herself for letting her past mar her present. They'd agreed that the past was finished and shouldn't affect them, but it was so easy to say, and difficult to do.

The ceremony at the church seemed to pass by in a dream for Faith. Strangers crowded the church courtyard to get a glimpse of her when she arrived, the next Duchess of Rothford.

Looking at Adam in his dark blue frock coat and tan trousers, smiling at her so tenderly, it finally felt real. She saw her first glimpse of his two friends, Blackthorne and Knightsbridge, standing next to him before the altar. They were big men, with the same competent ease that Adam had, men who knew their capabilities and had tested their own self-worth. Charlotte, Jane, and Sophia were there for her, looking lovely in gowns of various shades of blue.

The ceremony itself was a blur, and she focused on his face, on the tenderness in his eyes, the proud smile he wore, as if he'd really won a prize marrying her. It touched her heart. He was her husband now, and it was strange and wonderful and frightening all at once. Soon she was alone in a carriage with Adam for the short drive back to his home—their home.

He grinned and then gave her a possessive kiss. "Hello, Duchess."

She was speechless at the title, but he just laughed and kissed her again.

At Rothford Court, the orange flowers in her hair were reproduced in sugar atop the wedding cake. The wedding breakfast was more of a dinner than morning fare, cold lobster salad and chicken, ham and game pie, jellies and sweets. And at last, Adam was able to introduce her to his friends from the army.

Viscount Blackthorne, the lone one of the three still with the Eighth Dragoon Guards and a sergeant, not an officer, had a broad face and stark cheekbones beneath his brown hair. His expression serious and intelligent, he bowed over her hand. "Best wishes, Your Grace."

Faith almost turned around to see if Adam's mother was behind her. The shiver she felt was mostly nerves. "Thank you so much, my lord."

His wife, whom he'd married while half a world apart, also pressed her hand and smiled. She was the former Lady Cecilia Mallory, daughter of the Earl of Appertan, the late commander of the Eighth Dragoons. She was the picture of innocent English beauty, with blond hair and vivid blue eyes, but she was a woman who'd managed her father's great estates, and planned to do the same for her husband.

"Your Grace," Lady Blackthorne said, "I am so glad you were married before our ship departs. We are leaving for India within the month, so my husband can return to his regiment."

"Oh, I do hope we haven't kept you from all you must do!" Faith said.

"Nonsense," Lord Blackthorne said. "Cecilia already has everything well organized. I'm glad for the excuse to make her relax and enjoy a good party."

"It seems you married your match, Michael," said the other man, Lord Knightsbridge, in a dry, amused voice.

He was a handsome man with deep black hair and vivid green eyes, the latter of which fondly returned to his wife, who held his arm. Lady Knightsbridge, her light brown hair styled simply, looked in Faith's general direction, but her beautiful amber eyes were blank. It was her smile that made her striking, full of happiness and confidence. She was obviously no invalid, as so many of the blind were usually treated. She was a woman who'd been widowed, secluded deliberately by her family, and then had moved to an inherited property and managed her own life.

Faith could only be in awe of both these women, running estates like men, yet had found love with men who respected them. She felt herself mildly envious, because she didn't know if she'd ever join the ranks of well-loved women. She didn't know what her future would hold. And it was frightening.

"So how did you two meet?" Lady Knightsbridge asked. She tilted her head in Faith's direction. "My husband was not very good at discovering the romantic details."

"There weren't many romantic details to tell," Adam said. "I offered her a position as lady's companion with my aunt."

Faith blushed, knowing they all understood that living within the same household had contributed toward the hasty marriage. But all their expressions remained pleasant and interested.

"None of us were romantic," Lady Blackthorne said. "I asked my husband to marry me in a letter to India, since I needed access to my inheritance. I never thought we'd even meet."

Lady Knightsbridge chuckled. "And I needed an escort away from my family, so my dear Robert offered to pretend to be my fiancé."

Faith almost gaped at the forthright women, noticing how all the men just watched them fondly before exchanging amused glances with each other. She realized that, just like Adam, Blackthorne and Knightsbridge also wanted to make up for the mistakes they'd made in India. It had obviously worked out for all of them.

She just couldn't imagine such a happy ending for her and Adam. Faith had secrets to hide that must never be revealed. But at least Adam knew, which made her feel a little less deceptive.

She eventually mingled with other guests, all of whom she'd met either in Society or at her engagement party. She noticed the revolving partners that whirled around Sophia, Lord Shenstone as her false suitor, Mr. Percy as her "friend" who was beginning to behave like a martyr, and Lady Emmeline, glorying in the sympathy of every man who knew her. It was like a Shakespearean comedy, only Faith could not see how any happy endings would result.

At one point, when Adam left her alone, his

mother came up to point out someone she'd felt that Faith had slighted with attention so far. Faith thanked her and was about to do her bidding, when the dowager duchess stopped her.

"Faith," she said, using her Christian name for the first time, "my son tells me you did not wish to take a wedding trip."

"No, Your Grace. You all have done too much for me. I would rather stay here and continue my help with Lady Duncan's speeches."

"But you should also think of yourself now. You must be tired from the exertions of a hurried wedding."

Faith tried not to frown, knowing she'd done nothing more than nod her head in approval to anything the duchess wanted.

"Do go and see Rothford Castle. You might find yourself preferring it to London. Adam will be so busy now that he's taking a more active role in the House of Lords."

And then Faith realized that the woman was trying to get rid of her. After everything she'd done these past weeks to make up for her accidental entry into this family, accepting questionable menu choices for her wedding breakfast, allowing the pale pink gown when another had caught her fancy, Faith had had enough.

"Your Grace, I will see Rothford Castle when Adam wishes me to. And even then, I imagine we will see it together. We are newlyweds, after all."

Adam's mother stared at her narrow-eyed for

a moment, perhaps sizing her up, before giving a reluctant nod and moving away.

Faith's heart was still pounding from the encounter, but she chanced to see Adam staring at her from ten feet away, wearing an approving smile.

"Very impressive," said a woman from much closer.

Faith turned to find Lady Knightsbridge sitting alone at the nearest table, her head cocked in an attitude of listening.

She felt herself blushing. "My lady, I hope you do not think me rude to the woman who is now my mother-in-law."

"Oh, no, it was really quite entertaining. She obviously needed to be reminded that you are her son's choice."

"But not hers," Faith said in a rueful voice.

"Do sit down, Your Grace."

Faith did so. "It seems strange to be called that. I've always simply been Faith."

"And I am Audrey. I, too, was a commoner when I married Robert, but there was no one to object, for he was very alone, with little close family. That is your own family situation, too, am I correct?"

Faith nodded, then remembered Audrey couldn't see her. "Yes. My brother died serving with the Eighth Dragoons."

"As did my late husband, as well as Cecilia's father. We women are connected in a way, are we not? Three honorable men wanted to help us, and in some ways recover their own self-worth. I don't know about you, but it was very difficult to separate the need to help from the true emotion of love."

"I don't think I'm there yet," Faith admitted, then winced. She didn't even know this woman.

Audrey's smile was soft but determined. "Be patient with yourself and with him. Though I cannot see, I can hear the respect and admiration in the duke's voice when he speaks of you. Close quarters can only increase that and deepen emotion. That happened for me. I will pray that the same happens for you. Who knows, maybe it already has, and you're afraid to admit it."

Faith could only blink in astonishment.

"There, you're tongue-tied," Audrey said, her smile growing into a sly grin. "I must be close to the truth. But don't answer. You must believe it yourself."

Since the bride and groom usually left for a wedding trip after the breakfast, Faith felt a little silly and self-conscious just moving aimlessly about the house until the coming wedding night. Surely she'd feel eyes watching her, and many not happily, so she headed for her room. The duchess had been civil after Faith held her own in conversation, but Lady Tunbridge hadn't even bothered to congratulate her on the wedding.

But at least she'd allowed Frances to attend,

dressed in a beautiful new gown Faith had asked to have made for her. She was still surprised Lady Tunbridge had accepted.

When she arrived in her room, she found the door open and all of her personal effects gone.

Ellen rose from a chair near the hearth and smiled. "Good afternoon, Your Grace."

Faith shook her head even as she returned the smile. "That is so strange to hear."

"I moved all your things for you, but thought you'd forget and come here first."

"You're starting to know me too well, Ellen."

The girl blushed. "Come with me—wait until you see your beautiful suite!"

And it was truly beautiful, with a brass bed, a dressing table with a heart-shaped mirror, wardrobe, chest of drawers, and a chaise longue at the foot of the bed. The paintings were lush landscapes of gardens and green rolling hills.

"I'm told those are the grounds of Rothford Castle, ma'am," Ellen said. "It was built many centuries ago. I'm excited to visit."

Faith smiled at the now-talkative maid. "I imagine we'll go soon, but I don't know when. I guess we'll try to be patient."

Ellen walked her through the rest of the suite, her dressing room and bathroom, a shared sitting room, then they entered the master bedroom, with its dressing room and bath on the far side. The bed was massive, a four-poster with heavy curtains and a counterpane that matched a nearby sofa. Faith caught Ellen deliberately look-ing away from it, which amused and helped her relax. Then she retreated to her own bedchamber with its lovely writing desk full of little drawers, and started a dutiful letter to her mother about the wedding.

Later that afternoon, as she was trying to decide what to wear to dinner after her bath, Ellen came in and said, "Oh, no, Your Grace, the duke has or-dered dinner brought to your sitting room."

"Oh. How thoughtful." And private. She couldn't decide if she was glad to avoid the rest of the household or sad she wouldn't have the dis-traction.

One would think she was a virgin, the way she was so nervous!

"Your Grace, let us choose a gown that's easy to remove."

"Ellen!" Faith exclaimed, but she was laughing and blushing at the same time.

The maid put her hands on her hips. "Well, you won't want me to come back after dinner, now will you?"

Chapter 21

Faith remained in her bedroom until a maid respectfully announced that dinner was served in the duke's sitting room. Taking a deep breath, she walked slowly to the door, telling herself that at least for tonight, she'd try to do nothing to remind her groom that there had been two men before him—one he didn't even know about because she could not allow him to regularly look upon Timothy and know he'd taken Faith's virginity. So she would be quiet in her passion, restrained and dignified, even if it took every bit of her control. And it would, for she'd been drawn to Adam almost from the first moment of seeing him, and her anticipation had only continued to rise until it was like an ache that just wouldn't go away.

She entered the sitting room and found that a small table had been set with beautiful china and linens, and tall candles blazed in the center. She stood there admiring it until the far door opened and Adam came in, his hair damp from the bath, shirt open at the collar, trousers and bare feet. They really were having an informal dinner, she thought, hiding a smile.

"What?" he asked, grinning.

"With your bare feet, you are making me feel terribly overdressed."

His smile faded, and he came to her. "You're very overdressed."

And then he pulled her into his arms hungrily, bringing her up on her tiptoes until she twined her arms around his neck for their kiss.

He kissed every part of her face, nuzzled behind her ear, then murmured, "Take down your hair."

She almost asked about dinner, and realized she'd only be betraying her nerves. And she, a woman with experience.

Reaching up, she began to pull the pins from her hair, and he watched with the rapt attention of a man about to win a prize he'd long coveted.

"It was hell watching you all day and not touching," he said in a hoarse voice, once her dark hair fell about her shoulders. He put his hands deep in her hair and lifted it to his face. "Heavenly." Then he fisted it gently to pull her back against him. "Can dinner wait? I'm only hungry for you."

"You make me blush with such flattery," she said, smiling with pleasure.

He put his hands on the buttons at her throat. "May I make you blush another way?"

Her breath caught, and at first all she could do was nod. "I can remove this, if you'd like."

"Let me. Convenient buttons, by the way."

"The gown was chosen for ease."

He chuckled. Each movement of his dexterous hands from button to button was as arousing as if he stroked her. At last he spread wide her bodice, and inhaled sharply upon just seeing her silky chemise.

"You're not wearing a corset," he said hoarsely.

"You're not displeased?"

"God, no."

He slid his hands up the side of her rib cage, just touching the outer curves of her breasts, making her shudder. At her shoulders, he pushed the gown back and down her arms, which made her arch forward. The neckline of the chemise revealed the upper slopes of her breasts, with no girlish frills to distract, and he was staring there, those blue eyes narrowed and intent. It was as if he forgot about pulling her hands out of her tight sleeves, leaving her almost trapped, bound.

His hands did a slow slide from her waist over her rib cage and up, just cupping her breasts, as if feeling their weight. She threw her head back and stared up at him, begging him with her eyes to do more, to touch more, to make her . . . feel.

And then his thumbs brushed her nipples, and she jerked at the shock of pleasure that centered between her thighs. She whispered his name, even as he began to stroke her more rhythmically through the silk, rubbing and plucking until she was mindless with urgency.

"Let me hold you, let me touch you," she gasped, still constrained by her sleeves and the back of the sofa behind her.

But as if he hadn't heard, he bent and pressed light kisses along the bodice of her chemise, then went farther, taking her nipple into his mouth through the garment.

She cried out at the exquisite pleasure. "Please, oh, please," she begged, knowing exactly what she needed.

At last her arm came free and she reached up to pull down her chemise, to rip the strap if she had to.

He stopped her hand. "No, let me."

She had a momentary feeling of apprehension, as if she'd done something wrong, revealed her experience.

"I need to do this," he said against her throat. "I've been waiting so long."

She melted at those words, tried to put away her fears. He pulled her bodice down and the gown pooled at her feet, leaving just the sheer chemise. And then he caressed her body through it, as if delaying the reveal like a package at Christmas. But at last she was able to touch him, to run her hands up his arms, to sink her fingers into his thick, silky hair and hold him to her.

She felt a draft on the backs of her thighs and knew he was fisting the chemise in both hands, pulling it slowly upward. She lifted her arms and it came right off.

She was nude, and without thinking, she folded her arms at the top of her head, displaying herself provocatively. It didn't matter that he was still fully clothed; her heavy breasts and rounded hips seemed to please him, and that excited her.

"To think you once hid this magnificence behind shapeless gowns," he said with fervor.

For just a moment, her eyes stung at such generous praise. It was so hard to believe herself worthy of it.

"You're thinking again," he said. "Don't think."

And then he pulled his shirt over his head and she didn't want to think about anything but him. She'd never seen a man whose body rivaled what she'd seen in museum statues—she'd almost thought they had to be exaggerated, but now she knew otherwise. He was perfectly proportioned, chest well muscled and scattered with light brown hair, which continued down over the ridges of his abdomen. There were puckered scars of course, the marks of war, but none that looked deep or nearly fatal. She let her hands roam over him, knowing he found as much pleasure in it as she did. And then he brought her up hard against him, bare flesh to bare flesh, her nipples teased by the hair on his chest. She put her hands on his trousers and unbuttoned with too much expertise, but she was beyond caring now. When his trousers and underclothes fell to the floor, she took his heavy cock in her hand and stroked.

With a groan, he stopped her by lifting her off her feet and carrying her into his bedroom. He laid her back on the bed, and she let her hair fall all around her, reaching for him.

He came down beside her and began a slow exploration that near drove her out of her mind with wanting. Every caress was so filled with tenderness and admiration, as if her pleasure were more important than his own. Much as she'd enjoyed the act before, this was a revelation, a true mark of his care for her.

She rolled onto her side to face him, leaning in to kiss him even as his fingers slid between her thighs.

"Oh," she moaned, raising her knee, letting him explore, as she focused her own teasing touch on his erection.

They kissed with hungry mouths, making love sounds that only heightened her arousal. She whimpered as he circled the most pleasure-sensitive part of her, then delved deep inside. She tightened her sheath around his fingers, and he met her eyes in shock.

"Take me, Adam," she breathed, eyes half closed in arousal. "Please. I'm ready."

He rolled her onto her back and settled between her thighs. She lifted her legs off the bed, clutched him with her knees, doing her best to guide him where she wanted.

He laughed against her mouth. "Impatient, are you?"

"Yes, yes, impatient for you."

And then he sank into her, and it was as if she'd been waiting for this joining from the moment they'd met. They were together, together forever, and he looked down into her eyes even as he moved against her forcefully. She moved her body with his, knowing what she wanted, feeling the spiraling rise of desire overwhelm her before she could even think to make it last. She shuddered beneath him, the pleasure expanding outward until every part of her body seemed a part of his.

She opened her eyes and found him staring at her, intent, as he picked up speed, moving his body, changing the angle of his hips, as if he were trying to bring her to climax with him.

And he succeeded, groaning as he released his seed, and they shuddered together in mutual passion.

His weight was a pleasant heaviness, and she almost pouted when he rolled off. But he didn't go far, pulling her up along his body and into the crook of his arm. Sighing with happiness, she let her hands trail through his chest hair.

And then her stomach growled.

Eyes wide, she looked up at him, and they both laughed.

"Now I know what's important to you," he said. "I have to feed every one of your body's demands."

"You fed the important one first," she said. Then her smile faded, and so did his.

"Tell me I made you happy," he said softly.

"You did," she answered with the same quiet reflection. "I think I'm rather shocked by how much I enjoyed it."

He cupped her face. "He treated you poorly?"

She was surprised that he'd openly spoken of her protector in their marriage bed—but then again, he was a man who did what he wanted, often not thinking first.

"No, not that. He was good to me. I . . . made myself forget the enjoyment, I think. I've been so afraid that there was a part of me that was made for such wicked deeds, that I was . . . bad, because I liked how he made me feel. It worried me that in some way I was most suited to being a mistress, that I liked it. But you have made me see that it can be natural and right when two people—" She found herself stumbling then, adding, "when two people are married."

If he thought anything of the abrupt change in direction, he didn't mention it, only said, "Faith, everything we do and feel and experience together is right. I don't want you to think I feel like I'm in some kind of competition with your past. I am your present, your future, and it's up to me to make them the best years of your life."

They kissed again, deeply, seriously, intently, before he led her naked to the table where she couldn't help giggling as they fed each other. But she couldn't forget her hesitation on "when two people"—had she been about to say "love each other"? That wasn't true for them, not yet, maybe not ever. But she was thinking about it more and more. Maybe she did love him, but deep inside, she was worried that a man who felt he had to constantly save her—from poverty, from herself—could never respect her enough to truly love her as his equal.

And she wanted to be loved, perhaps more than she wanted to be saved.

Adam awoke to the most pleasant morning of his life. His bed was full of the warm softness of Faith—his wife. Forever she would be at his side.

Stroking her hair as she slept, he thought about their wedding day, and his first glimpse of her in the fine gown with orange blossoms in her hair and a veil that made her mysterious. Her eyes had been large when she'd met him at the altar, as if she thought he planned to change his mind. Marrying her did not seem to make her fully trust him, but somehow he'd convince her.

He was still relieved and amazed that the day had gone so well. Perhaps he'd secretly thought the blackguard would somehow interrupt, but no one had. He'd feared it during the ceremony, though, when he'd seen Timothy Gilpin at the back of the church. He'd wanted to throw him out, but anyone could be in a public church. And if he threw out Gilpin, he might have to do the same to Shenstone, who'd glowered at him and his best men as if Adam had never asked him to stand up with him.

But at least Shenstone had attended, which somehow made Adam feel better.

He liked seeing Faith with Michael, Robert, and their wives. It was amazing that three friends had returned from war, scarred and grieving and trying to atone, and somehow managed to find happiness. And the two couples had love, too, which was obvious just being near them. Would he and Faith someday inspire people with the same emotions?

As if his thoughts disturbed her, she suddenly stirred. He was able to see her dark lashes fan her cheeks, then slowly rise to meet his, revealing eyes as gorgeous gray as clouds heralding a storm. He liked to think no day would ever be the same with her, as if her mood and temper could change with every thought. Right now she still held herself back, though, as if afraid to reveal herself.

But not the previous night.

He was hard just remembering how she'd met him equally, not a shy bride afraid or ignorant on her wedding night. It obviously bothered her to be that way, but not him. He appreciated her lusty qualities, and hoped she would never again think she was "bad" for enjoying their marriage bed.

She arched and stretched, and the blanket fell down to her waist. He stared at her breasts as if he'd never seen a woman before. She rose up on her elbow, her dark hair falling about her shoulders, her smile languid and knowing, even as she slid her hand beneath the sheets until she felt the rigid length of him.

He inhaled sharply. "Faith," he said on a groan.

And then she rose up and straddled him, sliding along his cock with the warm wet depths of herself. Before he could do more than gasp, he was inside her, and she sat back on his hips until he was fully sheathed.

"My God," he said hoarsely, then reached up and took her breasts in his hands.

She sat still for an achingly long time, eyes half closed as she enjoyed his caresses. He could feel the spasms inside her when she reacted to each touch, and he thought he'd go mad staying so still. As if reading his mind—or perhaps his cock—she began to move, strong thighs lifting her up and down, breasts bouncing into his palms. He sat up to take one breast deep into his mouth, and she moaned and held him to her. They strained into each other, gasping, aching, and when he felt her come, he arched up inside her and gave her everything he had.

It was her turn to roll to the side and collapse, and they looked at each other, wearing silly grins.

"Words . . . fail me," he said long minutes later, still breathing heavily.

Her grin turned wicked, her hair wild from their exertions. My God, he could have taken her again, she so roused every part of him.

And then she covered her red face with her hand. "How am I supposed to face your family like this? No wonder people take wedding trips, just so everyone can become used to the changed circumstances."

"Should I whisk you away?"

She dropped her hand, and her smile faded. "No, I wasn't suggesting that. I should be here."

"Whatever you want."

"Will it always be so easy?" she teased. "Or perhaps this morning was a good example of why you're trying to keep me happy."

"I have more plans to keep you happy. But today, let's just stay here and be together. We'll have all our meals sent up."

"No! That would be so . . . obvious."

"So?"

She winced even as she looked intrigued. "Are you certain?"

"I'm certain."

So that's what they did. And when they finally emerged from their apartments, they spent a few days doing things together: horseback riding along Rotten Row in Hyde Park, to reacquaint Faith with horses after years without them; walks in the conservatory on rainy days, and they even had a picnic there, which Frances joined, giggling the whole time at the novelty of it all.

At last they emerged back into Society together, first attending the opera in the Rothford box. Faith told him it was like letting everyone ogle them all at once, and getting it out of the way. Privately, he thought his anonymous blackguard needed to see that none of his threats mattered.

At intermission they hosted many visitors, and

he found himself separated from her, but still watching.

Shenstone made an appearance, which surprised him, smiling his way through the dozen guests, and then that smile fading when his gaze met Adam's.

"Rothford," he said, still in that measured tone so unlike him. "You seem besotted with your bride."

"I am. Marriage is a happy state. Perhaps someday you'll try it."

And somehow that was the wrong thing to say, for his brows lowered in a frown, and he soon made his excuses. Adam sighed—when would he figure out how to repair his relationship with his old friend? Or if he even should, considering Shenstone was under suspicion for being the anonymous blackguard just by his behavior alone. And perhaps that was a mistake. Would someone hiding his identity be so openly antagonistic? That actually gave him a brief moment of hope.

That night, alone in their suite, he watched Faith brush out her hair after her lady's maid left. This simple, peaceful moment always brought him a quiet joy at the end of the day.

"Adam, did you see Lady Emmeline and Lord Shenstone together tonight? It is . . . a strange friendship. She seems so unhappy about losing the dream of marrying you—even despondent, according to Sophia. I cannot decide if Lord Shenstone is trying to cheer her up or—I hate to say it—take advantage of her weakened state to benefit his own interests."

Adam sighed. "He's never been one to abuse an innocent. But lately, I don't feel like I know what he's thinking anymore."

Faith paused, eyes downcast, her manner far too hesitant.

"What is it?" he asked. "You know you can tell me anything."

"Do you think Lady Emmeline would sink so low that she might try to become your mistress? She seems focused on you."

Adam blinked at her. "You cannot be serious."

"I know something of desperation," she reminded him.

"But she is not desperate the same way you were, sweetheart."

But the forlorn expression wouldn't leave her face, as if Emmeline's plight were her own.

"She will forget about me," Adam said, coming to stand behind her and resting his hands on her shoulders. "She has a fortune, beauty, and the beginnings of a caring nature."

He said the last as a joke, but Faith didn't laugh, only continued to look troubled.

"Put this out of your mind, Faith. I want you to be happy. You're my duchess now. I did my best to *make* you happy, and I think I was right."

She met his eyes again and frowned. "Why did you emphasize *making* me happy?"

He paused for only the briefest moment. "I

don't understand what you mean. I wanted you to be happy as my bride."

Her frown grew somber and suspicious. "Adam, what is the 'right thing' you're happy we did? We were found alone together, kissing. Is that?"

"I know it started out precariously, but I always knew we suited, and that our marriage would be good. Are we not happy?"

And now her mouth fell open before she whispered. "Did you—did you deliberately compromise me, Adam? Is that how you made me happy?"

Chapter 22

Faith's unease blossomed into a cold sensation of fear as she looked into Adam's eyes through the mirror. She was almost afraid to turn around, afraid to see that the mirror wasn't distorting what she saw with her own eyes. He clenched his jaw, and it was like the clean thrust of a knife through her ribs.

"Oh Adam, what did you do?" she whispered hoarsely.

He'd asked her to marry him, over and over again, and she'd refused every proposal. Had he taken the matter into his own hands?

"Did you know your family's exact schedule that night?" she demanded.

When he still said nothing, she jumped up to face him, but put distance between them, because if he touched her, she might scream. Every dream of happiness, of feeling respected and cherished, was slowly burning into ashes.

"Then I'll go to Sophia and find out!"

"No, there is no need."

He spoke impassively, but there was a light of righteousness in his eyes.

"Then answer my question!" Her voice sounded shrill, but she didn't care.

"I knew they would be coming in—not all of them. I thought only Sophia and Aunt Theodosia, who could be trusted."

"You—you deliberately humiliated me," she whispered, hand to her throat as the lump there grew and grew, demanding to be cried out with angry, painful tears.

"I didn't want you to feel that way. I knew we'd be embarrassed, but don't you see? We need each other, we want each other. I wanted you as my duchess and no other."

"You wanted to save me from my sins," she said bitterly.

"I want to protect you, to keep you safe and happy and give you children!"

She saw the incomprehension and frustration on his face, which only made her angrier.

"No—you wanted to save *yourself* from your sins," she countered. "This is about your guilt, and your need to be in control. You had all the power over me. Do you know how I blamed myself for besmirching your honorable reputation? How I thought my own unseemly lust forced you into this marriage?"

"That's not true, none of it!"

"I cried myself to sleep, thinking I was every kind of sinner my mother called me—"

"Faith, no." His eyes went somber and sad. "I wanted to make things better for both of us."

"You can tell yourself you were trying to help me, but it wasn't *about* me—it was about you and the guilt you cannot let go of." She gave a harsh laugh. "And to think I hoped we could someday actually love each other."

"I want that," he said with urgency.

"This can't be love, Adam. You want me like a possession, something you have to have for yourself. You're *smothering* me! You've taken away my freedoms from the beginning—my God, you tricked me into renouncing my first position, and I forgave you, thinking you'd learned your lesson. I forgave you for the mistakes that led to my brother's death. I was such a fool."

Wildly, she headed for the door, then realized she was in her own room. She turned and pointed to the far door. "I need you to leave."

"Faith—"

"I can't talk anymore. Please go."

"I will, but we will be finishing this discussion in the morning."

When he left, she started packing without even giving it another thought. She couldn't stay there in a loveless marriage where her husband had no problem manipulating her.

There was a knock on her door.

Frowning, she said, "Who is it?"

"Ellen, ma'am. His Grace sent for me, said you might have need of me."

And he was right, though he probably didn't know what for. "Come in."

Ellen came to a stop on seeing the clothes spread out all over the bed. "Your Grace?"

"I'm leaving, Ellen. For good."

"Then I'm coming with you."

Faith stared at her. "But . . . I don't even know where I'm going. You don't need to—"

"You believed in me, ma'am. That's all I care about. Now move aside and let me fetch your satchel."

For endless minutes, Faith had been trying not to cry, and now this girl's kindness had her eyes stinging. "Thank you, Ellen," she said, her voice choked.

"Let me do this, while you go speak with Lady Duncan."

Faith almost protested, not wanting anyone to stop her, but she owed an explanation. "You're right. I'll be back."

At the countess's door, she knocked softly, wondering if the elderly woman was still awake. When she heard her respond, she opened the door to find the room ablaze with lights, the lady seated at her writing table, turban on her head, wrapped in a voluminous dressing gown.

"Faith, what a pleasant surprise!"

"Good evening, Lady—Aunt Theodosia."

As she came into the light, Aunt Theodosia's smile faded. "What is it, dear?"

The first tears fell down her cheek. "I have to leave," she said in a broken voice. "I can't stay here with him anymore."

Aunt Theodosia reached for her hand and pulled her to the chair nearest her own. "You've been so happy! You're both radiant together. I never imagined seeing Adam so at peace."

"I—I do not want to speak ill of your nephew, my lady. Suffice it to say that he lied to me about something gravely important. I can't be with a man who doesn't respect me."

"Surely you can discuss it calmly."

She shook her head, the tears continuing to drip from her cheeks to her bodice.

Aunt Theodosia handed her a handkerchief. "I insist you tell me or, harsh as it is, I shall not permit you to go. And if you're going, you'll need my help, for where else will you stay?"

Faith started to cry, and the whole tale about the compromise spilled out.

Aunt Theodosia put her arms around her for a fierce hug. "There, there, dear. I totally understand how you're feeling. And though you don't want to hear it, I understand my nephew's thinking as well, foolish as it is. He loves you, and is desperate to hold on to you and keep you safe."

"That's not love, Aunt. And even if he believes it *is* love, he hasn't learned one thing from it. He humiliated me, more than once, and I won't stand for that. I'll go to a hotel if I have to, although I imagine that would cause talk."

"It would," Aunt Theodosia said with a sigh.

"Could you not just move back to your old room while you work this out?"

"And stare at the duchess's smirking face every day? Let Adam believe I'll just accept whatever he does? No."

"Then you should go to Mrs. Evans's. You remember her from the women's rights meetings?"

"I do."

"She thought you a diligent worker and a gifted writer. And she'd do anything for me, of course."

"Will she mind if Ellen goes with me?"

"Of course not. But she does retire early. I believe you should wait until morning."

Faith bit her lip. "I'm afraid he might make a scene trying to keep me here. He always thinks he knows best," she added bitterly.

"I will make sure he does not. If you leave at dawn, Mrs. Evans will certainly be awake. And she will be discreet."

"Thank you. If you need me before then, I will be in my old room."

Aunt Theodosia sighed, her wrinkled face drooping in sorrow. "I'm so sorry, dear. But promise me you will not refuse to see him, that you will give your marriage the chance to recover."

She hesitated. "I might need time to get over this terrible grief. How can I talk to him if I'm doing nothing but crying?"

"You must truly love him."

Faith felt the stark pain of that. "What does it matter? My love is not returned."

Sleeping in her old bedroom, she tossed and turned through the night. At dawn, she and Ellen flagged down a hackney, and then Rothford Court was behind her. It was for the best, even though her heart thought otherwise.

Adam wasn't even dressed when he heard a knock. His spirit lightened until he realized it wouldn't be Faith, because it came from the outer door.

"Come in," he said, tightening the belt on his dressing gown.

Aunt Theodosia stood there, hands on her hips. "You great big fool, she's left."

He blinked. "I know she returned to her old room, but—"

"No, *left*. She's out front, looking for a hackney."

"What? Did you know sooner?" He ran for the bellpull and gave it a yank.

"Last night. Don't worry, I know where she's going, but she left even earlier than I imagined."

"She needs a man with her."

"You can send one to Mrs. Evans's town house."

He grimaced. "That old bat? She'll fill Faith's head full of nonsense."

Aunt Theodosia puffed out her bosom. "The nonsense that both Faith and I believe in? No wonder she left you!"

"What did she say to you?"

"Everything—that you manipulated her ruin."

"That is a terrible way to put it."

"But it's the truth, isn't it?"

He sighed, hands on his hips.

"You made an awful mistake," she said gently, sadly.

"I see that now. I'll fix things."

"I don't know if you can."

He froze on the way to his dressing room, then said over his shoulder, "Don't say that, Aunt."

His valet arrived, and Adam requested Hales to attend him. He wished Aunt Theodosia would leave and take her condemning stare with her, but he wouldn't throw her out. He walked into his dressing room and started to change. Hales was there before he'd done more than put on trousers, so he sent the young man to stand outside Mrs. Evans's residence and watch over Faith.

He felt sick with worry, despondent that he'd made so many thoughtless mistakes, assuming he knew best. What the hell did he know—he couldn't even find one persistent blackguard.

Faith's rejection stung him in a way he hadn't felt in years. He'd grown up with rejection, had brothers who ganged up against him, so one would have thought he'd be immune to it. He was not going to let this happen. He and Faith belonged together.

He wasn't certain how any of this had happened. He'd worked hard to help Faith without being that impulsive man again, that man who jumped into an idea without enough thought.

He'd taken deliberate steps to protect her from the blackguard, had gotten her away from terrible employers. And then he'd realized he was falling in love with her. He'd spent days trying to get her to marry him, before succumbing to a last-resort solution.

And they were happy—*he'd* been happier than he'd ever been in his whole life.

He emerged from his dressing room to find his aunt calmly seated, both hands resting on her cane.

"I still can't believe you let her go alone," he grumbled.

"She's not alone—Ellen is with her."

He rounded on his aunt. "You know I've been suspicious of that girl. And I received another note threatening to call my duchess a whore in front of all of London."

He expected the old girl to flinch, but she only narrowed her eyes.

And then he remembered. "Wait. Faith told Ellen she was keeping her on permanently, even before I received the final note. Ellen was relieved and happy, or so I've been told."

"Then she wouldn't have written such a terrible letter, Adam. I can't believe it of her—this person hasn't even asked for money, which could be the only motive for a poor girl like her."

He nodded, but inside, everything that had happened was finally sinking in. He'd driven Faith away without telling her she might be in danger, all because he'd wanted to keep her in a happy little cocoon of innocence. He hadn't been able to protect her innocence from her brother's death, and now he hadn't been able to protect *her*. He'd driven her away, when all he'd wanted was to be married to her, to be happy.

Was compromising her truly all about him, as she'd accused?

But he couldn't name and reflect on his sins, not now. Her protection was all that mattered.

"Aunt Theodosia, it's time to confront the suspects once and for all. Since I can't get proof—I can only judge them in person."

"Perhaps you should inform Faith at last."

That went against everything inside him. "I can't cause her any more pain than I already have. Let me first make this last attempt."

She nodded, her expression skeptical.

"Tell the family whatever you think best about Faith."

"I think it's best to be somewhat honest."

"Fine," he said coolly.

Shenstone wouldn't agree to meet with him that day unless he fenced, so, gritting his teeth, Adam stood in the entrance hall and put on his gloves midmorning, ready to go confront his old friend. So far he'd avoided his mother and everyone else, so he didn't have any idea who knew what about his marriage.

"But why did she leave?"

Adam froze upon hearing the plaintive voice of his ten-year-old niece. She was in the family drawing room, the door partially ajar.

"Faith is upset."

The voice belonged to none other than Marian, speaking in the kindest tones he'd ever heard from her.

"She and your uncle had a disagreement. I'm certain they will talk soon and resolve everything."

"Are you sure?" Frances demanded, her voice anguished.

"No one can ever be sure, dear, but we will pray for them."

Pray that I can overcome being a fool, he thought.

At the academy, Adam changed into breeches and a loose shirt, then entered the practice room he'd requested. Shenstone was already there, rapier in his hand, chest protector and mask carelessly piled on a bench.

Adam held up his mask questioningly, but Shenstone shook his head. Gritting his teeth, angry that this confrontation was even necessary, Adam tossed his own mask away.

"Can we talk before we fence?" he demanded.

"Say what you need to say," Shenstone said idly, his curly auburn hair already damp with perspiration, as if he'd been practicing.

Adam sensed something being held back, and he was sick of it. "Then I'll just say it. I've been get-

ting notes from someone anonymous, threatening
to reveal something from my wife's past."

Shenstone's eyes narrowed, his sword stilled,
but he said nothing.

"This blackguard doesn't want money, just
wants to feel his power over me, and maybe humiliate my wife by revealing everything."

"And you didn't think to confide this in me
before?" Shenstone demanded.

"You've been so angry with me, and I couldn't
see why. So I can't help asking—are you the one
sending those letters, bribing little street urchins
to bring them to me?"

His dark eyes went wide. "You think I—your
oldest friend—would—that I would—"

With a groan of frustration, he thrust his sword
wildly. Though the tip was buttoned, if Adam
hadn't parried, he still might have been seriously bruised. But maybe that's what Shenstone
wanted, after goading him into not wearing his
chest protector.

"Is that a yes?" Adam demanded between gritted teeth, launching his own attack.

Shenstone fell back. "No!" he shouted, thrust-
ing forward again. "If I had such a problem with
you, I would come to you directly!"

"How can I believe that?" Adam demanded,
slashing stroke after stroke, forcing his friend on
the defensive. "You've been angry for weeks over
something you refuse to talk to me about."

"That's different. It's over a woman!"

"And my wife is a woman!" He slashed Shenstone along the upper arm, catching himself enough to leave a welt beneath his damaged shirt, but not pierce the skin.

Shenstone stepped back, breathing heavily. "I didn't . . . do this thing . . . Rothford," he said between breaths. "And I'll tell you right now . . . why I am furious with you—it's over Lady Emmeline."

Adam slowly let his sword tip sink to the floor. "Emmeline? Sophia's friend? What does she have to do with anything?"

"You used her badly!"

"I did not!" Adam shouted back. "I never courted the girl, never let her think anything other than that we were friends. She was a child when I was gone, and I've barely been back."

"I was courting her, and you returned and it was as if I didn't exist anymore," Shenstone said grimly.

Adam straightened. "That is what you're upset about? I've never wanted her, would never have taken her away from you. I could have told you all of this if you'd asked."

Shenstone groaned and spun away, slashing the air with his sword. "It's all her. She's *fixated* on you and your damned title. You've always gotten whatever woman you fancied."

"And did you not want me to have Faith?" Adam asked, lowering his voice as relief began to replace his anger.

"I didn't give a damn about Faith. I'm glad you

have her. But Emmeline—she's still distraught, and nothing I say makes a difference."

"Maybe you should give her some time to realize I was never going to be hers."

Shenstone mumbled something and slashed the air again, but all the fight between them sizzled and died.

"What about Sophia?" Adam asked.

Shenstone hesitated. "That, you need to talk to her about. It's . . . not what you think." He sighed. "So what's this about anonymous notes you thought I wrote?"

"Well, I didn't really *believe* it, but you were acting so angry, and I didn't have a clue why. I'm relieved you didn't write them." And he briefly elaborated, minus the more incriminating notions about Faith. "So all I can do is confront the people who've behaved oddly. There's a childhood friend of Faith's I'm still investigating."

"Did you have me investigated?" Shenstone asked, lip curling with amusement.

"No, though I did have you followed."

"I shook him off."

"You did not. You didn't even see him."

They slowly grinned at each other.

Adam held out a hand. "Forgive me my idiocy?"

Shenstone took it. "Forgive me my jealousy?"

They shook a little too hard, gripping tight, until at last Shenstone winced. "Damn, your grip strengthened in India. Is it something in the water?"

Adam smiled, but it faded quickly. "I've already blown everything, you know. Faith left me."

"The lady's companion left a *duke*?"

"I'm not much of a prize," Adam said, shrugging. "I'll find a way to make up for my sins and bring her home. And I'll stay away from Emmeline while I do."

Shenstone rolled his eyes and said dryly, "Wonderful. Thanks."

Adam clapped his friend on the back, but already his mind was thinking ahead. One by one, he'd ruled people out—except Timothy Gilpin.

Chapter 23

That first morning at Mrs. Evans's, Faith found herself alone most of the time, the lady respectful of her mourning for her marriage. She paced her bedroom for hours, thinking she'd been alone for the last few years, had briefly become part of a family, and now she was alone again.

She'd felt almost safe, even . . . loved, strange as it seemed, though he'd never said the words. And she really must love him, or his behavior wouldn't hurt so much. It was as if her future had turned dark with foreboding, barren and lifeless without his warmth, without his smile.

Oh, she was absolutely maudlin in her infatuation.

Late in the afternoon, there was a knock on the door and she tensed, but it was only Ellen. Much as the girl had wanted to attend her, she seemed distraught in the unfamiliar house.

Ellen peered out the window, obviously trying

to be subtle, but not succeeding. "That man is still out there, Your Grace."

Faith frowned and joined her at the window.

"I went down the block a ways," Ellen said hesitatingly, "and came back upon him unawares. He's one of our footmen—Hales—so you don't have to worry."

Not worry? Faith thought. Of course she was worried. Adam was controlling, but she was positive his aunt would have told him where Faith was going. Why did he feel the need to watch out for her? And he'd started sending a footman with them wherever they went. Was something else going on, something he hadn't told her?

No surprise there, she thought with bitter exasperation.

"Oh, ma'am," Ellen said, glancing at her, "you have a visitor."

And she hadn't said that right away? "Who is it?"

"Lady Sophia. She's in the front parlor."

The family assault had begun. But Faith wasn't about to cower behind her bunker. She descended to the parlor on the first floor and found Sophia looking somber, staring out the window—at their footman?

She turned when Faith entered, but her smile didn't lighten her sad eyes. "Faith. Oh, Faith." She pressed a handkerchief to her mouth and blinked furiously.

"Don't cry," Faith said gently, crossing the room to take her hand. "You didn't do anything."

"Yes, I did! If you only knew—"

"You agreed to walk in on us alone, so we'd be compromised."

Her watery green eyes went wide. "You knew?"

"I guessed and he confirmed. You only did what your brother asked. He can be very persuasive."

"You sound so bitter. Oh, Faith." Sophia covered her eyes with the handkerchief.

It was strange how much Faith wanted to console her, when Sophia really had behaved inappropriately.

"I just knew how much he loved you, and—"

"Did he tell you that?"

"No, of course not. He would never speak freely of his feelings. Not the way we were raised. I was young, and my older brothers left me alone, but they tortured Adam, picking on him, ridiculing him from the time he was a little boy, and they were so much older—old enough to know better. Adam learned not to show he liked anything, because it would be taken away or ruined."

"I had heard that your brothers resented your father's focus on his new wife and younger children, but I guess I didn't realize they'd started tormenting him so young." She'd pretty much imagined that a child of a duke must have a magical upbringing, even if he didn't get along with his brothers.

"As a third son, he knew he'd have to support himself, but our father refused to believe that his other sons would ever stoop so low as to cut off their brother." Sophia sighed. "Papa was always quick to believe the worst, once my brothers convinced him of Adam's wild ways. I was young, but even I could see Adam acted out just to be noticed, just to matter, because once upon a time Papa had adored him. And my brothers made that all go away." Sophia gave her a hesitant glance. "I don't know that telling you all this matters. I just know that it won't be easy for him to be open with anyone. I had thought, at last, he'd been able to do that for you."

"No, he never even came close. It wasn't about love or vulnerability. It was about guilt and power."

"No, Faith, not power, never that. What does he care about power? He's the duke now, and I'm not sure he really even cared about that. But guilt? I don't know."

"If it's not power, why is he having me followed?"

Sophia looked confused. So Faith pointed out the window.

"Don't you see your footman?"

"Oh. No, I didn't even see him. I don't understand."

"I don't either. But I don't want to talk about that anymore. Talk to me about something else, anything else."

"Then . . . you forgive me?"

"I do."

A tear slipped down her cheek and she wiped it away. "Thank you. Even though I don't deserve it, thank you. But what else can I tell you that even matters?"

"What about Mr. Percy?"

Sophia's smile turned brittle. "I am done trying to make him love me."

"But you were so hopeful!"

"But I was foolish and I should have simply held to the truth. Mr. Percy visited to gently break the news that Lord Shenstone might be misleading me, since he was courting another woman. I'm almost certain he meant Emmeline, but he didn't want to hurt me with it. As if I haven't noticed Lord Shenstone's fascination with her."

Faith blinked in astonishment. *She* hadn't noticed at all, but then she might have been distracted . . .

"And with all the mistakes I've recently made," Sophia continued, "I couldn't lie anymore, so I told him the truth, that I'd asked Lord Shenstone to show an interest in me when Mr. Percy was around, to make him jealous."

"What did he say?" Faith asked, curious in spite of her own melancholy.

"He seemed truly surprised I would do something like that for him. But it didn't matter. He said he could not in good conscience court my favor, and did I not see from your situation how marrying above one's station could only make . . ." Her voice faded away. "Oh, Faith, I'm so sorry."

"Don't be. I'm sorry to set such a bad example to Mr. Percy. And naturally you could not tell him that the difference in rank had absolutely nothing to do with our problems."

"Well, no, I would never reveal your private business. In some ways, I'm coming to the realization that if Mr. Percy believes he cannot take the pressure of our different backgrounds, then perhaps he really is not the man for me."

She was trying to be strong, but Faith could see the hurt underneath, the fear that Sophia worried she wasn't worth fighting for.

At least Faith didn't have to worry about that. Adam fought *too hard* for her.

"Enough about me," Sophia said. "You haven't asked about Adam."

"You know I won't. I only left this morning."

"He avoided us all at breakfast, when Aunt Theodosia told us you were gone."

"I imagine the duchess was quite satisfied."

"You know she cannot bear anything harming her son," Sophia chided. "She seemed worried about him. And Marian—she worried about how to tell Frances."

"Well, at least they weren't gleefully dancing a jig together." She blanched. "I'm sorry to speak of your mother this way."

"Pshaw," Sophia said, sounding like her aunt. She took Faith's hand. "What will you do now, Faith? Please tell me you'll think and maybe discuss things with Adam, and then come home."

"It's not my home, Sophia," she said gently. "It's his. I don't know what I'm going to do. I feel . . . betrayed."

But Faith couldn't forget about the man Adam had watching Mrs. Evans's home, and by the evening, when even Adam hadn't called on her, she sent a missive to Aunt Theodosia to meet somewhere. To her surprise, the lady came over immediately.

After the two old women exchanged the day's gossip, the lady of the house retreated so they could be alone.

"Aunt Theodosia, in no way did I mean you to rush over here," Faith said.

"I know, my dear, but I've spent the day concerned about the two of you, and I could not stay silent another minute, not when Adam is so worried, but determined to be strong and silent and protect you."

"And that footman outside is supposed to do it?"

"Ah, I knew that would not get past you. Yet you did not ask Adam directly."

Faith sighed. "I am not ready to speak to him."

"Meaning you're afraid you will be quite overpowered with emotion."

She lifted her chin. "And I don't want to be, so I will give myself time."

"To stop loving him?"

Faith said nothing.

"He will be angry I told you this," Aunt The-odosia said, "but he's still not thinking clearly. He's been receiving anonymous notes about your past, almost since you first took the posi-tion with me."

Faith's mouth dropped open.

"He didn't want to worry you, knew you'd probably flee if whatever is in your past came to notice. He did not tell me your secrets, of course, nor would I want him to."

"My God, everything I feared has come to pass," Faith said, finding her voice at last. She felt ill. "My sins are haunting me, threatening all of you."

"No one knows your sins, my dear. No one has come forward and done anything, except try to hurt Adam, to convince him to cast you off. He wouldn't back down, has vowed to figure all of this out."

"But he told you rather than me?"

"He did not tell me willingly. And what would your response have been if he'd told *you*?"

Faith stiffened. "It doesn't matter—it would have been *my* response, my choice."

"And he was convinced you'd flee, possibly putting yourself in danger."

"Instead he exposed all of you to terrible scan-dal. If you only knew—"

"I don't want to know. We've all made mistakes, and apparently, yours didn't bother Adam."

She flinched. How many men could have accepted that the woman they were involved with had been a mistress? She could not fault Adam for that.

"But his mistakes bothered you," Aunt Theodosia continued.

"He manipulated me into marriage! No one wants to be forced against their will."

"I don't remember seeing a gun."

Faith gasped. "I couldn't let him suffer for dishonoring me—you know that."

"And he didn't want you to suffer, knowing there was someone out there who wanted to hurt him by hurting you."

Faith let out her breath. The battle wasn't with Aunt Theodosia, but with Adam. "Does he have anyone he suspects?"

"He suspected everyone who knew you, and has gone to great pains to rule many out."

"How many people do I know who . . ." Her voice faded off. "Timothy," she breathed, then immediately wished she could take it back.

"You know that man better than anyone. Should you discuss him with Adam?"

"I'll think about it," Faith said after a long moment.

"Good." Aunt Theodosia braced her hands on her knees to rise, before finding her cane. "Do let me know what you decide, won't you?"

After the old woman had left, Faith sat still, the last few weeks rushing over her as if she could see them in a new light. She already knew he'd looked into her past, knew what she'd done, and still wanted to marry her, to protect her. But he'd risked his family with this anonymous threat. He'd done that—for her. It didn't make right the wrongs he'd done, but she couldn't stay here, practically a prisoner with a guard, and do nothing to save his family from the scandal of her past.

She had to go back. Though he'd manipulated her, he was also willing to put his family's reputation on the line for her. And she wasn't certain what that meant.

The next morning, Adam ate breakfast with his family, who cast sidelong glances at him as if waiting for him to explode. But no one mentioned Faith.

Until Sophia dropped the napkin from her hand and cried, "Faith!"

He turned around and she was standing there, dark hair demurely caught back as if she hadn't been wild in bed with him not two nights ago. He stood up. She was wearing one of those old shapeless gowns, too, rebuking everything he'd done for her.

And she looked—wonderful. The ache that had not left him since their argument eased the smallest bit. She'd come home to him. Maybe she even loved him.

Because he loved her. Every moment without her had been full of the never-ending fear that he'd ruined any chance to show her how much.

But she didn't look at him. She looked at Sophia, who was softly crying as if at the return of the sister she'd always wanted. Faith smiled at her, then went around the table and gave her a bolstering hug.

"Faith!" Aunt Theodosia said a bit too heartily. "How is my dear friend, Mrs. Evans? I do hope you were able to be of help with her speeches."

As if Faith had only gone off on an errand of assistance.

"She is well, Aunt," Faith said in a quiet voice. She nodded to his mother. "Ma'am."

And to his surprise, the dowager duchess said, "It is good to see you, Faith. It has been rather quiet without you."

"Thank you, ma'am."

As if she couldn't help herself, Faith shot him a questioning glance, which he felt like an arrow, but he managed to give only an imperceptible shrug.

Marian said nothing, busily eating as if she had far too much to do that day than waste her time on reunions. If it was a reunion. He found he couldn't let himself hope for that, not with the tension and coolness Faith gave off like steam from one's breath on a winter morning.

"Adam, may I speak with you privately?" Faith asked.

At last, the crux of the matter. He walked with her across the entrance hall, light shining through the stained glass far above as if the day would be beautiful.

Or maybe it would be the day his marriage ended. But he wouldn't give up without a fight.

"Faith!" Frances leaned over the balustrade on the next floor up.

Faith's smile bloomed so beautifully that his breath caught at the splendor. She would make a wonderful mother. Maybe she already carried his child. He'd worked at it often enough in just a few days. Then she'd *have* to stay with him.

But he didn't want her to feel like that, forced and unwilling. He wanted her devotion and love. He wanted the Faith who met his passion in bed, who challenged him to make a better man of himself.

Instead, she'd seemed cold and distant until Frances escaped her governess and came running down the stairs to throw her arms around Faith.

"I've missed you, Aunt Faith," the girl said, her words smothered in Faith's bodice.

"I was only gone a day," Faith said, chuckling.

Keeping her arms around her, Frances looked up. "It was a long day, and I was afraid you weren't coming back."

Faith kissed her brow. "I'm sorry to frighten you. We'll talk later. Off to your lessons."

Frances didn't even pout, just waved good-bye and ran back up the stairs.

In his study, she didn't bother taking a seat, only turned to face him and spoke coolly. "Don't think I've forgiven you. I only returned because your aunt told me about the anonymous notes you kept from me."

He grimaced. "I didn't want you hurt like this."

"Adam, you are not to decide what truths hurt me. I've told you that over and over."

"This is different," he insisted. "You are my wife."

"And they are your family," she said, pointing to the door. "You risked scandal on their good names for me."

"I'd do it again. They'd expect it of me."

She arched a brow.

"Most of them," he conceded. "So tell me— what should I have done? What would *you* have done?"

"I would have discussed it with you immediately."

"Would you?" he scoffed. "If it would have sent me fleeing alone into danger?"

She inhaled, then let it out.

"Now you see my dilemma. I know you, Faith, much as you think I don't. What if I couldn't have found you? What if this blackguard did?"

"From what Aunt Theodosia told me, he hasn't exactly threatened me."

"The notes are threatening enough, and they've escalated in tone."

"Let me see them."

He spread them out on the desk, and side-by-side, they looked at them: the rough, plain paper, the crude scrawl that made guessing the sex of the blackguard impossible.

Faith is lovely. Wherever she goes, you can't stop looking at her. But I'm watching you.

She's still there, in your home. You don't know anything about her. Your obsession is showing.

You risk much to have her—she's not worth it. I know what she is, what she's done.

You'll be sorry when everyone finds out your new duchess is a whore.

He saw her face pale as she put a hand over her mouth. But she didn't turn away, even leaned closer as she read them all again.

"Until the last note," she said slowly, "it's all mostly aimed at you, isn't it, even though it's about me?"

He nodded. "I believe someone is enjoying having power over me. But I haven't gratified them by giving in."

"And getting rid of me."

He met her stare with a confident one.

"Instead, you married me," she mused, without any emotion showing. "When did this last one come?"

"A week or so before the wedding."

"You risked this person revealing my secret."

"I know. I've risked much from the beginning. What would you have done differently? Should I have sent you away? I could have taken you away on the wedding trip, but that would have simply delayed whatever was going to happen. I felt I needed to be here."

Her eyes narrowed. "So whom do you suspect?"

"Shenstone has been so angry with me that I confronted him yesterday about it. He denied any role in it, and I believe him. Turns out, he's been angry over Emmeline's 'attachment' to me. He thought he was making progress courting her, then I returned and apparently ruined it all," he said with faint sarcasm. "We've settled our differences. Well, except about Sophia, but he wouldn't reveal her confidences."

Faith waved a hand. "Sophia asked him to pretend to court her to make Mr. Percy jealous. It didn't work, so she ended the charade."

Adam stared at her.

"I know it was foolish, but who are we to pass judgment? Back to your suspects."

He released a heavy sigh. "There's Ellen—"

"Ellen?" she interrupted, her eyes wide.

"She wasn't exactly happy to be your maid, was she? Anyone else would have removed her from the position due to her attitude and poor skills."

"Yes, but she was merely insecure."

"How was I to know that? You told me how excited she was to be your permanent lady's maid, and then another note came."

"So we can rule her out," Faith said.

"I hope so. I even had your past employer, as

well as Miss Ogden and Miss Atherstone investigated."

"Jane and Charlotte? They would never—"

"But you've only known them a few months, haven't you? What if one of them became jealous of my attachment to you?"

He saw her considering. "Charlotte was quite disapproving at the beginning, but I believe it was because she thought you had devious intentions."

"Maybe you agree with her."

She didn't look at him. "Not those intentions. I don't like what you did, but never once did you hint that my past only entitled me to be a man's mistress."

"Then I did something right," he murmured, and touched her shoulder.

She stepped away. "And then there's Timothy. After the way he behaved for a while there, he would seem the likeliest suspect. But . . . we were friends for so long, Adam. I know he's changed, but . . ."

"He was at our wedding," Adam said coldly.

Her wide-eyed gaze collided with his. "I didn't see him. But then I was only focused on you."

"I will take that as promising, rather than implying that I *wasn't* focused on you."

"Of course I didn't mean that," she said quietly. "So what did he say when you confronted him?"

"I haven't yet. That was on today's calendar."

She bit her lip, and for just a moment her eyes

almost twinkled. "Today's calendar? Did you write in 'confront suspect'?"

He smiled at her, but she turned away again, as if she didn't want to smile back.

And then the words he hadn't meant to say tumbled out in a hoarse voice. "It's taking everything in me not to draw you back against me, to put my arms around you and promise everything will be all right."

Her arms crept about to hold herself, but she said nothing.

"I want to inhale the scent of your hair, taste your fresh, sweet-smelling skin. I'm lost without you, sweetheart. But you don't want to hear that."

"Not now, Adam. I need time. I don't know . . . what I want."

He nodded although she couldn't see.

She cleared her throat and stepped away from him toward the door, saying over her shoulder. "I shall leave a card at the Gilpins today in hopes they'll visit us tomorrow. I think I need to look into my old friend's eyes."

Chapter 24

After a night in the ducal apartments—but in her own room—Faith came down to breakfast, determined to find out once and for all if her oldest friend hated her so much that he'd try to ruin her life.

But when she reached the breakfast parlor, all the family was assembled, and they looked at her with sad, angry, or wary expressions—depending on the person.

"What happened?" she asked, her stomach clenching.

Adam held up the ironed newspaper, now folded back to the Society pages. He pointed to a paragraph.

> What scandal brews? One hears that the D— of R— *had* to marry. Are there more secrets to be revealed?

Faith felt light-headed. Did that mean the blackguard had begun to follow through on his threats, and now meant to reveal the rest? She stared into Adam's grim eyes, but there were no answers there.

Sophia was the first to speak, her voice shrill. "Who would *say* such a thing, let alone write it?"

"I always feared the circumstances of your marriage would come out, son," the dowager duchess said. "You can keep nothing from the servants."

"None of it matters," Adam said dismissively. "They can say anything they'd like—you're my duchess, Faith, and those in Society who wish to remain in my good graces will never mention this."

Lady Tunbridge smothered what might have been a snort, but Adam didn't call her on it.

Faith was no longer hungry, couldn't seem to move. Except for Aunt Theodosia, no one here knew there were any more secrets to be uncovered. They all thought this was the only ugly rumor to matter.

But she had to think logically—would Timothy know the worst of her sins? No one in her village knew; her mother had seen to that. Timothy had never shown any interest in her when she was barely getting by. And when she had agreed not to ask his father for a letter of reference, he'd been relieved and seemed to think nothing more. It wasn't until he'd come to London, his marriage ailing, and seen her again did she sense a problem. But would he have paid investigators like Adam had to research her past? What would have been the point?

Though she wasn't hungry, she ate a small breakfast alongside Sophia, doing her best to appear not overly concerned. She certainly didn't want anyone to suspect there was more going on. After a morning of working with Aunt Theodosia writing letters—which the old lady insisted a duchess shouldn't do, and Faith overruled her— Faith had lunch sent up to her room on a tray, and awaited the arrival of the Gilpins. Precisely at three, Seabrook alerted them both to their callers, whom he'd shown to the family drawing room, since the dowager duchess and the other ladies would be receiving callers in the public room.

Faith wore one of Sophia's gowns, white with tiny green stripes, a touch of elegance, but nothing of the newest fashion that might make Timothy feel she was out to impress them.

Adam met her in the corridor outside their apartments, then held out an arm. "Ready?"

She nodded, placed her hand on his arm and allowed him to escort her downstairs. She was surprised that rather than nervous, she felt—bold, alive, ready to face the challenge.

Was this how Adam had felt in India, when he'd left his terrible brothers behind and could face challenges on his own?

In the drawing room, Timothy and his wife stood together near the hearth. In the moment before introduction, Faith thought Timothy looked nervous and didn't meet Adam's forthright gaze, but she knew well what he could be fearing—that Adam might know he'd been the one to have her innocence.

"Mr. Gilpin," Faith said pleasantly. "I'm so glad that you and your wife could attend us at Rothford Court. Have you met my husband? Allow me to introduce His Grace, the Duke of Rothford. Rothford, this is Mr. Gilpin, the man from my village I told you about."

She saw Timothy give an uneasy start and shoot a nervous glance at his wife. Mrs. Gilpin didn't notice, tense and alert and smiling too much. Her hair and eyes were both brown, and with her little upturned nose, Faith was put in mind of an eager kitten.

"Gilpin," Adam said impassively, nodding his head.

Timothy swallowed. "Your Graces, may I present Mrs. Gilpin."

Adam bowed over her hand. "I believe you'll someday be Lady Gilpin?"

Blushing, she nodded eagerly. "My husband is the heir to his father's barony, Your Grace. Are you not, Mr. Gilpin?"

"You are right, of course, my dear," he murmured.

Faith was surprised at how . . . subdued Timothy was, not at all a man in control of his life. As they all sat down, it was Mrs. Gilpin who did most of the talking, commenting on the opera and the latest musicale and someone's upcoming ball. Timothy nodded and made the appropriate affirmations in monosyllables. Faith got the sense that he wasn't doing this because of Adam's presence, but simply out of habit. She was surprised by how little interest he seemed to have in their socializing. It was rather sad—no wonder he was unhappy with his life, if he didn't speak up, or get a word in edgewise.

"Mr. Gilpin has told me such fine things about you and your late brother, Your Grace," Mrs. Gilpin said chattily to Faith, then her smile faded. "Oh, dear, do you mind if I mention him?"

"Of course not, Mrs. Gilpin. I wish I had more people who remembered him that I could talk to."

She glanced at Timothy, who opened his mouth, but was interrupted again by his wife.

"He talks fondly of the games you all played as children, how you used to love to read. Do you still feel the same?"

Adam smiled. "She does. I do believe she might have fallen in love with my library first."

Mrs. Gilpin laughed loud and merrily, and her husband started as if he was overly sensitive to her voice.

"Oh, this is delightful," she said. "I've been insufferable I'm sure, asking Mr. Gilpin when we might call upon his old friend, the duchess."

Adam settled his steady gaze on Timothy. "Did you send me several notes recently?"

Faith held her breath, trying to look interested but not too curious. She hadn't known Adam was going to be so direct.

Timothy frowned. "I did not, Your Grace. Are you certain you do not have me confused with someone else?"

Adam shrugged. "I guess I do."

Through it all, Faith watched Timothy carefully. She'd known him her whole life, had been able to read his expressions as a child, and these last few months, had had no problem understanding how unhappy he was.

But he seemed totally clueless about the anonymous notes. And she believed him. The relief she felt that it wasn't her childhood friend was soon replaced by a renewed worry—if it wasn't Timothy, then who was it?

Precisely a quarter hour after they arrived, the Gilpins took their leave. Timothy didn't meet her eyes as he bowed to them both and followed his wife out the door.

Adam closed the drawing-room door and leaned against it. "He's a milksop."

"He doesn't know a thing, Adam."

"You would know him better than I, but I have to agree. Dammit, Faith, if it's not him, then who could it be?"

"I hate to suggest it, but could it be someone even closer than we've ever imagined?"

His blue eyes were wintry. "You mean family?"

She said nothing, only bit her lip. "My mother took great pains to hide my sins from the world."

"I cannot imagine my mother or Sophia or my aunt wanting to harm us, but . . ."

His voice faded away, even as she stiffened.

"Lady Tunbridge?" she whispered.

He ran a hand through his sandy hair. "My brother hated me. He tried to poison the whole family against me—maybe he succeeded with her."

"Oh, Adam, she's a good mother to Frances. Why would she do this?"

"I don't know, unless it's just to hurt us, since I'm now the duke and her husband is dead."

"She's thought I was beneath you from the beginning. But to have me investigated in depth?"

He started pacing, head bent, brows furrowed. "She was too . . . calm after you left, no gloating, no arrogance. At the time, I was just thankful for the peace, but now . . . I don't know. Let's ask Aunt Theodosia if she's seen anything suspicious."

He took her hand and pulled her from the room, and she could barely keep up to his pace. At the public drawing room, he slowed just before reaching the door. They could hear many voices.

"If we go in there, it'll be at least an hour before we can escape," Adam said. He turned to Hales, who waited dutifully. "Wait until we're gone five minutes, and then please ask my aunt to attend us in our apartments."

He continued to hold her hand all the way up the stairs, and at the top, she said, "I do know my way—you don't need to lead me."

He looked startled, then lifted up their joined hands. "It simply felt right."

She extricated hers and walked ahead of him. She wasn't thinking about the two of them, not now. In their sitting room, she was the one who paced, and Adam lounged back in a chair and just watched her.

Finally she rounded on him. "Must you stare so?"

He smiled. "Yes, I am newly married, and the sight of my wife quite arouses me."

She felt herself blushing, though she struggled to will those dark, sensual memories away. "Can you not concentrate on what we must do? The reputation of your family is at stake."

"*My* family?" he said, slowly rising to his feet and then coming toward her.

She wanted to back away, and she wanted to strain toward him. It didn't matter how disappointed and hurt she was—her body remembered the pleasure and the struggle and the release.

"It's your family, too," he said huskily.

And then Aunt Theodosia swept in before he could touch her, and she breathed a sigh of relief.

"And what do we have here?" she asked, limping forward and positively beaming at them.

Faith stepped away. "We have a suspect."

Her happy expression faded into determination. "That Gilpin fellow?"

"No," Adam said, "we've both concluded that it just didn't feel right. And then we began to wonder if there was anyone closer to us both, whom we'd overlooked."

"Closer?" his aunt echoed, looking both puzzled and worried.

"Marian," Adam said coldly.

Aunt Theodosia's eyes narrowed.

"She's the only person that makes sense," he continued, "the one who wants to punish me for having lived when her husband died. She couldn't stand Faith from the beginning, and since my return from India, she's veered often into disrespect."

The elderly lady slowly sank into a chair, looking older than she had but a moment ago. "Oh, Adam, I can't believe it . . . I don't want to believe it."

"We need proof," Faith said. "I would never humiliate someone by simply accusing."

"She has no problem humiliating us," Adam countered. "If it *is* her, she put that notice in the paper, and maybe plans another."

Faith shivered, and when he put an arm around her waist, she didn't pull away. She felt shocked and hurt and so sad. Frances's mother—could she really have done this?

Faith struggled to put her emotion aside. "She would have had to contact the man who paid the little boys to bring the letters," she mused. "Does she go out alone?"

"Not often," Aunt Theodosia said. "But I have seen her do so recently, without calling for the carriage—which is *very* unusual, as she takes pride in the ducal insignia on the door."

"She could be walking to a friend's," Faith pointed out.

"She never walks anywhere," Adam said. "I've heard her say walking is for common people."

"Well, I like to walk," Faith said dryly. "I imagine she believes her theory quite proven by me."

"I hate to suggest it, but I'd like us to talk to Frances," Adam said somberly. "With gentle restraint, of course. She might have seen something than can help us."

"If it's true," Aunt Theodosia said with a quavering voice, "the poor girl." Then she straightened. "Marian has gone out. I can't wait much longer to know the truth. Now that you've returned, Faith, she might become desperate. I do not know what other secrets she hints at—and I do not wish to know your private business, because we all have secrets—but I imagine it will only harm you both to have them revealed. I suggest we send for Frances now."

Faith lifted both hands. "Wait. If she sees us all here, she'll be quite upset, do you not think? What if I bring her to the conservatory for a walk? She loves it there."

Adam nodded. "Excellent idea. We'll meet you there."

"I shall find my book of flowers," Aunt Theodosia said absently, her expression still so sad.

For the next hour, Adam found himself watching his wife, the gentle way she had with Frances, never speaking down to her, always treating her as the smart, funny girl she was. He felt both angry and sad that Marian might have risked everything and hurt her child in the process, all for an old grudge that hadn't even begun with her.

They looked at flowers and examined the fish in the fountain, until Adam thought he'd explode with impatience. But Faith never once betrayed any concerns, until at last she began to talk about writing to her mother.

"It is a duty to write to one's mother, of course, but sometimes it's sad."

"Why are you sad?" Frances asked, still trailing her fingers in the fountain.

Adam was seated on a nearby bench, pretending to look at the flower book with Aunt Theodosia, but his ears were straining. He'd thought he would have a difficult time restraining his own questions, but Faith had everything under control.

Now she was saying, "My mother and I aren't as close as your mother and you are. It's hard to know what to say to her. Does your mother write to her mother?"

Frances nodded. "She writes letters every day."

"Ladies often do," Faith said, nodding. "I must admit, since coming to live here, the ducal stationery makes it a pleasure to write. Such pretty paper. Your mother must like it."

Adam tensed, never having thought to connect her to the paper the notes were on.

Frances wrinkled her little nose. "She has this ugly paper she uses sometimes. When I tried to read it once, she took it away."

Faith nodded, then splashed a few drops on Frances, who laughed. But Faith met Adam's eyes with a determined, triumphant expression.

"I'll be right back," Adam said to his aunt.

Anger seethed inside him like a hot summer storm. He took the stairs two at a time to Marian's apartments, and then searched every drawer and beneath and within every piece of furniture. He found a yellowed calling card she'd once kept safe and waiting for the day she'd be duchess, the day that never came. At last he found the paper hidden behind her giant wardrobe—and there was a new letter ready to post to the newspaper. Faith appeared in the doorway, and her eyes went wide when she saw what he held.

Gritting his teeth so hard his cheek spasmed, he ripped it open. Faith crowded against him so they could read it together.

The D—s of R—'s secrets are revealed. She was a special "friend" to the late Lord R— of Fenton in Northumberland.

Faith gasped. "She doesn't care if she hurts Lord Reyburn's son!"

Adam gripped her shoulders and looked into her eyes, feeling triumphant. "And now she'll never hurt you. I'll see to that."

"Adam, wait. Let me talk to her."

He hesitated, everything inside him demanding revenge and justice. She was his wife, she was his love, and he wanted to protect her, to keep her safe.

"She disdains me," Faith insisted. "I am nothing to her but a means to an end. I think she'd be more on her guard with you."

"We don't have to care—we have the proof," he said, holding up the letter.

"But don't we want to hear her say it? This is Frances's mother, your sister-in-law. You will be deciding her fate—don't you want to know it all?"

And then he realized that it was about *her* past, *her* future—and she should be the one to see it through.

"You're right," he said.

She blinked at him. "Really? You're giving in?"

"I told you I could learn from my mistakes, didn't I?"

She watched him warily, but he thought there might be the faintest trace of amusement in her eyes.

And that gave him hope.

Chapter 25

A quarter hour later, Faith waited in the private drawing room, keeping a close watch on the entrance hall as well as the street. The duchess continued to entertain visitors, and Faith ducked out of the way at arrivals and departures. The folding doors were closed, separating the drawing room into two smaller rooms, and Adam and Aunt Theodosia listened on the far side.

Soon enough, Marian entered through the front door, handing off parcels to footmen as if she simply expected them to be there.

Faith took a deep breath. "Lady Tunbridge? May I speak with you for a moment?"

She frowned as she removed her shawl and bonnet, looked up the massive stairs as if something important awaited her, but with a sigh, she acquiesced.

Faith closed the door, then pulled a calling card from her pocket and held it out. "A maid brought this to me. She found it when cleaning your apartments."

Marian read the card, then her eyes briefly widened before narrowing as she studied Faith, disdain barely hidden. "What does this matter? It was made when my husband yet lived, when it seemed that the old duke was sickly."

"Yet you kept it, knowing there would be another duchess. And now I'm here."

"Well, the little kitten has claws," Marian said, her smile not touching her eyes. "It seemed you didn't want to be the duchess just two days ago."

"We had an argument. It's settled."

"So you run at the first sign of a problem? Not very dignified of you."

"You mean not dignified as a duchess should be. You think you would have handled things better?"

"I know I would. I far deserved the title, spent my youth and adulthood knowing it would come to me, and preparing for it. If my husband had lived an hour longer, I'd have *been* the duchess for life. You? You don't deserve the honor. You're nothing but a whore."

Faith didn't even flinch. "How interesting. That is the same word used in the anonymous letters Adam has been receiving. The cowardly ones."

Adam folded the door back, and Marian saw him there, with Aunt Theodosia looking pale and disappointed.

Marian's eyes blazed with hatred. "I have nothing more to say." She turned to leave.

Adam stepped between her and the door, then held up the latest note. "You won't be sending this. I suggest you tell me everything, before I send you far from here."

"There's nothing you can do, you fool," she hissed, her eyes malevolent.

"I wonder what Frances would think."

That simple sentence made her choke, her face going red before pale. "You would not hurt her like that."

"No. Strangely enough, you've done well as a mother. But I'm about to send you to my most northern property in Scotland, where you will live out your days in far more prosperity than you deserve. But Frances—what you do now will decide her fate. Will she have the large dowry promised to her? Will she spend some time each year with Faith and me in London?"

Marian's lips parted with anguish. "You threaten a child?"

"I threaten *you*. Frances will be fine. She will have the dowry left to her by her father. But I will give her so much more, present her to Society, see her well married. But it all depends on you."

"What do you want?" Marian asked haughtily.

"The truth, all of it. And your promise to never speak of this again. Frances doesn't need to know the ugly things you've done here."

Marian's gaze went from Adam's cold, unyielding expression to Aunt Theodosia's scorn and sorrow, then to Faith, who met that gaze with calm indifference.

Marian actually seemed to sag from within. "I sensed from the beginning you were not of the same moral fiber as your brother, Rothford, and it showed the moment you met this commoner."

"Insults to my beloved won't win you my indulgence," Adam warned.

She winced at "beloved," but sighed and said, "I overheard Mr. Gilpin pressuring your 'beloved,' and realized there was something in her past. I hired an investigator who discovered that you're not worthy for the honor of being a duchess," she said scornfully to Faith. "Why should I have spoken of it when I could torment you, Adam?" She chuckled. "I wish I could have seen your face when you opened each one. I actually saw you chase those little boys, and I laughed until my eyes ran with tears."

"It'll be a long time before you laugh again," Adam said impassively. "The Highlands are bitterly cold in winter, and full of biting midges in the summer. You'll enjoy the rest of your life there, far from Society."

"What care I for this stupid city if I cannot rule Society as I was destined? *I* should have been the duchess, not you!" she shouted, pointing a finger in Faith's face.

Adam took her arm and bent it behind her back until she gasped. Inches from her face, he said, "I don't plan to ever hurt a woman, but you're the first who tempts me to do so. You will be escorted to your rooms and you will not leave until the carriage is ready to take you away. Enjoy the rest of your life. I hope it was worth it."

He let her go, and she staggered, then righted herself.

Adam opened the door and quietly said, "Hales, escort her ladyship to her chambers and remain outside the door. She needs to stay within, and if she does not, come tell me."

Marian's last scornful look raked them all, but Faith did not miss that her shoulders slumped as she left the room.

It was over. Faith was glad that the worry Adam had been living with for months was gone.

"I—I'm tired," she said, starting to move past him.

"Faith, will you join us for dinner?" he asked softly.

"I think I'll have a tray sent up. I have much thinking to do."

He nodded, and she sent a brief smile to Aunt Theodosia, who watched her with concern.

Faith felt a bit in a dream as she went slowly up the stairs. What was next for her? She was no innocent, she knew, and could not continue to be angry with Adam forever. Her own choices had affected her past, and would affect her future, too. Would she always choose correctly? No, no one was perfect.

She'd only met Adam because of her brother. The grief she'd long suppressed over what his death had done to her family had at long last faded away. She smiled wryly when she thought how surprised he'd be by all that had happened to her because of him.

She'd forgiven Adam his part in that—how could she not do the same now? And could she not learn to forgive herself for what she'd been forced to do to survive?

"Faith?"

As if she'd called him to mind, he was coming down the corridor just as she'd meant to close the door. He looked so handsome, so concerned, lines in his forehead that bespoke a maturity through hard work and sacrifice.

"Will you let me in?" he asked.

She opened the door wide and gestured. He looked relieved, as if he doubted her, perhaps doubted everything she felt.

"I was afraid if you sat up here alone," he began, not coming any closer, "you'd think of all the stupid things I've done, all the ways I've hurt you."

"Perhaps I'm thinking of all the stupid things *I've* done," she said softly.

He looked taken aback. "Faith, you have done nothing wrong. You've spent your life buffeted by the decisions of others, and you've only done your best."

"And you tried to do your best," she said. "Even if you were misguided."

He stared hard at her. "Faith—"

"Regardless of your mistakes, I think you've

changed, Adam. You let me in, you let me help, even when you worried it might hurt me. You let me make my own choice about confronting Marian."

"But I didn't give you much of a choice about marrying me. I'm trying to do the right thing now," he said huskily, coming a step nearer.

She reached for his hand, and his face softened as he gently brought her hand to his mouth.

"Faith," he whispered. "I want to prove I've changed—for you, for myself. I can't promise I'm perfect, but I see now the mistakes I kept making. But the one thing I can't regret, that won't ever be a mistake, is falling in love with you."

She inhaled, closing her eyes, trying to savor those words she thought she might never hear.

"I don't know when or how it happened, but I only realized how much I needed you when you left me, how barren the future looked without you. I want to prove myself worthy of your love, to prove I'm not the wastrel of my youth, the floundering former soldier. I have skills and knowledge, and ferreting out Marian made me realize that there's still a place for me that isn't just attending balls or dinners—though of course I'd escort you anywhere you wanted to go."

She laughed and touched his cheek with her free hand. "So what do you want to do?"

"Offer my skills to the War Department. I don't wish to travel much, but I can help train men, read correspondence, offer my advice. I learned a lot in India, especially how to understand the enemy. And maybe it'll keep me from interfering in anyone else's life," he added wryly.

She smiled.

His own faded into a determination. "I love you. I've never met anyone more resilient and brave. There aren't many people who do what they must to survive and come out stronger."

The first tear fell from her lashes, and he cupped her face to wipe it away with his thumb.

"Oh, Adam, I've fallen in love with you, too," she whispered.

He took a deep breath, briefly closing his eyes as if he'd never even hoped. She was touched and flattered, and so warm with love for him.

"You've wanted to change, and you have—although maybe not as fast as I'd have liked. You made mistakes, but for the right reasons, and I know that. I honestly believe you respect me, that you'd never again do what you think best for me without my knowledge," she added dryly.

"Never." He let his hands slide down her shoulders and arms, then took both her hands in his. "Will you stay with me, Faith, raise children with me, love me?"

She smiled through her tears. "I will. Let these be our real wedding vows, Adam, now that there is love."

Epilogue

"I'm here!"

Upon hearing Frances's voice, Faith rushed as quickly as she could from the family drawing room. Frances was in the entrance hall, flinging her shawl aside even as she flung herself at Faith.

"Hey, careful," Adam said, catching her about the waist and swinging her around until she squealed. "You don't want to bump the baby."

When Frances landed back on the floor, she gasped at Faith's large stomach. "Can I touch the baby?"

"He might even kick you," Faith said, taking her niece's hand and holding it to her belly.

Frances's mouth fell open. "He kicked me! Is it really a boy?"

"We're just guessing. It doesn't matter to us."

"He wants to meet you," Adam said. "We're glad you came back from Scotland in time. Did you have fun?"

"I love it there! There are horses to ride and puppies to play with, and I can see mountains from my room. It's so wonderful to read lying in fields of flowers. Oh—Mother says she's sorry she couldn't come."

Faith and Adam exchanged a relieved glance. So far, Marian had kept her word.

"Frances!" Sophia cried, rushing forward to hug her niece. "I'm so glad you'll be here for the wedding."

"It's about time you and Mr. Percy married," Aunt Theodosia said with a sniff. "He couldn't let Faith be the only brave one to take on our family."

Sophia blushed and smiled at Faith. For several months, Faith had been denying that she'd inspired Mr. Percy to come forward after the ugly hints in the newspaper. She thought it was Sophia's beauty and kindness that had finally made him realize he'd never find another woman like her.

And weddings must be in the air, because at last, when Lord Shenstone had stopped pursuing Lady Emmeline, she'd realized she might actually miss him and consented to be his wife.

Resting her hands on her belly, Faith smiled as Frances hugged each member of her family.

Faith's family. She smiled at her husband, so grateful that he'd come to find her that day in Hyde Park, that he'd made her his duchess, a mother—but mostly, his wife.

Next month, don't miss these exciting new love stories only from Avon Books

Kiss of Wrath by Sandra Hill
It's been centuries since Mordr the Berserker was turned into a Viking vampire angel and now he has a new assignment: protect lust-worthy Miranda Hart. Miranda needs a miracle to keep her late cousin's five children safe from her cousin's dangerous husband. But Miranda wants nothing to do with a hunk who claims to be a Viking. Together they must decide if they fit in each other's worlds . . . before their enemies close in.

All I Want Is You by Toni Blake
Christy Knight thinks maybe it's time for her to leave Destiny, Ohio, and find a guy who's smart, sexy, and solvent. Her rugged handyman neighbor fits the bill. Jack DuVall hasn't been entirely honest—he's not really a handyman and he's not broke, but he finds gorgeous, feisty Christy irresistible. When secrets are exposed, the seaside town of Coral Cove could be the perfect place to find a red-hot destiny of their own.

The Once and Future Duchess by Sophia Nash
After a debauched bachelor party, the Prince Regent demands that the Duke of Candover be brought to heel—and he believes Isabelle Tremont, the Duchess of March, is the lady up to the challenge. For Candover, there's no shortage of other candidates, but if he and Isabelle can put aside pride and duty, then a love once denied might be their destiny.

Visit www.AuthorTracker.com for exclusive information on your favorite HarperCollins authors.

REL 0514

Available wherever books are sold or please call 1-800-331-3761 to order.

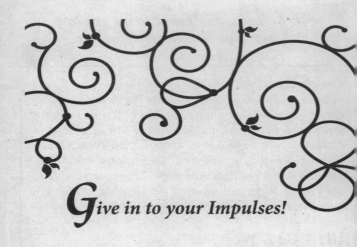